Also by Leni Zumas

Farewell Navigator

The Listeners

RED CLOCKS

LENI ZUMAS

b
THE BOROUGH PRESS

The Borough Press

A catalogue record for this book is available from the British Library

ISBN: 978-0-00-820986-5

This novel is entirely a work of fiction.
The names, characters and incidents portrayed in it are
the work of the author's imagination. Any resemblance to
actual persons, living or dead, events or localities is
entirely coincidental.

Printed and bound in the UK by CPI Group (UK) Ltd, Croydon CR0 4YY

MIX
Paper from
responsible sources
FSC™ C007454

This book is produced from independently certified FSC™ paper
to ensure responsible forest management.

For more information visit: www.harpercollins.co.uk/green

for Luca and Nicholas
per sempre

For nothing was simply one thing. The other Lighthouse was true too.

Virginia Woolf

~~Born in 1841 on a Faroese sheep farm,~~

~~The polar explorer was raised on a farm near~~

In the North Atlantic Ocean, between Scotland and Iceland, on an island with more sheep than people, a shepherd's wife gave birth to a child who would grow up to study ice.

Pack ice once posed such a danger to ships that any researcher who ~~knew the personality of this ice~~ could predict its behavior was valuable to the companies and governments that funded polar expeditions.

In 1841, on the Faroe Islands, in a turf-roofed cottage, in a bed that smelled of whale fat, of a mother who had delivered nine children and buried four, the polar explorer Eivør Mínervudottír was born.

THE BIOGRAPHER

In a room for women whose bodies are broken, Eivør Mínervudottír's biographer waits her turn. She wears sweatpants, is white skinned and freckle cheeked, not young, not old. Before she is called to climb into stirrups and feel her vagina prodded with a wand that makes black pictures, on a screen, of her ovaries and uterus, the biographer sees every wedding ring in the room. Serious rocks, fat bands of glitter. They live on the fingers of women who have leather sofas and solvent husbands but whose cells and tubes and bloods are failing at their animal destiny. This, anyway, is the story the biographer likes. It is a simple, easy story that allows her not to think about what's happening in the women's heads, or in the heads of the husbands who sometimes accompany them.

Nurse Crabby wears a neon-pink wig and a plastic-strap contraption that exposes nearly all of her torso, including a good deal of breast. "Happy Halloween," she explains.

"And to you," says the biographer.

"Let's go suck out some lineage."

"Pardon?"

"Anagram for blood."

"Hmm," says the biographer politely.

Crabby doesn't find the vein straight off. Has to dig, and it hurts. "Where *are* you, mister?" she asks the vein. Months of needlework have streaked and darkened the insides of the biographer's elbows. Luckily long sleeves are common in this part of the world.

"Aunt Flo visited again, did she?" says Crabby.

"Vengefully."

"Well, Roberta, the body's a riddle. Here we go—*got* you." Blood swooshes into the chamber. It will tell them how much follicle-stimulating hormone and estradiol and progesterone the biographer's body is making.

There are good numbers and there are bad. Crabby drops the tube into a rack alongside other little bullets of blood.

Half an hour later, a knock on the exam-room door—a warning, not a request for permission. In comes a man wearing leather trousers, aviator sunglasses, a curly black wig under a porkpie hat.

"I'm the guy from that band," says Dr. Kalbfleisch.

"Wow," says the biographer, bothered by how sexy he's become.

"Shall we take a look?" He settles his leather on a stool in front of her open legs, says "Oops!" and removes the sunglasses. Kalbfleisch played football at an East Coast university and still has the face of a frat boy. He is golden skinned, a poor listener. He smiles while citing bleak statistics. The nurse holds the biographer's file and a pen to write measurements. The doctor will call out how thick the lining, how large the follicles, how many the follicles. Add these numbers to the biographer's age (42) and her level of follicle-stimulating hormone (14.3) and the temperature outside (56) and the number of ants in the square foot of soil directly beneath them (87), and you get the odds. The chance of a child.

Snapping on latex gloves: "Okay, Roberta, let's see what's what."

On a scale of one to ten, with ten being the shrill funk of an elderly cheese and one being no odor at all, how would he rank the smell of the biographer's vagina? How does it compare with the other vaginas barreling through this exam room, day in, day out, years of vaginas, a crowd of vulvic ghosts? Plenty of women don't shower beforehand, or are battling a yeast, or just happen naturally to stink in the nethers. Kalbfleisch has sniffed some ripe tangs in his time.

He slides in the ultrasound wand, dabbed with its neon-blue jelly, and presses it up against her cervix. "Your lining's nice and thin," he says. "Four point five. Right where we want it." On the monitor, the lining of the biographer's uterus is a dash of white chalk in a black swell, hardly enough of a thing, it seems, to measure, but Kalbfleisch is a trained professional in whose expertise she is putting her trust. And her money—so much money that the numbers seem virtual, mythical, details from a story about money rather than money anyone actually has. The biographer, for example, does not have it. She's using credit cards.

The doctor moves to the ovaries, shoving and tilting the wand until he gets an angle he likes. "Here's the right side. Nice bunch of follicles..." The eggs themselves are too small to be seen, even with magnification, but their sacs—black holes on the grayish screen—can be counted.

"Keep our fingers crossed," says Kalbfleisch, easing the wand back out.

Doctor, is my bunch actually nice?

He rolls away from her crotch and pulls off his gloves. "For the past several cycles"—looking at her chart, not at her—"you've been taking Clomid to support ovulation."

This she does not need to be told.

"Unfortunately Clomid also causes the uterine lining to shrink, so we advise patients not to take it for long stretches of time. You've already done a long stretch."

Wait, what?

She should have looked it up herself.

"So for this round we need to try a different protocol. Another medication that's been known to improve the odds in some elderly pregravid cases."

"Elderly?"

"Just a clinical term." He doesn't glance up from the prescription he's writing. "She'll explain the medication and we'll see you back here on day nine." He hands the file to the nurse, stands, and makes an adjustment to his leather crotch before striding out.

Asshole, in Faroese: *reyvarhol.*

Crabby says, "So you need to fill this today and start taking it tomorrow morning, on an empty stomach. Every morning for ten days. While you're on it, you might notice a foul odor from the discharge from your vagina."

"Great," says the biographer.

"Some women say the smell is quite, um, surprising," she goes on. "Even actually disturbing. But whatever you do, don't douche. That'll introduce chemicals into the canal that if they make their way through the cervix can, you know, compromise the pH of the uterine cavity."

The biographer has never douched in her life, nor does she know anyone who has.

"Questions?" says the nurse.

"What does"—she squints at the prescription—"Ovutran do?"

"It supports ovulation."

"How, though?"

"You'd have to ask the doctor."

She is submitting her area to all kinds of invasion without understanding a fraction of what's being done to it. This seems, suddenly, terrible. How can you raise a child alone if you don't even find out what they're doing to your area?

"I'd like to ask him now," she says.

"He's already with another patient. Best thing to do is call the office."

"But I'm here *in* the office. Can't he—or is there someone else who—"

"Sorry, it's an extra-busy day. Halloween and all."

"Why does Halloween make it busier?"

"It's a holiday."

"Not a *national* holiday. Banks are open and the mail is delivered."

"You will need," says Crabby slowly, carefully, "to call the office."

The biographer cried the first time it failed. She was waiting in line to buy floss, having pledged to improve her dental hygiene now that she was going to be a parent, and her phone rang: one of the nurses, "I'm sorry, sweetie, but your test was negative," the biographer saying thank you, okay, thank you and hitting END before the tears started. Despite the statistics and Kalbfleisch's "This doesn't work for everyone," the biographer had thought it would be easy. Squirt in millions of sperm from a nineteen-year-old biology major, precisely timed to be there waiting when the egg flies out; sperm and egg collide in the warm tunnel—how could fertilization *not* happen? *Don't be stupid anymore,* she wrote in her notebook, under *Immediate action required.*

* * *

She drives west on Highway 22 into dark hills dense with hemlock, fir, and spruce. Oregon has the best trees in America, soaring and shaggy winged, alpine sinister. Her tree gratitude mutes her doctor resentment. Two hours from his office, her car crests the cliff road and the church steeple juts into view. The rest of town follows, hunched in rucked hills sloping to the water. Smoke coils from the pub chimney. Fishing nets pile on the shore. In Newville you can watch the sea eat the ground, over and over, unstopping. Millions of abyssal thalassic acres. The sea does not ask permission or wait for instruction. It doesn't suffer from not knowing what on earth, exactly, it is meant to do. Today its walls are high, white lather torn, crashing hard at the sea stacks. "Angry sea," people say, but to the biographer the ascribing of human feeling to a body so inhumanly itself is wrong. The water heaves up for reasons they don't have names for.

Central Coast Regional H.S. seeks history teacher (U.S./World). Bachelor's degree required. Location: Newville, Oregon, fishing village on quiet ocean harbor, migrating whales. Ivy League–educated principal is committed to creating dynamic, innovative learning environment.

The biographer applied because of *quiet ocean harbor* and no mention of teaching experience. Her brief interview consisted of the principal, Mr. Fivey, plot-summarizing his favorite seafaring novels and mentioning twice the name of the college he had gone to. He said she could do the teacher-certification course over two summers. For seven years she has lived in the lee of fog-smoked evergreen mountains, thousand-foot cliffs plunging straight down to the sea. It rains and rains and rains. Log trucks stall traffic on the cliff road, locals catch fish or make things for tourists, the pub hangs a list of old shipwrecks, the tsunami siren is tested monthly, and students learn to say "miss" as if they were servants.

She starts class by following her daily plan, but when she sees chins mashing into fists, she decides to abandon it. Tenth-grade global history, the world in forty weeks, with a foolish textbook she is contractually obliged to use, can't be stood without detours. These kids, after all, have not been lost yet. Staring up at her, jaws rimmed with baby fat, they are perched on the brink of not giving a shit. They still give a shit, but not, most of them, for long. She instructs them to close their books, which they are happy to do. They watch her with a new stillness. They will be told a story, can be children again, of whom nothing is asked.

"Boadicea was queen of a Celtic tribe called the Iceni in what is now Norfolk, England. The Romans had invaded a while back and were ruling the land. Her husband died and left his fortune to her and their daughters, but the Romans ignored his will, took the fortune, flogged Boadicea, and raped the daughters."

One kid: "What's 'flog'?"

Another: "Beat the frock out of."

"The Romans had screwed her royally"—somebody laughs softly at this, for which the biographer is grateful—"and in 61 CE she led her people in rebellion. The Iceni fought hard. They forced the Romans all the way back to London. But bear in mind that the Roman soldiers had lots of incentive to win, because if they didn't, they could expect to be cooked on skewers and/or boiled to death, after seeing their own intestines being pulled out of their bodies."

"That rules," says a boy.

"Eventually the Roman forces were too much for the Iceni. Boadicea either poisoned herself to avoid capture or got sick; either way, she died. The win column isn't the point. The point is..." She stops, aware of twenty-four little gazes.

Into the silence the soft laugher ventures: "Don't frock with a woman?"

They like this. They like slogans.

"Well," the biographer says, "*sort* of. But more than that. We also have to consider—"

The bell.

A burst of scraping and sliding, bodies glad to go. "Bye, miss!" "Have a good day, miss."

The soft laugher, Mattie Quarles, idles near the biographer's desk. "So is that where the word 'bodacious' comes from?"

"I wish I could say yes," says the biographer, "but 'bodacious' originated in the nineteenth century, I think. Mix of 'bold' and 'audacious.' Good instinct, though!"

"Thanks, miss."

"You really don't need to call me that," says the biographer for the seven thousandth time.

After school she stops at the Acme, grocery and hardware and drugstore combined. The pharmacist's assistant is a boy—now a young man—she taught in her first year at Central Coast, and she hates the moment each month when he hands her the white bag with the little orange bottle. *I know what this is for,* his eyes say. Even if his eyes don't actually say that, it's hard to look at him. She brings other items to the counter (unsalted peanuts, Q-tips) as if somehow to disguise the fertility medication. The biographer can't recall his name but remembers admiring, in class, seven years ago, his long black lashes—they always looked a little wet.

Waiting on the hard little plastic chair, under elevator music and fluorescent glare, the biographer takes out her notebook. Everything in this notebook must be in list form, and any list is eligible. *Items for next food shop. Kalbfleisch's necktie designs. Countries with most lighthouses per capita.*

She starts a new one: *Accusations from the world.*

1. You're too old.
2. If you can't have a child the natural way, you shouldn't have one at all.
3. Every child needs two parents.
4. Children raised by single mothers are more liable to rape/murder/drug-take/score low on standardized tests.
5. You're too old.

6. You should've thought of this earlier.
7. You're selfish.
8. You're doing something unnatural.
9. How is that child going to feel when she finds out her father is an anonymous masturbator?
10. Your body is a grizzled husk.
11. You're too old, sad spinster!
12. Are you only doing this because you're lonely?

"Miss? Prescription's ready."

"Thank you." She signs the screen on the counter. "How's your day been?"

Lashes turns up his palms at the ceiling.

"If it makes you feel any better," says the biographer, "this medication is going to make me have a foul-smelling vaginal discharge."

"At least it's for a good cause."

She clears her throat.

"That'll be one hundred fifty-seven dollars and sixty-three cents," he adds.

"Pardon me?"

"I'm really sorry."

"A hundred and fifty-seven dollars? For ten pills?"

"Your insurance doesn't cover it."

"Why the eff not?"

Lashes shakes his head. "I wish I could, like, slip it to you, but they've got cameras on every inch of this bitch."

The polar explorer Eivør Mínervudottír spent many hours, as a child, in the sea-washed lighthouse whose keeper was her uncle.

She knew not to talk while he was making entries in the record book.

Never to strike a match unsupervised.

Red sky at night, sailor's delight.

To keep her head low in the lantern room.

To pee in the pot and leave it, and if she did caca, to wrap it in fish paper for the garbage box.

THE MENDER

From the halt hen two eggs come down, one cracked, one sound. "Thank you," the mender tells the hen, a Dark Brahma with a red wattle and brindled feathers. Because she limps badly—is not one of the winners—this hen is the mender's favorite. A daily happiness to feed her, save her from foxes and rain.

Sound egg in her pocket, she pours the goats' grain. Hans and Pinka are out rambling but will be home soon. They know she can't protect them if they ramble too far. Three shingles have come off the goat-shed roof; she needs nails. Under the shed there used to sleep a varying hare. Brown in summer, white in winter. He hated carrots and loved apples, whose seeds, poisonous to rabbits, the mender made sure to remove. The hare was so cuddly she didn't care that he stole alfalfa from the goats or strewed poo pellets on her bed when she let him inside. One morning she found his body ripped open, a sack of furry blood. Rage poured up her throat at the fox or coyote, the bobcat, *you took him,* but they were only feeding themselves, *you shouldn't have took him,* prey is scarce in winter, *but he was mine.* She cried while digging. Laid the hare beside her aunt's old cat, two small graves under the madrone.

In the cabin the mender stirs the egg with vinegar and shepherd's purse for the client who's coming later, an over-bleeder. The drink will staunch her clotty, aching flow. She's got no job and no insurance. *I can pay you with batteries,* her note said. Vinegary egg screwed tight in a glass jar and tucked into the mini fridge, beside a foil-wrapped wedge of cheddar. The mender wants the cheese right now, this minute, but cheese is only for Fridays. Black licorice nibs are for Sundays.

* * *

She mostly eats from the forest. Watercress and bitter cress, dandelion, plantain. Glasswort and chickweed. Bear grass, delicious when grilled. Burdock root to mash and fry. Miner's lettuce and stinging nettle and, in small quantities, ghost pipe. (She loves the white stalks boiled with lemon and salt, but too much ghost pipe can kill you.) And she gleans from orchards and fields: hazelnuts, apples, cranberries, pears. If she could live off the land alone, without person-made things, she would. She hasn't figured out how yet, but that doesn't mean she won't. Show them how Percivals do.

Her mother was a Percival. Her aunt was a Percival. The mender has been a Percival since age six, when her mother left her father. Which was because her father went away most Friday afternoons and didn't come back until Monday and never said why. "A woman wants to know why," said the mender's mother. "At least give me that, fuckermo. Names and places! Ages and occupations!" They drove west across Oregon's high desert, over the Cascade Mountains, mother smoking and daughter spitting out the window, to the coast, where the mender's aunt ran a shop that sold candles, runes, and tarot packs. On the first night, the mender asked what that noise was and learned it was the ocean. "But when does it stop?" "Never," said her aunt. "It's perpetual, though impermanent." And the mender's mother said, "Pretentious much?"

The mender would take pretentious any day over high.

She lies naked with the cat by the stove's heat, hard steady rain on the roof and the woods black and the foxes quiet, owlets asleep in their nest box. Malky leaps from her lap, paws at the door. "You want to get soaked, little fuckermo?" Gold-splashed eyes watch her solemnly. Gray flanks tremble. "You have a girlfriend you need to meet?" She shakes off the blanket and opens the door, and he flashes out.

* * *

Whenever Lola came over, Malky hid; she thought the mender lived in the cabin alone. "Don't you get frightened," said Lola, "all the way up here in the middle of nothing?"

Silly bitch, trees are not nothing. Nor are cats, goats, chickens, owls, foxes, bobcats, black-tailed deer, long-eared bats, red-tailed hawks, dark-eyed juncos, bald-faced hornets, varying hares, mourning cloak butterflies, black vine weevils, and souls fled from their mortal casings.

Alone *human*-wise.

She hasn't heard from Lola since that day of the shouting. No notes left in her mailbox at the P.O., no visits. It was more than shouting. A fight. Lola, in her adorable green dress, was fighting. The mender was not. The mender barely said a word.

Past noon, but the goats aren't home yet. Cramp of worry. Last year they wrecked a campsite near the trail. Not their fault: some dumb tourist left food all over the woods. When the mender found them, the guy was pointing a rifle at Hans. "You better keep them on your property from here on out," he said, "because I love goat stew."

In Europe they once held trials for misbehaving animals. Wasn't just the witches they hanged. A pig was sent to the gallows for eating a child's face, a mule roasted alive for having been penetrated by its human master. For the unnatural act of laying an egg, a rooster was burned at the stake. Bees found guilty of stinging a man to death were suffocated in the hive, their honey destroyed, lest murder honey infect the mouths that ate it.

She with murder honey on her teeth shall bleed salt from where two curves of thigh skin meet. Tasting honey from the body of a bee with devil-face shall start this salty blood. Faces of bees who have done murder do resemble those of starving dogs, whose eyes grow more human looking as they starve. *Apis mellifera, Apis diabolus.* If a town be swarmed by bees with devil-face, and those bees do drip honey into open mouths, the body of a woman with honey tooth, bleeding thigh salt, shall be lashed to whatever stake will hold her. The bee swarm shall be gathered in a barrel and dumped upon the fire that eats her. The honey teeth do catch flame first, sparks of blue at the white before the red tongue catches too, and the lips. Bees' bodies when burning do smell of hot marrow; the odor makes onlookers vomit, yet still they look on.

You needed a boat to reach the lighthouse, a quarter mile from shore, and if a storm hit, you slept overnight in a reindeer bag on the watch room's slanted floor.

During storms the polar explorer stood on the lantern gallery, holding its rail as if her life depended on it, because her life did. She loved any circumstance in which survival was not assured. The threat of being swept over the rail woke her from the ~~lethargy~~ sluggery she felt at home chopping rhubarb, cracking puffin eggs, peeling the skin off dead sheep.

THE DAUGHTER

Grew up in a city born of the terror of the vastness of space, where the streets lie tight in a grid. The men who built Salem, Oregon, were white Methodist missionaries who followed white fur-trade trappers to the Pacific Northwest, and the missionaries were less excited than the trappers by the wildness foaming in every direction. They laid their town in a valley that had been fished, harvested, and winter-camped for centuries by the Kalapuya people, who, in the 1850s, were forced onto reservations by the U.S. government. In the stolen valley the whites huddled and crouched, made everything smaller. Downtown Salem is a box of streets Britishly named: Church and Cottage and Market, Summer and Winter and East.

The daughter knew every tidy inch of her city neighborhood. She is still learning the inches in Newville, where humans are less, nature is more.

She stands in the lantern room of the Gunakadeit Lighthouse, north of town, where she has come after school with the person she hopes to officially call her boyfriend. From here you can see massive cliffs soaring up from the ocean, rust veined, green mossed; giant pines gathering like soldiers along their rim; goblin trees jutting slant from the rock face. You can see silver-white lather smashing at the cliffs' ankles. The harbor and its moored boats and the ocean beyond, a shirred blue prairie stretching to the horizon, cut by bars of green. Far from shore: a black fin.

"Boring up here," says Ephraim.

Look at the black fin! she wants to say. *The goblin trees!*

She says, "Yeah," and touches his jaw, specked with new beard. They kiss for a while. She loves it except for the tongue thrusts.

Does the fin belong to a shark? Could it belong to a whale?

She draws back from Ephraim to look at the sea.

"What?"

"Nothing."

Gone.

"Wanna bounce?" he says.

They race down the spiral staircase, boot soles ringing on the stone, and climb into the backseat of his car.

"I think I saw a gray whale. Did you—?"

"Nope," says Ephraim. "But did you know *blue* whales have the biggest cocks of any animal? Eight to ten feet."

"The dinosaurs' were bigger than that."

"Bullshit."

"No, my dad's got this book—" She stops: Ephraim has no father. The daughter's father, though annoying, loves her more than all the world's gold. "Anyway," she says, "here's one: A skeleton asks another skeleton, 'Do you want to hear a joke?' Second skeleton says, 'Only if it's humerus.' "

"Why is that funny?"

"Because—'humerus'? The arm bone?"

"That's a little-kid joke."

Her mom's favorite pun. It's not her fault he didn't know what a humerus was.

"No more *talking*." He goes to kiss her but she dodges, bites his shoulder through the cotton long sleeve, trying to break the skin but also not to. He gets her underpants down so fast it feels professional. Her jeans are already flung to some corner of the car, maybe on the steering wheel, maybe under the front seat, his jeans too, his hat.

She reaches for his penis and circles her palm around the head, like she's polishing.

"Not like that—" Ephraim moves her hand to grip the shaft. Up down up down up down. "Like *that*."

He spits on his hand and wets his penis, guides it into her vagina. He shoves back and forth. It feels okay but not great, definitely not as great as they say it should feel, and it doesn't help that the back of her head keeps slamming against the door handle, but the daughter has also read that it takes some time to get good at sex and to like it, especially for the girl. He has an orgasm with the same jittery moan she found weird at first but is getting used to, and she is relieved that her head has stopped being slammed against the door handle, so she smiles; and Ephraim smiles too; and she flinches at the sticky milk dribbling out of her.

The explorer went to the lighthouse whenever allowed, at first, and once she could handle the boat alone, even when forbidden. Her uncle Bjartur felt bad that her father was dead and so let her come, although she bothered him with her questions; he was a lighthouse keeper, God knows, because he preferred his own company, but this little one, this Eivør, youngest of his favorite sister, he could find it in his chewed heart to let her run up the spiral stairs and dig through his trunk of ships' debris and on drenched tiptoes watch the weather.

THE WIFE

Between town and home is a long twist of road that hugs the cliffside, climbing and dipping and climbing again.

At the sharpest bend, whose guardrail is measly, the wife's jaw tenses.

What if she took her hands off the wheel and let them go?

The car would jump along the top branches of the shore pines, tearing a fine green wake; flip once before building speed; fly past the rocks and into the water and down forever and—

After the bend, she unclenches.

Almost home.

Second time this week she has pictured it.

Soon as the groceries are in, she'll give herself a few minutes upstairs. It won't kill them to watch a screen.

Why did she buy the grass-fed beef? Six dollars more per pound.

Second time this week.

They say grass-fed has the best fats.

Which might be entirely common. Maybe everyone pictures it, maybe not as often as twice a week but—

A little animal is struggling across the road. Dark, about a foot long.

Possum? Porcupine? Trying to cross.

Maybe it's even healthy to picture it.

Closer: burnt black, scorched to rubber.

Shivering.

Already dead, still trying.

What burned it? Or who?

"You're making us crash!"—from the backseat.

"We're not crashing," says the wife. Her foot is capable and steadfast. They will never crash with her foot on the brake.

Who burned this animal?

Convulsing, trembling, already so dead. Fur singed off. Skin black rubber.

Who burned you?

Closer: it's a black plastic bag.

But she can't unsee the shivering thing, burnt and dead and trying.

At the house: unbuckle, untangle, lift, carry, set down.

Unpack, put away.

Peel string cheese.

Distribute string cheese.

Place Bex and John in front of approved cartoon.

Upstairs, the wife closes the sewing-room door. Sits cross-legged on the bed. Fixes her stare on the scuffed white wall.

They are yipping and pipping, her two. They are rolling and polling and slapping and papping, rompling with little fists and heels on the bald carpet.

They are hers, but she can't get inside them.

They can't get back inside her.

They are hurling their fists—Bex fistier, but John brave.

Why did they name him John? Not a family name and almost as dull as the wife's own. Bex had said, "I'm going to call the baby Yarnjee."

Is John brave, or foolish?—he squirms willingly while his sister punches. The wife doesn't say *No hitting* because she doesn't want them to stop, she wants them to get tired.

She remembers why John: because everyone can spell and say it. John because his father hates correcting butchered English pronunciations of his own name. The errors of clerks. John is sometimes *Jean-voyage;* and Ro calls him Pliny the Younger.

In the past hour, the kids have

Rolled and polled.

Eaten leftover popcorn stirred into lemon yogurt.

Asked the wife if they could watch more TV.

Been told no.

Slooped and chooped.

Tipped over the standing lamp.

Broken an eyelash.

Asked the wife why her anus is out in space when it should be in her butt.

Slapped and papped.

Asked the wife what's for dinner.

Been told spaghetti.

Asked the wife what does she think is the best kind of sauce for butt pasta.

The grass-fed beef grows blood in a plastic bag. Does contact with the plastic cancel out its grass-fedness? She shouldn't waste expensive meat in spaghetti sauce. Marinate it tonight? There's a jar of store sauce in the—

"Take your finger out of his nose."

"But he likes it," says Bex.

And broccoli. Those par-baked dinner rolls are delicious, but she isn't going to serve bread with pasta.

Sea-salt-almond chocolate bar stowed in the kitchen drawer, under the maps, please still be there, please still be there.

"Do you like having your sister's finger stuck up your nose?"

John smiles, ducks, and nods.

"When the fuck is dinner?"

"What?"

Bex knows her crime; she eyes the wife with a cunning frown. "I mean when the gosh."

"You said something else. Do you even know what it means?"

"It's bad," says Bex.

"Does Mattie ever say that word?"

"Um . . ."

Which way will her girl's lie go: protect or incriminate?

"I think maybe yes," says Bex dolefully.

Bex loves Mattie, who is the good babysitter, much preferred over Mrs. Costello, the mean. The girl when she lies looks a lot like her father. The hard-sunk eyes the wife once found beguiling are not eyes she would wish upon her daughter. Bex's will have purplish circles before long.

But who cares what the girl looks like, if she is happy?

The world will care.

"To answer your question, dinner is whenever I want it to be."

"When will you want it to be?"

"Don't know," says the wife. "Maybe we just won't have dinner tonight."

Sea-salt-almond. Chocolate. Bar.

Bex frowns again, not cunningly.

The wife kneels on the rug and pulls their bodies against her body, squeezes, nuzzles. "Oh, sprites, don't worry, of course we'll have dinner. I was joking."

"Sometimes you do such bad jokes."

"It's true. I'm sorry. I predict that dinner will happen at six fifteen p.m., Pacific standard time. I predict that it will consist of spaghetti with tomato sauce and broccoli. So what species of sprite are you today?"

John says, "Water."

Bex says, "Wood."

Today's date is marked on the kitchen calendar with a small black *A*. Which stands for "ask."

Ask him again.

From the bay window, whose frame flakes with old paint possibly brimming with lead—she keeps forgetting to arrange to have the kids tested—the wife watches her husband trudge up the drive on short legs in jeans that are too tight, too young for him. He has a horror of dad pants and insists on dressing as he did at nineteen. His messenger bag bangs against one skinny thigh.

"He's home," she calls.

The kids race to greet him. This is a moment she used to love to picture, man home from work and children welcoming him, a perfect moment because it has no past or future—does not care where the man came from or what will happen after he is greeted, cares only for the joyful collision, the *Daddy you're here*.

"Fee fi fo fon, *je sens le sang* of two white middle-class Québécois-American children!" Her sprites scramble all over him. "A'right, a'right, settle down, eh," but he is contented, with John flung over his shoulder and Bex pulling open the satchel to check for vending-machine snacks. She's got his salt tooth. Did she get everything from him? What is in her of the wife?

The nose. She escaped Didier's nose.

"Hi, *meuf,*" he says, squatting to set John on the floor.

"How was the day?"

"Usual hell. Actually, not usual. Music teacher got laid off."

Good.

"Hello, hell!" says Bex.

"We don't say 'hell,'" says the wife.

I'm glad she's gone.

"Daddy—"

"I meant 'heifer,'" says Didier.

"Kids, I want those blocks off the floor. Somebody could trip. Now! But I thought everyone loved the music teacher."

"Budget crisis."

"You mean they're not replacing her?"

He shrugs.

"So there won't be any music classes at all?"

"I must pee."

When he emerges from the bathroom, she is leaning on the banister, listening to Bex boss John into doing all the block gathering.

"We should get a cleaner," says Didier, for the third time this month. "I just counted the number of pubic hairs on the toilet rim."

And soap heel crusted to the sink.

Black dust on the baseboards.

Soft yellow hair balls in every corner.

Sea-salt-almond chocolate bar in the drawer.

"We can't afford one," she says, "unless we stop using Mrs. Costello, and I'm not giving up those eight hours." She looks into his blue-gray eyes, level with hers. She has often wished that Didier were taller. Is her wishing the product of socialization or an evolutionary adaptation from the days when being able to reach more food on a tree was a life-or-death advantage?

"Well," he says, "*somebody* needs to start doing some cleaning. It's like a bus station in there."

She won't be asking him tonight.

She will write the *A* again, on a different day.

"There were twelve, by the way," he says. "I know you have stuff to do, I'm not saying you don't, but could you maybe wash the toilet once in a while? Twelve hairs."

Red sky at morning, sailor take warning.

THE BIOGRAPHER

Can't see the ocean from her apartment, but she can hear it. Most days between five and six thirty a.m. she sits in the kitchen listening to the waves and working on her study of Eivør Mínervudottír, a nineteenth-century polar hydrologist whose trailblazing research on pack ice was published under a male acquaintance's name. There is no book on Mínervudottír, only passing mentions in other books. The biographer has a mass of notes by now, an outline, some paragraphs. A skein draft—more holes than words. On the kitchen wall she's taped a photo of the shelf in the Salem bookstore where her book will live. The photo reminds her that she is going to finish it.

She opens Mínervudottír's journal, translated from the Danish. *I admit to fearing the attack of a sea bear; and my fingers hurt all the time.* A woman long dead coming to life. But today, staring at the journal, the biographer can't think. Her brain is soapy and throbbing from the new ovary medicine.

She sits in her car, radio on, throat shivering with hints of vomit, until she's late enough for school not to care that her eye–foot–brake reaction time is slowed by the Ovutran. The roads have guardrails. Her forehead pulses hard. She sees a black lace throw itself across the windshield, and blinks it away.

Two years ago the United States Congress ratified the Personhood Amendment, which gives the constitutional right to life, liberty, and property to a fertilized egg at the moment of conception. Abortion is now illegal in all fifty states. Abortion providers can be charged with second-degree murder, abortion seekers with conspiracy to commit murder. In vitro fertilization, too, is federally banned, because the amendment outlaws the transfer of embryos from laboratory to uterus. (The embryos can't give their consent to be moved.)

She was just quietly teaching history when it happened. Woke up one morning to a president-elect she hadn't voted for. This man thought women who miscarried should pay for funerals for the fetal tissue and thought a lab technician who accidentally dropped an embryo during in vitro transfer was guilty of manslaughter. She had heard there was glee on the lawns of her father's Orlando retirement village. Marching in the streets of Portland. In Newville: brackish calm.

Short of sex with some man she wouldn't otherwise want to have sex with, Ovutran and lube-glopped vaginal wands and Dr. Kalbfleisch's golden fingers is the only biological route left. Intrauterine insemination. At her age, not much better than a turkey baster.

She was placed on the adoption wait-list three years ago. In her parent profile she earnestly and meticulously described her job, her apartment, her favorite books, her parents, her brother (drug addiction omitted), and the fierce beauty of Newville. She uploaded a photograph that made her look friendly but responsible, fun loving but stable, easygoing but upper middle class. The coral-pink cardigan she bought to wear in this photo she later threw into the clothing donation bin outside the church.

She was warned, yes, at the outset: birth mothers tend to choose married straight couples, especially if the couple is white. But not all birth mothers choose this way. Anything could happen, she was told. The fact that she was willing to take an older child or a child who needed special care meant the odds were in her favor.

She assumed it would take a while but that it would, eventually, happen.

She thought a foster placement, at least, would come through; and if things went well, that could lead to adoption.

Then the new president moved into the White House.

The Personhood Amendment happened.

One of the ripples in its wake: Public Law 116-72.

On January fifteenth—in less than three months—this law, also known as Every Child Needs Two, takes effect. Its mission: *to restore dignity, strength, and prosperity to American families.* Unmarried persons will be legally prohibited from adopting children. In addition to valid marriage licenses, all adoptions will require approval through a federally regulated agency, rendering private transactions criminal.

Woozy with Ovutran, inching up the steps of Central Coast Regional, the biographer recalls her high school career on the varsity track team. "Keep your legs, Stephens!" the coach would yell when her muscles were about to give out.

She informs the tenth-graders they must scrub their essay drafts clean of the phrase *History tells us*. "A stale rhetorical tic. Means nothing."

"But it does," says Mattie. "History is telling us not to repeat its mistakes."

"We might reach that conclusion from *studying* the past, but history is a concept; it isn't talking to us."

Mattie's cheeks—cold white, blue veined—go red. Not used to correction, she's easily shamed.

Ash raises her hand. "What happened to your arm, miss?"

"What? Oh." The biographer's sleeve is pushed way up above the elbow. She yanks it down. "I gave blood."

"It looks like you gave, like, gallons." Ash rubs her piglet nose. "You should sue the blood bank for defamation."

"Dis*figure*ment," says Mattie.

"You got straight disfigured, miss."

By noon the cloudy throb behind her eyebrows has dialed itself back. In the teachers' lounge she eats maize puffs and watches the French teacher fork pink thumbs out of a Good Ship Chinese takeout box.

"Certain kinds of shrimp produce light," she tells him. "They're like torches bobbing in the water."

How can you raise a child alone when all you're having for lunch is vending-machine maize puffs?

He grunts and chews. "Not these shrimp."

Didier has no particular interest in French but can speak it, the tongue of his Montreal childhood, in his sleep. Like being a teacher of walking or sitting. For this predicament he blames his wife. During his first conversation with the biographer, years ago, over crackers and tube cheese in the lounge, he explained: "She says to me, 'Aside from cooking you have no skills, but at least you can do this, can't you?'—so *ici. Je. Suis.*" The biographer then imagined Susan Korsmo as a huge white crow, shading Didier's life with her great wing.

"Shrimp are sky-high in cholesterol," says Penny, the head English teacher, deseeding grapes at the table.

"This room is where my joy dies," says Didier.

"Boo hoo. Ro, you need nourishment. Here's a banana."

"That's Mr. Fivey's," says the biographer.

"How can anyone be sure?"

"He wrote his name on it."

"Fivey will survive the loss of one fruit," says Penny.

"Ooosh." The biographer holds her temples.

"You okay?"

Thudding back down into the chair: "I just got up too fast."

The PA system sizzles to life, coughs twice. "Attention students and teachers. Attention. This is an emergency announcement."

"Please be a fire drill," says Didier.

"Let us all keep Principal Fivey in our thoughts today. His wife has been admitted to the hospital in critical condition. Principal Fivey will be away from campus until further notice."

"Should she be telling everyone this?" says the biographer.

"I repeat," says the office manager, "Mrs. Fivey is in critical condition at Umpqua General."

"Room number?" yells Didier at the wall-mounted speaker.

The principal's wife always comes to Christmas assembly in skintight cocktail dresses. And every Christmas Didier says: "Mrs. Fivey's gittin sixy."

* * *

The biographer drives home to lie on the floor in her underwear.

Her father is calling again. It has been days—weeks?—since she answered.

"How's Florida?"

"I am curious to know your plans for Christmas."

"Months away, Dad."

"But you'll want to book the flight soon. Fares are going to explode. When does school let out?"

"I don't know, the twenty-third?"

"That close to Christmas? Jesus."

"I'll let you know, okay?"

"Any plans for the weekend?"

"Susan and Didier invited me to dinner. You?"

"Might drop by the community center to watch the human rutabagas gum their feed. Unless my back flares up."

"What did the acupuncturist say?"

"*That* was a mistake I won't make twice."

"It works for a lot of people, Dad."

"It's goddamn voodoo. Will you be bringing a date to your friends' dinner?"

"Nope," says the biographer, steeling herself for his next sentence, her face stiff with sadness that he can't help himself.

"About time you found someone, don't you think?"

"I'm fine, Dad."

"Well, I *worry,* kiddo. Don't like the idea of you being all alone."

She could trot out the usual list ("I've got friends, neighbors, colleagues, people from meditation group"), but her okayness with being by herself—ordinary, unheroic okayness—does not need to justify itself to her father. The feeling is hers. She can simply feel okay and not explain it, or apologize for it, or concoct arguments against the argument that she doesn't *truly* feel content and is deluding herself in self-protection.

"Well, Dad," she says, "you're alone too."

Any reference to her mother's death can be relied on to shut him up.

There was Usman for six months in college. Victor for a year in Minneapolis. Liaisons now and again. She is not a long-term person. She likes her own company. Nevertheless, before her first insemination, the biographer forced herself to consult online dating sites. She browsed and bared her teeth. She browsed and felt chest-flatteningly depressed. One night she really did try. Picked the least Christian site and started typing.

What are your three best qualities?

1. Independence
2. Punctuality
3.

Best book you recently read?

Proceedings of the "Proteus" Court of Inquiry on the Greely Relief Expedition of 1883

What fascinates you?

1. How cold stops water
2. Patterns ice makes on the fur of a dead sled dog
3. The fact that Eivør Mínervudottír lost two of her fingers to frostbite

But the biographer didn't feel like telling anyone that. Delete, delete, delete. She could say, at least, she had tried. The next day she called for an appointment at a reproductive-medicine clinic in Salem.

Her therapist thought she was moving fast. "You only recently decided to do this," he said, "and already you've chosen a donor?"

Oh, therapist, if only you knew how quickly a donor can be chosen!

You turn on your computer. You click boxes for race, eye color, education, height. A list appears. You read some profiles. You hit PURCHASE.

A woman on the Choosing Single Motherhood discussion board wrote, *I spent more time dead-heading my roses than picking a donor.*

But, as the biographer explained to her therapist, she did *not* choose quickly. She pored. She strained. She sat for hours at her kitchen table, staring at profiles. These men had written essays. Named personal strengths. Recalled moments of childhood jubilance and described favorite traits of grandparents. (For one hundred dollars per ejaculation, they were happy to discuss their grandparents.)

She took notes on dozens and dozens—

Pros:

1. Calls himself "avid reader"
2. "Great cheekbones" (staff)
3. Enjoys "mental challenges and riddles"
4. To future child: "I look forward to hearing from you in eighteen years"

Cons:

1. Handwriting very bad
2. Commercial real-estate appraiser
3. Of own personality: "I'm not too complicated"

—then narrowed it to two. Donor 5546 was a fitness trainer described by sperm-bank staff as "handsome and captivating." Donor 3811 was a biology major with well-written essay answers; the affectionate way he described his aunts made the biographer like him; but what if he wasn't as handsome as the first? Both of their health histories were perfect, or so they claimed. Was the biographer so shallow as to be swayed by handsomeness? But who wants an ugly donor? But 3811 was not necessarily ugly. But was ugly even a problem? What she wanted was good health and a good brain. Donor 5546 claimed to be bursting with health, but she wasn't sure about his brain.

So she bought vials of both. She wouldn't stumble upon 9072, the just-right third, for another couple of months.

"Do you feel undeserving of a romantic partner?" asked the therapist.

"No," said the biographer.

"Are you pessimistic about finding a partner?"

"I don't necessarily *want* a partner."

"Might that attitude be a form of self-protection?"

"You mean am I deluding myself?"

"That's another way to put it."

"If I say yes, then I'm not deluded. And if I say no, it's further evidence of delusion."

"We need to end there," said the therapist.

The polar explorer liked to stand on the turf roof of the two-room cottage and think of her feet being precisely above the head of her mother, who was stirring or cutting or pounding; and how many inches of grass and soil lay between them; and how she was *above*, her mother *below*, reversing the order, flipping the world, with nobody able to tell her it couldn't be flipped.

Then she would be called in to help boil the puffin.

THE MENDER

Walks home from the library the long way, past the school. The three o'clock bell is big over the harbor, flakes of bronze dropping slow to the water, bell in her mouth, bell in her scabbard. The blue school doors open: boots and scarves and shouts. Part-hid behind a bitter cherry, the mender waits. A string of Aristotle's lanterns—the spiky teeth of sea urchins—hangs on her neck as protection. Last week she stood here an hour until the last child came out and the doors stopped; but the girl she was waiting for did not appear.

The mender herself performed quite poorly at Central Coast Regional, which she left, fifteen years ago, without a diploma. *Fails to meet minimum standards. Acts deliberately uninterested in what goes on in class.* Oh bitches, it was no act. Her brain wasn't even in the room. In class the mender made sure never to talk except to fled souls or a bulb moon blown down into the stomach of the ocean. Her brain cells thrumming in their helmet went off to the forest road, where lay mole mother torn open by owl, her spent babies like red seeds; or to frondlets of sea lawn dragged into mazes by crabs. Her body stayed in the room, but her brain didn't.

They come through the blue doors, little and big, bundled for weather: fishermen's children, shopkeepers' children, waitresses' children. Girls with white cheek paint and black eyelids and crimson lips who are not the girl she is waiting for. The girl she is waiting for doesn't wear makeup, at least not that the mender can tell. She smells smoke. Her aunt Temple's brand. Is Temple close? Has Temple come—? Stupid, stupid, they don't come back. It's the blond weasel, who teaches at the school. His hair and his teeth go in all directions. She has seen him with his daughter and son on the cliff path, pointing at the water.

"Looking for someone?" he says.

She gives him the side-eye.

The blond weasel sucks and blows. "Seems like you are."

"No," she says, and goes.

She shouldn't be seen trying to see the girl. People already think she's unhinged, a forest weirdo, a witch. She is younger than the broomy witches people know from TV, but that doesn't stop them whispering.

Up the cobbly lane to the cliff path. Then back and back into the trees. A Douglas-fir was felled on a hillside, sawn into logs, truck-hauled to a mill. Boards were cut and trimmed, planed true. A man bought the boards and notched them together to make a cabin. Two rooms and a toilet closet. Wood stove. Double sink. A cupboard north and a cupboard south. The lamps and mini fridge run on batteries. Showerhead outside, nailed up. Wintertime she sponge bathes or stinks. The goat shed and chicken coop sit behind the cabin on either side of a dead black hawthorn, lightning split. In its cleft the mender has built nest boxes for the owls, swallows, marbled murrelets, golden-crowned kinglets.

She ought to be more careful. Can't let people see her watching. The yellow-haired, tumble-toothed weasel looked suspicious. It is no crime to watch someone, but humans like to name *these* things normal and *those* things peculiar.

Clementine comes to the mender's door with a picnic cooler and a pain. Her last complaint was vicious burning when she peed; today's pain is new. "Pants off and lie down," says the mender, and Clementine unzips herself, kicks away the jeans. Her thighs are white and very soft, underwear the size of a shoelace. She plumps back on the mender's bed and opens her knees.

A vesicle on Clementine's south lip, the inner fold, white-red in the browny pink: how much does it hurt?

"Oh God, a lot. Sometimes at work I'm like 'Eeesh!' and they think I'm—Anyway, do I have syphilis?"

"No. Plain old cunt wart."

"My vadge isn't having a good year."

The ointment: emulsion of purslane, bishopswort, and devil's claw in sesame oil. She dabs a few drops on the wart, recaps the vial, hands it to Clementine. "Put this on it twice a day." More warts are likely to join it, possibly a lot more, but she doesn't see cause to say this.

After Clementine leaves, the mender misses her, wants back the soft white thighs. She likes her ladies big-sirenic, mermaids of land, pressing and twisting in fleshful bodies.

Out in the shed she pours a scoop of grain and waits for Pinka and Hans to come galloping. Hans nuzzles the mender's crotch, and Pinka lifts a front hoof to be shaken. *Hello, beautifuls.* Their tongues are hard and clean. First time she saw a goat's pupil—rectangular, not round—she felt a stab of recognition. *I know you, strangeness.* They will never be taken from her. They know to behave, now, after that mischief near the trail.

Clementine brought black rockfish as payment. Her brothers are fishermen. The mender lifts it from the cooler, plops it into a bowl, picks up the little knife. She feeds the flesh to Malky and crunches the bones in her own mouth. The eyes she throws into the woods. Malky needs protein for all the hunting he does. Gone for days and comes back thin. Fish bones shouldn't be feared; you just have to chew them right so they won't pierce your throat walls or stomach lining.

"Your science teacher will tell you," said Temple, "fish bones are pure calcium and can't be digested by the human body, but let me assure you, that's not the whole story." One of the things the mender loved best about her aunt was "let me assure you." That and she cooked regular meals. Not once while living with Temple did the mender have to eat sautéed condiments for dinner. Temple became her guardian after the mender's mother left a note saying *Your better off with auntie don't worry I will send letters!* The mender was eight years old and herself not the best speller, but she noticed that the first word of the note was wrong.

Temple said the things she sold in her shop, Goody Hallett's, were props for tourists; but if her niece happened to be interested in the true properties of alchemy, she could teach her. Magic was of two kinds: natural and artificial. Natural magic was no more than a precise knowledge of the secrets of nature. Armed with such knowledge, you could effect marvels that to the ignorant seemed miracles or illusions. A man once cured his father's blindness with the gall bladder of a dragonet fish; the beat of a drum stretched with the skin of a wolf would shatter a drum stretched with the skin of a lamb.

The mender bottled her first tincture soon after her mother left. Per Temple's instructions, she gathered dozens of stalks of flowering mullein, yellow and shaped cheerfully. She picked the flowers and laid them to dry on a towel. Scooped them into a glass jar with chips of garlic, filled the jar with almond oil, left the jar on the sill for a month. Then she strained the oil into six small brown bottles, which she lined up on the kitchen counter—she was already tall enough—and brought Temple to see. Her aunt stood over her, aswirl with red hair, all that long, ropy, sparkling hair, and said, "Well done!" and it was the first time in her life the mender could remember being praised for doing something instead of for not doing it. (Not talking, not crying, not complaining when her mother took six hours to come back from the store.) "Next time your ear hurts," said Temple, "this is what you'll use." The promise of fixing and curing sent hot waves through the mender's belly. Show them how Percivals do.

When she wakes, the cabin is so dark from the rain and the trees, she doesn't know it is morning. But it is, and Malky is scratching, and the door is knocking.

* * *

She drinks a tea of horse-flavored ashwagandha. Eats brown bread. The new client wants nothing but water. Her name is Ro Stephens. Face dry and worried, hair dry and dull (feeble blood?), body thin (not perilously). She has lost people, the mender senses. A tiny smell, like a spoonful of smoke.

"I've been trying for a long time with Dr. Kalbfleisch at Hawthorne Reproductive Medicine."

The mender has heard of Kalbfleisch from other clients. One described him as a NILF: Nazi I'd Like to Fuck.

"So you've been taking their medications."

"A shit ton, yes."

"How's your cervical mucus?"

"Fine, I guess?"

"Does it resemble egg whites, near ovulation?"

"For a day or two. But my period's not—that regular. With the medications it gets better, but still it's not, like, clockwork."

She is so worried. And trying to hide the worry. Her face keeps twitching out of its behaving lines, cracking with *What if? What then?* then smoothing, obeying again. Deep down she doesn't believe the mender can help, no matter how much she wants to believe it. This is a person unaccustomed to being helped.

"Let's see your tongue."

White scum over the pink.

"You need to stop drinking milk."

"But I don't—"

"Cream in coffee? Cheese? Yogurt?"

Ro nods.

"Stop all of that."

"I will." But Ro looks like she's thinking *I didn't come here for nutrition tips.*

Eat warm and warming foods. Yams, kidney beans, black beans, bone broth. More red meat: the clock walls need building. Less dairy: the tongue is damp. More green tea: the walls are weakish still. All in the elementals, bitches. Everyone wants charms, but thirty-two years on earth have convinced the mender charms are purely for show. When the body is slow to do something, or galloping too fast toward death, people want wands waved. *Broth? That's it?* The mender teaches them to boil meat bones for days. To simmer seed and stem and dried wrack, strain it, drink it. Womb tea makes a cruel stench.

She pulls down the tea jar from the north cupboard. Shakes some into a brown bag, tapes it closed, hands it to Ro. "Heat this up in a big pot of water. After it boils, turn the heat down and simmer for three hours. Drink a cup every morning and every night. You won't like the taste."

"What's in it?"

"Nothing harmful. Roots and herbs. They'll make your lining lusher and your ovaries stronger."

"*Which* roots and herbs, exactly?"

She's one of those people who think they will understand something if they hear its name, when really they will only hear its name.

"Dried fleeceflower, Himalayan teasel root, wolfberry, shiny bugleweed, Chinese dodder seed, motherwort, dong quai, red peony root, and nut grass rhizome."

The tea tastes (the mender has tried it) like water buried underground for months in a bowl of rotted wood, swum through by worms, spat into by a burrowing vole.

The hair on Ro's upper lip. The irregular bleeding. The scummy tongue. The dryness.

"Has Dr. Kalbfleisch checked you for PCOS?"

"No—what's that?"

"Polycystic ovary syndrome. It affects ovulation, so it could be contributing." Seeing Ro flash with fear, she adds: "A lot of women have it."

"Wouldn't he have mentioned it, though? I've been seeing him for over a year."

"Ask for a test."

Ro has a gentle face—freckled, laugh lined, sad in the mouth corners. But her eyes are angry.

How to make boiled puffin (*mjólkursoðinn lundi*):

1. Skin puffin; rinse.
2. Remove feet and wings; discard.
3. Remove internal organs; set aside for lamb mash.
4. Stuff puffin with raisins and cake dough.
5. Boil in milk and water one hour, or until juices run clear.

THE DAUGHTER

Is seven weeks late, approximately, more or less.

She stares at the classroom floor, arranging linoleum tiles into groups of seven. One seven. Two seven.

But she doesn't feel pregnant.

Three seven. Four seven.

She would be feeling something by now, five seven, if she was.

Ash passes a note: *Who finer, Xiao or Zakile?*

The daughter writes back: *Ephraim.*

Not on list, dumblerina.

"So what are we talking about here?" goes Mr. Zakile. "We've got whiteness. The white whale. How come it's white?"

Ash goes, "God made it white?"

Six seven.

"Well, okay, that wasn't really what I was . . ." Mr. Zakile paws through his notes, likely ripped whole from online, searching in those cut-and-pasted sentences for the brain he wasn't born with.

Of all divers, said Captain Ahab, *thou hast dived the deepest.*

Has moved amid this world's foundations.

The daughter wants to float down into the murderous hold of this frigate Earth.

Hast seen enough to split the planets.

Seven seven.

And not one syllable is thine.

She's been late before. Everyone has. The anorexics, for instance, miss periods constantly, as starving shuts down the blood; or if you haven't been eating enough iron; or if you're smoking too much. The daughter smoked three-quarters of a pack yesterday. Ash's sister, Clementine, says tweaker girls have sex fearlessly because meth prevents conception.

Last year one of the seniors threw herself down the gym stairs, but even after she broke a rib she was still pregnant, and Ro/Miss said in class she hoped they understood who was to blame for this rib: the monsters in Congress who passed the Personhood Amendment and the walking lobotomies on the Supreme Court who reversed *Roe v. Wade.* "Two short years ago," she said—or, actually, shouted—"abortion was legal in this country, but now we have to resort to throwing ourselves down the stairs."

And, of course: Yasmine.

The self-scraper. The mutilator.

Yasmine, who was the first person the daughter became blood sisters with (second grade).

Yasmine, who was the first person the daughter ever kissed (fourth grade).

Yasmine, who made him use a condom but got pregnant anyway.

The daughter wishes she could talk to her mom about it. Get told "Seven weeks late is nothing, pigeon!"

In most areas, her mom is sensible and knowledgeable—

"My poo is furry!"

"Don't worry. It's from that green cleanse you did. It's mucoid plaque sloughing off the intestinal walls."

—but not in all areas.

Can you tell me what color eyes my grandmother had?

What color hair my grandfather had?

Were my great-aunts all deaf?

My great-great-uncles all lunatics?

Do I come from a long line of mathematicians?

Were their teeth as crooked as my teeth?

No, you can't tell me, and neither can Dad, and neither can the agency.

It was a closed adoption. Zero trace.

Are you mine?

* * *

Ephraim doesn't have an orgasm, he stops after a couple of minutes, says he isn't feeling it. Shifts his weight off her. The first thing she feels is relief. The second is fear. No male teenager ever passes up the chance for intercourse, according to her mom, who last year gave her A Talk that included, thank God, no anatomical details but did feature warnings about the sex-enslaved minds of boys. Yet here is Ephraim, sixteen going on seventeen, passing up a chance. Or stopping mid-chance.

"Did I, like, do something wrong?" she says quietly.

"Unh-unh. I'm just way tired." He yawns, as though to prove it. Pushes back his blond-streaked hair. "We're doing two-a-days for soccer. Hand me my hat?"

She loves this hat, which makes him look like a gorgeous detective.

But her own clothes: Black wool leggings. Red tube skirt. White glitter-paste long sleeve. Purple loop scarf. A pathetic outfit; no wonder he stopped.

"Want me to drop you at Ash's?"

"Yeah, thanks." She waits for him to say something about the next time, make a plan, allude to their future together, even just *You coming to our game Friday?* They get to Ash's and he hasn't. She says, "So..."

"See you, September girl," he says, and kisses, more like bites, her mouth.

In Ash's bathroom she drops the purple scarf in the trash and covers it with a handful of smushed toilet paper.

Eivør Mínervudottír's family lived on fish, potatoes, fermented mutton, milk-boiled puffin, and pilot whale. Her favorite food was the *fastelavnsbolle,* a sweet Shrovetide bun. ~~In 1771 the Swedish king ate fourteen *fastelavnsboller* with lobster and champagne, then promptly died of indigestion.~~

THE WIFE

Bex won't wear a raincoat. They will be in the *car* mostly and she doesn't *care* if her hair gets wet between the car and the store and she *hates* how the plastic feels on her *neck*.

"Fine, get wet" is Didier's answer, but the wife isn't having it. It's pouring. Bex will wear a raincoat. "Put. It. On," she bellows.

"No!" screams the girl.

"Yes."

"No!"

"Bex, nobody is getting in the car until you put it on."

"Daddy said I don't have to."

"Do you see how hard it's raining out there?"

"Rain is good for my skin."

"No, it's not," says the wife.

"Jesus, let's *go,*" says Didier.

"Please back me up on this."

"I would if I agreed with you, but we've been standing here for ten goddamn minutes. It's ridiculous."

"Enforcing rules is ridiculous?"

"I didn't know we had a *rule* about—"

"Well, we do," says the wife. "Bex? Do you want to keep holding everyone up, or are you ready to act like a six-year-old and wear your raincoat?"

"I'm not a six-year-old," she says, arms crossed. "I'm a little babykins. I need my diaper changed."

The wife slaps the raincoat across Bex's shoulders, yanks the hood into place, and ties the strings under her chin. Lifts up the girl's rigid body and carries her out to the car.

* * *

Her husband's hands sit on the wheel at ten and two, a habit that in their courting days shocked the wife: he had played in bands, done drugs, punched his father in the face at age fourteen. Yet he steered—steers—like a grandma.

She is glad not to be driving. No decisions to be made at the bend in the road.

Little animal black and twitching, burnt to death but not quite dead.

A scrap of tire struggling its way across.

Little animal, plastic bag.

But maybe it wasn't a plastic bag.

Maybe her first sight was correct.

Somebody lit it on fire, some bad kid, bad adult. Newville is not lacking in badness—

but it's beautiful here and your family's been coming here for generations and the sea air's full of negative ions. They boost the mood, remember?

Bex is chattering again by the time they reach the store.

Where's the doll section.

John's so lazy.

Somebody's mom came to class who's a dental hygienist and said even the nub of an adult tooth growing in still needs to be brushed.

"Perfects at two o'clock," hisses Didier, elbowing the wife's elbow.

Not them. Not today.

"Shell!" squeals Bex. "Oh my God, *Shelly!*"

The girls embrace dramatically, as though bumping into each other in the town where they both live were the most amazing surprise.

Bex: "Your dress is so pretty."

Shell: "Thanks. My mom made it."

"Hey, friends!" chirps Jessica Perfect. "Good to see you!"

"You too." The wife leans in for an air-kiss. "Brought the whole crew, huh?"

Shell's tanned, slender siblings stand in a row behind their tanned, slender parents.

"Yep, it's one of those days."

Those days at the Perfects' are probably a little different from *those days* on the hill.

On top of making dresses, Jessica knits sweaters out of local Shetland wool for all four children.

Cans jam from the wild berries they pick.

Home-cooks their wheat-free, dairy-free meals.

Chicken nuggets and string cheese never cross her threshold.

Her husband is a nutritionist who once lectured Didier on the importance of soaking nuts overnight.

"Blake." Didier nods.

"How's it hangin, buddy?"

"Long and strong," says her husband, with only a flicker of a smile.

"Look at *this* guy! He's getting so big! How old are you now?" Blake leans down toward John, who squirms in the shopping cart, shoving his face into Didier's stomach.

"Three and a half," says the wife.

"Wow. Time just *passes,* doesn't it?"

"I know," says Jessica, "and it's been forever since we had you over! We need to do that. It's hard to find a good night with the kids so busy after school. We've got soccer, cross-country, violin—gosh, what am I missing?"

The oldest child says, "My gifted-and-talented class?"

"That's right, my love. *This* one"—she nuzzles the boy's head—"tested off the charts last year, so he qualifies for an accelerated math and language-arts program. You guys aren't vegetarian, are you? We've been getting the most heavenly beef from our friends down the road. Their cows are grass-fed, no antibiotics whatsoever, just pure happy beef."

"You mean happy before they're slaughtered," says Didier, "or once they turn into food?"

She doesn't bat an eye. "So when you guys come over, I'll make steaks, and the chard will be ready soon. Gosh, we've got *acres* of it this year. Fortunately the kids love chard."

Still raining hard on the way home. Wipers furious.

"Shooting?" says Didier.

"Too quick," says the wife. "What's a very slow poison?"

"Hemlock, I think," he says, taking a hand off the wheel to caress the back of her neck. "No, wait—starvation! Hoist them on their own, like, whatevers."

"Petards," she says.

"What is a petard, anyway?"

"Can't remember. But I vote for starvation."

"'I notice you've got some unsoaked nuts on the premises, and I'm a little concerned. Frankly I wouldn't dream of feeding my children an unsoaked nut.'"

"What are you guys talking about?" says Bex.

"A TV show we saw," says Didier, "called *The World's Smallest Petard.* You would like it, Bexy. There's an episode where every time a person farts, you can actually see the fart—there's these little brown clouds trailing behind the characters."

Bex giggles.

The wife moves his hand from her neck down to her thigh and closes her eyes, smiling. He squeezes her jeaned flesh.

She remembers what she loves.

Not the fart jokes, but the sweetness. The solidarity against the Perfects of this world.

She will ask him tomorrow.

In the car-window fog she draws an *A.*

It was bad, yes, the last time he refused. She promised herself she wouldn't ask again.

But the kids adore him.

And he really is sweet sometimes.

I got the name of a person in Salem, she will say, *who's supposed to be fantastic, not that expensive, does late appointments. We can get Mattie to sit—*

And she has seen herself driving off the cliff road with the kids in the car.

When the polar explorer turned six, she was shown the best way to hold the knife and how to make a slice across the lamb's throat—just one, they don't feel it, do it hard, watch your brother. But when she had the knife, and her mother was squatting beside her with the little wriggler, she didn't want to. Eivør was ordered twice to cut it and twice she said *"Nei, Mamma."*

Her mother put a hand over hers and drew the knife under the lamb's face; its face fell off; Eivør fell with it, screaming; and her mother hoisted the animal above a washtub to bleed.

Eivør was beaten on her thighs with a leather strap used for hanging slit lambs in the drying shed. And she ate no *ræst kjøt* that Christmas or *skerpikjøt* that spring, apart from the occasional secret bite her brother Gunni saved in his shoe.

THE BIOGRAPHER

Doesn't know for a fact that Gunni saved pieces of fermented lamb in his shoe when Eivør wasn't allowed to have any, but she writes it in her book, because her own brother used to hide cookies in his napkin when their mother told the biographer she didn't need more dessert unless she wanted to get chubby. Archie would leave the cookies in his drawer for her to retrieve. Each time she opened the drawer and saw the grease-darkened napkin tucked among socks, a flame of happiness lit in her throat.

She wrote the first sentences of *Mínervudottír: A Life* ten years ago, when she was working at a café in Minneapolis and trying to help Archie get clean. When she wasn't driving him to meetings or outpatient appointments, she was dropping leafy greens into smoothies he didn't drink. She was checking his pupils for pinnedness, his drawers for needles, her own wallet for missing cash. Sometimes he would ask to read the manuscript. He liked the part where the polar explorer watches men drive whales to their deaths in a shallow cove.

As a hater of tradition, Archie would have applauded her solo pregnancy efforts. Would have tried to get his friends to supply sperm for free. (One dose of semen from Athena Cryobank costs eight hundred dollars.)

She has not told her father about the efforts.

She closes her computer and sets Mínervudottír's journal on a pile of books about nineteenth-century Arctic expeditions. Rolls her head toward one shoulder, then the other. Is a stiff neck another sign of polycystic ovary syndrome? She has researched PCOS online, a little, as much as she can stand. The pregnancy statistics aren't good.

But Gin Percival might not know what she's talking about. She didn't even graduate from high school, according to Penny, who was already teaching at Central Coast when Gin dropped out. The visit to her did not go badly, or particularly well. She liked Gin Percival fine. She came away with a bag of gruesome tea.

Speaking of: the biographer gets out the saucepan. While the tea heats, she braces for the flavor of a human mouth unbrushed for many moons and debates whether to change for dinner. It's only Didier and Susan and the kids; but these sweatpants, truth be told, have not been washed in a while.

Her white mug is streaked tan inside. Are her teeth this stained? Probably almost. Years of frequent coffee. Long hiatuses from dentistry. Could poor mouth hygiene be a cause of PCOS? Inflammation leaking from the gums into the bloodstream, a slow poison, her hormones dizzy and ineffectual?

If she *does* have PCOS, maybe Gin Percival can give her another concoction—to lower her testosterone levels, repair her blood. Her cells will jump to work, plumping and fluffing and densing, her FSH numbers will drop into the single digits, Nurse Crabby will call with her bloodwork results and say, "Wow! Just, wow!" and even Fleischy will give a golden nod of amazement. They'll shoot in the sperm of the rock climber or the personal trainer or the biology student or Kalbfleisch himself, and the biographer, at last, will conceive.

It's got to be mostly hokum, of course. Tree bark and frog's spit and spells. Mash up a few berries and seeds and call it a solution.

But what if it works? Thousands of years in the making, fine-tuned by women in the dark creases of history, helping each other.

And at this point, what else can she do?

You could stop trying so hard.

You could love your life as it is.

The Korsmos' place, horror-movie handsome on its hill, would make the biographer jealous if she were a house wanter, which she is not, as houses make her think of being stuck neck-deep in a mortgage; but she admires its lead-glazed panes and the ocellated trim work vining its porch. It was built by Susan's great-grandfather as a summer place. In winter they duct-tape the windows and stuff sweaters under the doors.

Didier smokes on the porch steps, yellow hair poking like hay from under his beanie. He is sunk-eyed and snaggletoothed yet manages somehow—the biographer can't figure out how—to be fetching. *Beau-laid*. He raises one beautiful-ugly palm in greeting.

"ROOOOOO!" yells Bex, running at the biographer across the lawn.

"Pipe the fuck down," says her father. He squashes the cigarette on his bootheel, tosses it into a large brown bush, and ambles over to lift the girl into the air. "Bexy, remember that 'fuck' goes in the special box. You hungry, Robitussin? Also, we invited Pete."

"I'm elated. What's the special box?"

"The box of words we never say to Mommy," says Bex.

"Or even near Mommy." Didier sets the girl down, and she scurries back toward the house. "I see you didn't bring anything, which is awesome."

"What?"

"My wife adheres to the twentieth-century belief that civilized people arrive with small gifts or contributions to an invited meal. And once again this proves her wrong because you're civilized but, as usual, you brought zilch."

The biographer foresees the wince, the disapproval filed away. Susan keeps track to the grave.

Pliny the Younger stomps behind while Bex gives the biographer yet another tour of her room. She is very proud of her room. The purple walls are thick with fairies, leopards, alphabets, and Pinocchio noses. When her brother dares to move a rabbit from the bed, Bex slaps his hand; he yowls; the biographer says, "I don't think you're supposed to do that."

"It was only a *soft* hit," says the girl. "See, I have one shelf for the monster and one shelf for the fish. Here's a squirrel mummy."

The biographer peers. "Is that a real squirrel?"

"Yeah, but it died. Which is, like, when..." Bex sighs, twists her hands together, and looks up at the biographer. "What is death?"

"Oh, you know," says the biographer.

Blond-brown, endearing, demanding, sometimes quite irritating—how eerily they resemble Susan and Didier. It's much more than the coloring: they are *shaped* like their parents, Bex with Didier's shadowy eye sockets, John with Susan's elfin chin—small faces imprinted by two traceable lineages. They are the products of desire: sexual, yes, but more importantly (in the age of contraception, at least) they come from the desire to recur. Give me the chance to repeat myself. Give me a life lived again, and bigger. Give me a self to take care of, and better. Again, please, again! We're wired, it's said, to want repeating. To want seed and soil, egg and shell, or so it's said. Give me a bucket and give me a bell. Give me a cow with her udders a-swell. Give me the calf—long eyes, long tongue—who clamps the teat and sucks.

Downstairs she trips on a plastic truck and slams elbow first into a side table. The floor is choked with toys. She kicks a blue train against the wall.

"They live in squalor," says Pete Xiao.

"I may have sprained my elbow."

"That aside, how are you?" Pete came to Central Coast Regional two years ago, to teach math, and announced he'd only be here for one year because he wasn't built for a hinterland. This year, too, is meant to be his last; and next year will undoubtedly be his last.

"Swell," she says. Swollen. The Ovutran bloats.

They gather in the dining room, which Susan's forebears rigged up in style: fat oak ceiling beams, hand-carved wall panels, built-in credenza. The little black roast is sliced and served. Munchings and slurpings.

"This year's parents," says Pete, "are even more racist than last year's. One guy goes, 'I'm glad my child is finally studying math with someone of your persuasion.'"

"Calm your yard, Pete-moss," says Didier.

"I have a yard?"

"It's in your pants, nestled like a teeny mouse."

"How very white of you to change the subject away from model-minority stereotypes."

"Hey, Roosevelt, are you using only white sperm donors out of racism?"

"Didier, *God,*" says Susan.

"White is the state color of Oregon," says Pete.

"The kid is already going to feel weird about his paternity situation," says the biographer, "and I don't want to add to the confusion."

"Once you have that kid, you won't be able to take a dump by yourself. And you'll become even less cool than you are now. As they say, 'Heroin never hurt my music collection, but parenthood sure has!' "

"No one says that," says Susan, reaching for another roll.

"I once did a research paper," says Didier, "on the history of words for penis, and 'yard' was a preferred term until a couple of centuries ago."

"Was that considered a research topic at your wattle-and-daub college?" says Pete.

"Not wattle and daub," says Susan, "so much as frosted glass block and drive-through window."

"What's wattle and daub?" says Bex.

Didier scratches his neck. "Even if it *had* been a community college, which it was not, so what? I mean, literally, *meuf,* why would it matter?"

Pete shouts, "Why does everyone say 'literally' so much these days?"

" 'When I lay with my bouncing Nell,' " recites Didier, " 'I gave her an inch, but she took an Ell: But... it was damnable hard, When I gave her an inch, she'd want more than a Yard.' Ell meant the minge, by the way."

"Yet he can't remember the name of the kids' pediatrician," says Susan.

Didier gives his wife a long look, rises from the table, heads for the kitchen.

He returns with a butter dish.

"We don't need butter," says Susan. "Why did you get out the butter?"

"Because," he says, "I want to put some butter on my potatoes. They happen to be a little *dry*."

"Daddy," says Bex, "your face just looked like a butt." Giggles. "Don't be a buttinski, you buttinski!"

"Use your NPR voice, *chouchou,*" says Didier.

"I hate NPR!"

"What Daddy means is you need to speak more quietly, or you're leaving the table."

Bex whispers something to her brother, then counts to three. "AAAAAAHHHHHH!" they roar.

"That's it," snaps Susan. "You're done. Leave the table."

"But John's not done! If you don't feed us it's, um, it's *child abuse*."

"Where did you hear that term?"

"Jesus," says Didier, "she prolly got it from TV. Relax."

Susan closes her eyes. For a few seconds, nothing moves. Then her eyes open and her voice comes out placid: "Let's go, sprites, time for bath. Say good night!"

Pete and Didier keep opening beers and ignoring the biographer. Their conversation topics include European soccer, artisanal whiskey, famous drug overdoses, and a multiplayer video game whose name sounds like "They Mask Us." Then Didier, suddenly remembering her, says: "Instead of driving a million miles to Salem, why don't you just go to the witch? I saw her the other day, waiting outside the school. At least I think it was her, although she looks less witchy than most of the girls at Central Coast."

"She's not a *witch*. She's—" Tall, pale, heavy browed. Eyes wide and pond-green. Black cloth pinned around her neck. "Unusual."

"Still," says Didier, "worth a try?"

"Nah. She'd give me a bowl of tree bark. And I'm already in massive debt." The biographer isn't sure why she's lying. She's not ashamed of her visit to Gin Percival.

"All the more reason to avoid single motherhood," says Didier.

Is she ashamed?

"So only couples in massive debt"—she raises her voice—"should have kids?"

"No, I just mean you have no idea how hard it's going to be."

"Actually I do," she says.

"You very much don't. Look, I'm the *product* of a single mother."

"Exactly."

"What?"

"You turned out fine," says the biographer.

"You're human evidence," adds Pete.

"Wait'll it's four a.m.," says Didier, "and the kid's puking and shitting and screaming and you can't decide if you should take him to the emergency room and there's no one to help you decide."

"Why would I need someone to help me decide?"

"Okay, what about when the kid has a guitar performance in assembly and you can't be there because of work and everyone laughs at him for crying?"

The biographer does the tiny violin.

Didier pats his shirt pocket. "Hell are my smokes? Pete, do you—?"

"I got you, brah." They head out together.

She thinks to start clearing the table—this would be a good thing to do, a courteous and helpful thing—but stays in her chair.

Susan, in the doorway: "They're finally down." Her narrow face, edged by blond waves, pulses with anger. At her kids for not settling faster? At her husband for doing nothing? She goes to hover behind a chair, surveying the mess of the table. Even angry she is shining, every piece of dining-room light caught and smeared across her cheeks.

The males clomp back in, smelling of smoke and cold, Didier laughing, "Which is what I told the ninth-graders!"

"Classic," says Pete.

Susan reaches for plates. The biographer gets up and hefts the roast pan.

"Thanks," says Susan, to the pan.

"I'll wash."

"No, it's fine. Can you get the strawberries out of the fridge? And the cream."

The biographer rinses, pats, and de-tops.

"I bought those specially for you," says Susan.

"In case I need some folic acid?"

"Are you—?"

"Another insemination next week."

"Well, distract yourself if you can. Go to the movies."

"The movies," repeats the biographer. Susan has a knack for commiserating with suffering she hasn't suffered. Which doesn't feel like compassion or empathy, but why not? Here is a friend trying to connect over a trouble. But the effort itself is insulting, the biographer decides. The first time Susan got pregnant, it wasn't planned. The second time (she told the biographer) they'd only just started trying again; she must be one of those Fertile Myrtles; she'd expected it to take longer, but lo and behold. If she told Susan about seeing the witch, Susan would act supportive and serious, then laugh about it behind the biographer's back. With Didier. Oh, poor Ro—first she's buying sperm online, now she's tramping into the forest to consult a homeless woman. Oh, poor Ro—why does she keep trying? She has no idea how hard it's going to be.

On her teacher's salary she will die holding notices from credit-card agencies, whereas Susan and Didier, who also live on a teacher's salary, are debt-free, as far as she knows, and pay no rent. Bex and John no doubt have trust funds set up by Susan's parents, fattening and fattening.

"The comparing mind is a despairing mind," says the meditation teacher.

Well, the biographer will figure out how to send her baby who does not exist yet to college. If the baby chooses to go to college, that is. She won't push the baby. The biographer herself liked college, but who's to say what the baby will like? Might decide to be a fisherperson and stay right here on the coast and eat dinner with the biographer every night, not out of obligation but out of wanting to. They will linger at the table and tell each other how the day went. The biographer won't be teaching by that point, only writing, having published *Mínervudottír: A Life* to critical acclaim and now working on a comprehensive history of female Arctic explorers; and the baby, tired from hours on the fishing boat but still paying attention, will ask the biographer intelligent questions about menstruating at eighty degrees below zero.

As a girl, I loved (but why?) to watch the *grindadráp.* It was a death dance. I couldn't stop looking. To smell the bonfires lit on the cliffs, calling men to the hunt. To see the boats herd the pod into the cove, the whales thrashing faster as they panic. Men and boys wade into the water with knives to cut their spinal cords. They touch the whale's eye to make sure it is dead. And the water foams up red.

THE MENDER

Malky's been gone three days. Long for him—she doesn't like it. The sun is dropping. Killers in the woods. Malky is a killer himself but no match for coyotes and foxes and red-tailed hawks. Every creature, prey to someone. The girl rides away from school in the car of a boy in an old-fashioned hat. (Does he believe the hat looks *good*?) Hat boy walks hips first, boom swagger swagger, pirate-like.

Not that the mender can warn her. She has been keeping away from town for fear the girl will catch her watching.

She wipes down the sink, the oak countertop. Tidies the seed drawer. Sets clean jars by a basket of eyeless onions.

Boom swagger boom.

A pirate slept off his dreadful deeds at a tavern on Cape Cod. He met the local beauty, not yet sixteen. Maria Hallett fell hard for this bandit. Then Black Sam Bellamy sailed away. She was packed with child. Child died the same night born—hid in a barn, choked on a piece of straw.

Or so went the story. Little did they know. The farmer's wife who raised the child told no one but her diary.

Goody Hallett was imprisoned. Or banned from the village. Became a recluse. Lived in a shack by a poverty grass. Waited on the cliffs for Black Sam Bellamy in her best red shoes. Rode the backs of whales, tied lanterns to their flukes, lured ships to crash on the shoals. Got a reputation: witch.

* * *

Black Sam was the Robin Hood of pirates. They rob the poor under the cover of law, he said, and we plunder the rich under the protection of our own courage. In 1717, after some Caribbean plundering, Captain Bellamy rode back up the Atlantic with his gang of buccaneers. Their stolen ship, *Whydah,* sailed into the worst nor'easter in Cape Cod history. Ship went to pieces. Dead pirates all over the beach. Black Sam's body was never recovered.

In 1984 the remains of *Whydah* were found off the coast of Wellfleet, Massachusetts. That same year Temple Percival bought a foreclosed tackle shop in Newville, Oregon, and arranged on the shelves some spooky trinkets and called it Goody Hallett's.

Now Temple's fingernails live in a jar on the cabin shelf. Lashes in a glassine packet. Head hair and pubic hair in separate paper cartons—both almost gone. The rest of her body in the chest freezer behind the feed trough in the goat shed.

Scratching on the doorstep. Malky slinks in without greeting or apology. She tries to sound stern: "Don't ever stay out that long again, fuckermo." He purrs tetchily, demanding supper. She gets a plate of salmon from the mini fridge. It is happiness to see his pink tongue lapping. Merry, merry king of the woods is he.

Two short knocks. Stop. Two more. Stop. One. Malky, who knows this knock, goes on eating.

"Is it you?"

"It's me."

She opens the door but stays on the threshold. Cotter is her only human friend, the kindest person she knows; doesn't mean she wants him in the cabin.

"New client," he says, holding up a white envelope. His poor pimpled cheeks are worse than usual. Toxins trying to exit. They should be leaving through the liver but are leaving through the skin.

The mender pockets the envelope. "You talk to this one?"

"Works at the pulp mill in Wenport. Ten weeks along."

"Okay, thanks." She needs to replenish coltsfoot and fleabane. Check her supply of pennyroyal. "Good night."

Cotter rubs his black wool cap. "You all right? You need anything?"

"I'm fine. Good night!"

"One more thing, Ginny—" He pulls off the cap, palms his forehead. "People are saying you brought the dead man's fingers back."

The mender nods.

"I'm just telling you," says Cotter.

She wants to sit by the stove with Malky in her lap and nothing in her head. No vigilance, no fear. "I'm tired."

Cotter sighs. "Get to bed early, then." He turns, is taken by the woods.

Cotter works at the P.O. Whatever people are talking about, he hears. But she knew before he told her. She's been getting notes in her post box. From fishermen, or fishermen's wives, frightened by the seaweed plague.

A lace of dried dead man's fingers does hang in a window of her cabin. Did Clementine report this to her fishermen brothers? Fishermen hate dead man's fingers for fouling hulls in the harbor, fastening to oysters and carrying them away.

U think its funny? Its our LIVING.

She adds pine branches to the stove. Where is Malky? "Come here, little mo." He can't be persuaded onto her lap, even though he knows how much she's missed him.

Cunt, quit hexing the water.

Her own cat does not obey her; why should seaweed?

Why could I stand to see the whales killed,
but not the lambs?

THE DAUGHTER

She thought it would go a different way. She thought the way it would go would not include taking the east stairwell to lunch and seeing Ephraim's hand in the shirt of Nouri Withers, whose eyes were shut and fluttering.

The daughter makes no sound. She creeps back up the stairs.

But she can't breathe.

Breathe, dumblerina.

She sits on the landing, spreading her rib cage to make room for air.

Breathe, ignorant white girl.

Still has to finish the day. Get through Latin and math. Go pick up her new retainer.

Nouri Withers? Maybe if you like tangled hair and black eye shadow and nail polish made from otter dung.

She has never missed Yasmine more than exactly right now.

Yasmine, lover of strawberries, queen of whipped cream.

Singer of hymns and smoker of weed.

Who'd say: *Forget that Transylvanian slut.*

Who'd say: *Are you even going to remember his ass in five years?*

Yasmine, who was smarter than the daughter but who got worse grades because of her "attitude."

Yasmine came out of the bathroom and held up the pee stick.

A month earlier the federal abortion ban had gone into effect.

The daughter was thinking: we need to get you to Canada. They hadn't closed the border to abortion seekers yet. The Pink Wall was still just an idea.

A year and a half later the Canadian border patrol arrests American seekers and returns them to the States for prosecution. "Let's spend the taxpayers' money to criminalize vulnerable women, shall we?" said Ro/Miss in class, and somebody said, "But if they're breaking the law, they *are* criminals," and Ro/Miss said, "Laws aren't natural phenomena. They have particular and often horrific histories. Ever heard of the Nuremberg Laws? Ever heard of Jim Crow?"

Yasmine would have liked Ro/Miss, who talks about history in a way that makes it memorable and who wears the clothes of a kid: brown cords, green hoodies, sneakers.

A tuft of cells inside her, multiplying. Half Ephraim, half her.

You can't be sure.

She carries the test around unopened in her satchel.

If she *is*—

She might not be. Her body feels pretty much like it always does.

But if she is, what the hell is she going to do?

Don't borrow worry. —Mom

Stay in your lane. —Dad

After all, she might not be.

In math Nouri Withers taps her steel-toed boot against the chair leg, from excitement probably; she's thinking of her next time with Ephraim. Where will they go? What will they do? *What have they already done?* Ash isn't there to comfort her; the daughter has no friends in this room; it's calculus, all eleventh- and twelfth-graders except for her. The tenth-graders think she's a snob because she moved here from Salem and takes AP classes and her dad's not a fisherman and she once said it was dumb to call the teachers "miss." To prove her lack of snobbery, she says "miss" now too.

After class Mr. Xiao pulls her aside for "a word." She is already shaky from the combination of eight weeks late plus Ephraim's hand up Nouri's shirt; the prospect of a reprimand from her second-favorite teacher makes her eyes water.

"Whoa, whoa! You're not in trouble. Jesus, Quarles, it's *cool*."

She dabs her eyes. "Sorry."

"Everything all right?"

"My period." Men teachers don't touch that excuse.

"Okay, well, I've got some good news for you. Do you know about the Oregon Math Academy?"

The daughter nods.

As if she shook her head, Mr. Xiao explains: "It's a weeklong residential program in Eugene. The most prestigious and competitive academic camp in the state. Nobody from Central Coast has ever been selected. And I'm nominating you for it."

She hears the words, but no feeling follows. "Thank you so much."

"I think your chances are good. You're bright, you're female, and as a little bonus, I went to undergrad with one of their admissions guys." He waits for her to look impressed.

The Matilda Quarles of last year—of last *month*—would be euphoric right now. Would be dying to get home and tell her parents.

"The deadline is January fifteenth," adds Mr. Xiao, who is not good at noticing how people feel unless they're crying or yelling and so believes the daughter is just as happy as she should be.

"I look forward to applying," she says.

She knows quite a lot, in fact, about the Oregon Math Academy. She has wanted to go since the seventh grade. She and Yasmine planned to apply together. In eighth grade Yasmine scored highest in their school on the math section of the state exam; the daughter was two points behind her.

Going to the academy would help her get into colleges with top marine-biology departments.

Her parents would be over the moon.

The academy happens in April, over spring break.

If she's three months pregnant now, she'll be eight months pregnant then.

How to make *skerpikjøt* ("sharp meat"):

1. Hang lamb's hind legs and saddle in drying shed (October).
2. Cut down saddle and eat as *ræst kjøt* ("semi-dried meat") (Christmastime).
3. Cut down legs and carve for serving (April).

THE WIFE

Herd crumbs into palm.

Spray table.

Wipe down table.

Rinse cups and bowls.

Place cups and bowls in dishwasher.

Open bill for Didier's dentist co-pay.

Open bill for plumber, who did not even fix the dripping tap.

Open overdue notice for John's trip to the ER, where all they did was give him an antinausea pill yet somehow it cost six hundred dollars.

Write check for dentist co-pay because it's only $49.84.

Slide plumber and hospital into folder labeled PAY NEXT MONTH.

Start a list on the back of an envelope: *Why we should go to counseling.*

Think of what to put first—not the strongest reason, nor the weakest.

In law school they teach you to end any litany on the most convincing item and bury in the middle the weakest.

Last spring, Didier's answer was five variations on "Because I don't want to."

At eleven a.m., the violet sedan pulls up.

Mrs. Costello bothers John less than she bothers Bex, and sweet John never complains on Tuesdays and Thursdays when the sedan deposits Mrs. Costello and her knitting bag. The wife is always ready with purse on shoulder, keys in hand. Four hours, twice a week, belong to her alone.

"There's fish sticks in the freezer, and baby carrots, and I got more PG Tips for you—"

"We'll be splendid," Mrs. Costello mournfully says.

And John lets her pet his blond head—John, who is nicer than the rest of the hill dwellers, who will snuggle against Mrs. Costello even though she smells like old-person teeth. Bex was an accident, but it took ten months of trying to conceive John; the wife had begun to despair; she cried every morning after Didier left for school; then, finally, it worked. And John came murmuring into the world, leaking what looked like milk. Little white drops kept forming on his nipples. Witches' milk.

The wife has until two forty-five, pickup time for Bex.

What should she do until pickup?

She isn't impressed with the first-grade teacher. Homework is a sheet of fill-in-the-blanks or some tame question they have to answer using a computer encyclopedia.

Does not want to shop or otherwise errand; the kids might as well be with her for that.

But what does she expect from a rural school district that can't afford music classes.

Does not like to stay at home, hidden from John, because she's home all the bleeding time.

The nearest private school is an hour away and Catholic and, though less expensive than the average private, still too expensive for the Korsmos. The wife's parents have nothing more to give them. Didier's mother is a part-time bartender, and his father he hasn't seen since he was fourteen.

She chooses the library. She was once a good researcher, at ease in the stacks, fetching, piling, skimming, choosing.

The rain is letting up.

The wife had her own carrel at the law library with its thirty-foot windows, black mirrors at night.

On a low stool by the newspaper rack is Temple Percival's niece, stinking of onion, twigs in her hair. That stool is her favorite.

The wife smiles, as she always does.

Guilty for finding her repulsive.

But she *is* repulsive.

Temple Percival once gave the wife a tarot reading, at her store: "The castle will fall."

At one of the two blond-wood tables, she spreads the paper before her.

"Excuse me, but are you done with the sports section?"

Armpits and aftershave. She turns. He teaches at the high school. What's his—

"Oh, hi," he says. "You're Didier's wife, yeah?"

"Susan. I think we met at the summer picnic. How are you?" It hurts her neck to look up at him, he's so long.

"*Sweaty*. I apologize." He pulls out the chair beside her. "The kids are taking bubble tests so I'm free until soccer practice, and I ill-advisedly went for a run."

"What do you teach?"

"English. For my sins." He is big, everything about him big: neck, forearms, shoulders, head, damp shining sprouts of black hair. A dimple when he smiles.

"Sorry, but I forgot your—"

"Bryan Zakile."

"Of course! My husband says you're, um, a great teacher."

"Didier's a good guy—kids love him."

"So he's always telling me," she says.

He fingers the corner of the newspaper. "I take it you're not reading the sports?"

"Can't say I'm a fan."

"Frivolous shit, I agree. But it keeps men's lizard cortexes occupied." The wife watches Bryan Zakile not take his eyes off her. In a lower voice: "So what *are* you a fan of?"

"Um," she says. "Various things."

They go two doors down to Cone Wolf. Over single-scoop chocolates she learns a few facts about Bryan.

He played Division I college soccer and was invited to try out for the U.S. Olympic team, but a knee injury put paid to that.

He has traveled in South America.

He is starting his third year at the high school, where he got the job because the principal is married to his second cousin.

"Mrs. Fivey's your cousin? How is she—?"

"Talking and moving around. Still in the hospital, but going home soon."

"Oh, that's good. Didier said they had to induce a coma?"

"She banged her head hella hard on those stairs. Got swelling on the brain. They couldn't wake her up until the swelling went down."

"How did she fall—do you know?"

Bryan shrugs. He licks his spoon, throws it on the counter, crosses his arms. "*That* was satisfying."

The wife did not find her teensy little marble of a scoop satisfying. "Delectable," she says, and blushes. The shop clock says 2:38. "I have to go pick up my daughter."

"How old?"—the first question he has asked her since the library.

"Six. I also have a three-year-old son."

"Wow, you're a busy woman."

The wife sees how he must see her. Shower-bunned blond hair. Drapey scarf to hide stomach. Black yoga pants. Mom clogs.

Over the course of human evolution, did men learn to be attracted to skinny women because they were not visibly pregnant? Did voluptuousness signal that a body was already ensuring the survival of another man's genetic material?

When Bex climbs into the booster seat, she's on a verge. The wife has come to fear this particular after-school look: reddened, scrunched. "Shell is so stupid."

"What happened?"

"I hate her."

"Seat belt, please. Did you and Shell fight?"

"I don't *fight,* Momplee. It's against the rules."

"I mean argue?" The wife turns off the ignition. The cars behind them in the pickup line will just have to go around.

The girl takes a long, shuddering breath. "She said I stole her bag of pennies and I didn't."

"What bag of pennies?"

"She had pennies in a bag which she wasn't supposed to because you can't bring money to school but she did and she couldn't find them and said I stole them. And I *didn't!*"

"Of course you didn't."

She might have.

She is her father's daughter.

The wife and Didier make fun of Ro's sperm donors, but what about Didier's genes, which may have deposited in Bex a puerile interest in drugs and a willingness to embezzle cash from a doughnut shop?

Two sets of instructions battle it out in the girl: well-shaped brown eyes vs. sunken blue-gray ones, orderly teeth vs. huge and crooked, solid SAT scores vs. never took the SAT.

When she got pregnant with Bex, at thirty, the wife felt as though she were sliding under a closing garage door.

Why did "thirty" loom like an expiration date?

She and Didier hadn't planned it; they weren't married; they'd been dating for seven months. But the wife felt old. It was August, her last year of law school was about to start, the home pregnancy test made a cross. *This is what I want, this!*—law school was nothing to this.

"She said I did steal," says Bex, "and so she isn't friends with me anymore."

"Give Shell some time to cool off."

"But what if she *never* cools off?"

"I think she will," says the wife. "Also, we need to talk about your research project! Have you decided on a topic yet?"

A small smile. "It's narrow to two."

"Oh, you narrowed it down?" The wife starts the ignition, flips her turn signal. Throat stab: she forgot to get any new books for Bex at the library.

"Wood sprite or ghost pepper, the hottest pepper known to man."

"Those are good choices, sweetpea."

"Shell's mom has ghost pepper from India at their house. They have seventy-three different spices in their spice cabinet."

"Oh, they don't have that many."

"Yes, they do—we counted. How many spices do *we* have, Momplee?"

"No idea."

In the rearview, some cow is waving at her to get moving.

The wife will take her sweet time.

If she constructs a solid argument, he'll be convinced.

But then you'd actually have to go to counseling with him.

Which might work!

Which would be the whole point.

To feel okay again. Even good.

To stop her throat from hurting when Bex asks "Do you and Daddy love each other?"

To stop reading online articles about the maladaptive coping mechanisms of kids from broken homes.

To stop *brokenhomebrokenhomebrokenhome* from reeling in her head.

To stop staring at the guardrails.

I brought aboard with me a sack of *sker-pikjøt,* which the Canadian sailors were interested to try. They called its taste "harrowing." I explained that if the lamb is dried during an unusually wet or warm season, it may ferment to the point of decay.

THE BIOGRAPHER

The biographer loves Penny at school, sharing snacks in the teachers' lounge, but she loves her best on Sunday nights, when they watch Masterpiece mysteries in her little house with its rose-dotted wallpaper and stone fireplace and wool rugs, rain pattering on the oriel windows.

Penny hands her a napkin, a fork, and a plate of shepherd's pie. "Tap water or limeade?"

"Limeade. But isn't it time?"

"Oh damn!" Penny hurries to the television. (She is always losing her clicker.) Settles with her own plate next to the biographer, tucks a napkin into the collar of her turquoise sweater. "Let's see what skills you've got for us, Sergeant Hathaway." The opening credits begin, theme song swelling over shots of Oxford's dreaming spires, a weak English sun turning Cotswold limestone the color of apricots. Penny intones, "Who will die tonight?"

"You should write mysteries instead of bra rippers," says the biographer.

"But I prefer the beating heart. Did I tell you I'm going to a romance writers' convention? They have agents you can pitch to."

"How much do they charge you for that privilege?"

"Well, they charge plenty. And why shouldn't they? The agents are being flown all the way from New York."

"Can I read your pitch?"

"Honey, I have it memorized. '*Rapture on Black Sand* opens at the end of World War I. Euphrosyne Farrell is a young Irish nurse so gutted by her sweetheart's death at the Somme that she emigrates to New York City. After becoming engaged to a middle-aged widower, she finds herself drawn to Renzo, the widower's nephew, whose magnetic Neapolitan eyes prove irresistible.' "

"Where does black sand come in?" asks the biographer.

"Euphrosyne and Renzo make love for the first time in a small cove on Long Island."

"But wouldn't it be more interesting and, um, maybe less clichéd if she got engaged to the nephew, then found his *uncle* irresistible?"

"Lord no! This isn't *Little Women*. Renzo's a Brooklyn stallion and his britches are strained to bursting."

Penny is a teacher of English and an inventor, she says, of entertainments. "They're a hoot," she answered when the biographer once ventured to ask why she wanted to write soap operas valorizing romantic love as the sole telos of a female life. Penny has written nine of them, all waiting for cover art showing bulge-groined men relieving bulge-chested women of their bodices. She intends to be a published author by her seventieth birthday. Three years to make it happen.

"Okay," she says, "here's Detective Sergeant Hathaway. Can't *buy* cheekbones like that."

Inspector Lewis and DS Hathaway trade jokes across a sheeted corpse; enjoy beers at The Lamb & Flag; and chase a murderous puppeteer through a faculty drinks party, leaving a wake of Oxford dons agape.

Then a large rosy meat bursts onto the screen. "It's never too early to reserve joy. Call today for your Christmas ham!" Having lost all of its government funding, because the current administration won't sanction the liberal bias of baking shows and mountaineering documentaries, PBS now airs long blocks of advertising. A spot for control-top hose ("Mom, you look extra beautiful tonight—is it your hair?" "No, my Tummy Tamers!") makes the biographer's nose sting.

"Hey, you're crying!" says Penny, returning from the kitchen with glasses of limeade.

"Am not."

Penny presses a napkin to the biographer's cheek.

"It's this new elderly-ovary medication," sobs the biographer.

"Blow your nose," says Penny. "Just use the napkin; I can wash it. Do the commercials with children make you—"

"No." The biographer blows and wipes, shoves the napkin between her knees. "They make me think about my mom."

In-breath.

Who would pity her daughter for these solo efforts, this manless life.

Out-breath.

But her mother, who went from father's house to college dorm to husband's house without a single day lived on her own, never knew the pleasures of solitude.

"What does your therapist say?" asks Penny.

"I quit seeing him."

"Was that such a smart move?"

"Poison is a woman's weapon," a grim lady tells Lewis and Hathaway. " 'I love the old way best, the simple way of poison, where we too are strong as men.' "

"Medea!" shouts the biographer.

"We should get you on a game show," says Penny.

Five thirty a.m., the air cold and gritty with salt. She can't face the drive to her day-nine egg-check appointment without coffee, even though caffeine is on Hawthorne Reproductive Medicine's *What to Avoid* handout. Teeth on her mug, she steers up the hill, under towering balsam fir and Sitka spruce, away from her town. Newville gets ninety-eight inches of rain a year. The inland fields are quaggy, hard to farm. Cliff roads dangerous in winter. Storms so bad they sink boats and tear roofs from houses. The biographer likes these problems because they keep people away—the people who might otherwise move here, that is, not the tourists, who cruise in on dry summer asphalt and don't give a sea onion about farming.

A billboard on Highway 22 is a stick drawing of a skirt-wearing person with a balloon for a stomach, accompanied by:

WON'T STOP ONE,

WON'T START ONE.

CANADA UPHOLDS U.S. LAW!

* * *

American intelligence agencies must have some nice dirt on the Canadian prime minister. Otherwise, why agree to the Pink Wall? The border control can detain any woman or girl they "reasonably" suspect of crossing into Canada for the purpose of ending a pregnancy. Seekers are returned (by police escort) to their state of residence, where the district attorney can prosecute them for attempting a termination. Healthcare providers in Canada are also barred from offering in vitro fertilization to U.S. citizens.

Unveiling these terms at a press conference last year, the Canadian prime minister said: "Geography has made us neighbors. History has made us friends. Economics has made us partners. And necessity has made us allies. Those whom nature hath so joined together, let no man put asunder."

Kalbfleisch calls her ultrasound "encouraging." The biographer has five follicles measuring twelve and thirteen, plus a gaggle of smallers. "You'll be ready for insemination right on schedule, I suspect. Day fourteen. Which is..." He leans back, waits for the nurse to open the calendar and count off the squares with her finger. "Wednesday. Do we have at least a couple of vials here?" As usual, he doesn't look at her, even when asking a direct question.

Four, in fact, are sitting in the clinic's frozen storage, tiny bottles of ejaculate from the scrota of a college sophomore majoring in biology (3811) and a rock-climbing enthusiast who described his sister as "extremely beautiful" (9072). She also owns some semen from 5546, the personal trainer who baked a cake for sperm-bank staff; but his remaining vials are still at the bank in Los Angeles.

"Start the OPKs tomorrow or the next day," says Kalbfleisch. "Fingers crossed." He rubs foaming sanitizer into his hands.

"By the way." She sits up on the exam table, covers her crotch with a paper sheet. "Do you think I might have polycystic ovary syndrome?"

Kalbfleisch stops mid-rub. A golden frown. "Why do you ask?"

"A friend told me about it. I don't have *all* of the symptoms, but—"

"Roberta, were you looking online?" He sighs. "You can diagnose yourself with anything and everything online. First of all, the majority of women with PCOS are overweight, and you are not."

"Okay, so you don't—"

"Although." He is looking at her, but not in the eye. More in the mouth. "You do have excessive facial hair. And, come to think of it, excessive body hair. Which is a symptom."

Come to think of it? "But, um, how does that account for genetics? Certain ethnic groups are naturally hairier. My mom's grandmothers both had mustaches."

"I can't speak to that," says Kalbfleisch. "I'm not an anthropologist. I do know that hirsutism is a sign of PCOS."

Wouldn't that be human biology, in which all physicians are trained, and not anthropology?

"When you come in on—" He glances at the nurse.

"Wednesday," she says.

"—I'll take a closer look at your ovaries, and we'll include a testosterone check with your bloodwork."

"If I have PCOS, what does that mean?"

"That the odds of your conceiving via intrauterine insemination are exceedingly low."

To justify being late to work, sometimes as often as twice a week, she scatters crumbs of mortal illness. Principal Fivey is annoyed—has broached the subject of unpaid leave. But he hasn't been around much since his wife went into the hospital.

Taking fresh blue books from the supply closet, the biographer asks the office manager how Mrs. Fivey is doing.

"Poor thing's still in very critical condition."

Is "critical" an adjective that can take an intensifying premodifier? "What happened, exactly?"

"Took a nasty tumble down the stairs."

"What stairs?"—picturing the *Exorcist* steps, the biographer's favorite ten minutes of a family trip to Washington, DC.

"At home, I think? We're circulating a card."

Mrs. Fivey always looks good in her Christmas costumes. Garish, true, but good. Also: why garish? Probably only because the biographer grew up in suburban Minnesota. A saying of her mother's was "Don't take your clothes off before they do." The muddy grammar always bothered the biographer. Should she not take her clothes off before the men removed their *own* clothes? Or should she keep her clothes on until the men took them off for her?

"Here's the card," says the manager. "And can you write something personal? Most people have only been signing their names."

"I don't—"

"Sheesh, I'll tell you what to say: 'Heartfelt hopes for a speedy recovery.' Is that so hard?"

"Hard? No. But my hopes are not heartfelt."

The two long jowls on the manager's face shake a little, as though in a breeze. "You don't want her to get better?"

"I do in my mind. Not in my heart."

In her mind she wants Mrs. Fivey to walk out of the hospital. In her heart she wants her brother to be alive again. In a place that is neither mind nor heart, or both at once, she wants an ashy line down the center of a round belly; she wants nausea. Susan's marks of motherhood: spider veins at the knee backs, loose stomach skin, lowered breasts. Affronts to vanity worn as badges of the ultimate accomplishment.

But why does she want them, really? Because Susan has them? Because the Salem bookstore manager has them? Because she always vaguely assumed she would have them herself? Or does the desire come from some creaturely place, pre-civilized, some biological throb that floods her bloodways with the message *Make more of yourself!* To repeat, not to improve. It doesn't matter to the ancient throb if she does good works in this short life—if she publishes, for instance, a magnificent book on Eivør Mínervudottír that would give people pleasure and knowledge. The throb simply wants another human machine that can, in turn, make another.

Sperm, in Faroese: *sáð*.

Three donors walk into a bar.

"What can I get you?" says the bartender.

Donor 5546, dumb and cocky and hot, says: "Whiskey."

Donor 3811, looking up the weather on his phone, says: "Hold on."

Donor 9072, who notices the bartender has his own glass going, says: "Whatever you're drinking."

Bartender points to 5546 and says: "You're a little too hot."

And to 3811: "You're a little too cold."

And to 9072: "But you're just right."

True to 9072's humble nature, he blushes, only deepening the bartender's sense that this man would make a first-class provider of genetic material. Throughout the evening, 9072 is sociable and composed, at ease with self and others. Meanwhile, 5546 hits on four different women before last call, and 3811 stays on a stool, swiping through his phone, aloof and alone.

The least confident of the four women takes 5546 to her house, where they have unprotected sex, and she happens to be ovulating, but because his sperm are too weak to puncture her egg, she doesn't get pregnant.

Donor 3811 leaves after two beers, without talking to any humans.

Donor 9072 strikes up a conversation with the most confident of the four women hit on by 5546. She is drawn to 9072's good health and good brain. They discuss his rock-climbing skills and his beautiful sister. He walks the woman to her car, where she tells him she wants to have sex, but he shakes his head politely.

"I'm a sperm donor," he explains, "and my sperm are exceptionally vigorous, which means I'm likely to impregnate whatever body receives them, whether through intercourse or intrauterine insemination. So I can't go around having a lot of sex. If too many children are conceived from my loin butter, especially in the same geographical area, some of them might meet each other and fall in love. Which would be bad."

The woman understands, and they part as friends.

But how can you raise a child alone when you can't resist twelve ounces of coffee?

When you've been known to eat peanut butter on a spoon for dinner?

When you often go to bed without brushing your teeth?

Ab ovo. The twin eggs of Leda, impregnated by Zeus in swan form: one hatched into Helen, who would launch ships. Start from the beginning. Except there is no beginning. Can the biographer remember first thinking, feeling, or deciding she wanted to be someone's mother? The original moment of longing to let a bulb of lichen grow in her until it came out human? The longing is widely endorsed. Legislators, aunts, and advertisers approve. Which makes the longing, she thinks, a little suspicious.

Babies once were abstractions. They were *Maybe I do, but not now.* The biographer used to sneer at talk of biological deadlines, believing the topic of baby craziness to be crap for lifestyle magazines. Women who worried about ticking clocks were the same women who traded salmon-loaf recipes and asked their husbands to clean the gutters. She was not and never would be one of them.

Then, suddenly, she was one of them. Not the gutters, but the clock.

The narwhal's blotchy hide has been likened to the skin of a drowned mariner. Its stomach has five rooms. It can hold its breath under the ice for outrageous lengths. And the male horn, of course — much could be said.

THE MENDER

Would kill to never make another trip to the Acme, yet her needs can't be met entirely by the forest, orchards, fields, or clients who trade with fish and batteries. For certain essentials she must use green cash. But the store lights hurt the mender's eyes. And the floors are so hard. And she notices—because even though the teachers at Central Coast Regional called her stupid, she is not stupid—that people stare at her in the Acme. They take their children's hands.

She is here for ginger, sesame oil, Band-Aids, thread, and a box of black licorice nibs. Passing the butcher counter, she is sickened to see the machine-pressed slices, the loaves of meat. Oils from the tissues of pig and cow and lamb glisten on the air. She has a long walk in front of her, in the rain, and night is coming. She speeds up toward the candy aisle, where her nibs—

"I know what you did"—a low snarl, nearly unhearable.

The mender keeps on.

Louder: "Dolores Fivey almost *died*."

She keeps on, staring at the end of the aisle, where she will turn right.

Loudest: "She was in the ICU! Do you care? Do you even *care?*"—voice lifting to the vast fluorescent beds, but the mender won't look, she won't grace them with a look.

"Find everything okay today?" says the cashier.

The mender nods, staring down.

"Cool necklace, by the way."

She always wears her Aristotle's lanterns to town.

Lola didn't almost die. It would have been in the newspaper at the library.

Ignore them, says Temple from the freezer. *People will believe any old crap.*

* * *

Her cloak is sopping by the time she reaches home. Wool socks squelch in her sandals. In the goat shed, pouring grain, nuzzled by the snouts of her beautifuls, she tells Temple: "I hate them all." Runs her hand over the lid of the chest freezer, listening, though she knows Temple won't come back.

Salem, Massachusetts, 1692: a "witch cake" was baked with rye flour and urine from girls said to have been stricken by spells. This fragrant cake was fed to a dog. When the dog ate it, the witch would suffer—so went the folk wisdom—and her yelps of agony would incriminate her.

"How did they get the girls' urine?" the young mender wanted to know.

"Unimportant," said Temple. "The important thing is that people will believe any old crap. Never forget that, okay? Any. Old. Crap."

The mender misses her aunt every day.

It's not true that she hates them all, but it makes her feel better to say it.

She doesn't hate the girl she watches for.

And she doesn't hate Lola. She misses the compliments—"You have the coolest eyes I ever saw." The sugar packets and shakers of salt Lola stole from restaurants for the mender. She misses Lola's finger in her slit, Lola's plump tits in her mouth.

No visits or notes in over a month. The mender has considered going back to the big sandstone house, when the husband's at work, to bring her a spray of fawn lily. But Lola might get confused again.

She had come to the cabin for help with a burn. The mender knew she was lying about how she got the burn.

* * *

She adds wood to the stove. Eats a cold white stalk of ghost pipe. Steps out of her wet clothes, stands naked by the stove until she is dry.

Who was that yelling in the Acme? What has Lola been telling people?

The last time, Lola wore a green dress, shoulders bare. The scar was knitting well, less puckery, but it would be on her forearm the rest of her life. Into the marked skin the mender rubbed elderflower oil infused with lemon, lavender, and fenugreek.

"That feels so good," said Lola.

"Okay," said the mender, wiping her hands on an old washcloth. Packed bottle and washcloth into her rucksack. "See you."

"But you just got here!"

The mender blinked at the flowered couch, bag of golf clubs, family photos running up the long staircase. Through the cork soles of her sandals she felt the wall-to-wall teeming with carpet-beetle larvae.

"He won't be back until five. We could . . . ?" Little plucked eyebrow twitched coaxingly. "I haven't seen you for two whole weeks," added Lola, coming closer. "I *missed* you. I have this friend in Santa Fe"—nudging the mender's toe with her shiny black boot—"who sells handmade piñon kokopellis. We could go there for a while. He'd never find—"

"I won't leave my animals."

Clumsily stroking the mender's biceps: "Maybe I could stay with you, then?"

Jab of heat in her throat. "You can't stay."

"Why not?" Lola stepped back, frowning. "I thought you liked me, Gin."

Humans always want more.

"I like you," said the mender.

"But—" A panicky smile. "Hold on, are you . . . ?"

"It's just," began the mender.

Devil flowers danced on the couch, jumping, blurring.

"What? *What?*"

But some feelings aren't fastened to words.

"It—isn't—I don't—" The mender's tongue was an oily toe.

"Can't you talk? Can't you even *say a sentence?*" Lola slid her hands up and down her thighs, bunching the green dress, smoothing it, bunching again. "You know everyone thinks you're crazy, right?"

"I'm not crazy."

"You're *bat*shit," hissed Lola.

The mender took the scar oil from her sack and set it on the coffee table. "You can keep the whole bottle. No charge."

Lola said, "Get the fuck out of my house."

She couldn't understand—and the mender wasn't good at helping her understand—how much the mender likes to be alone. Human-wise.

Sea-washed lighthouse built with:

Aberdeen granite
salt-tolerant poplar
hydraulic lime

Bells and sledgehammer = fog signal

THE DAUGHTER

Please be bloody. Please be a gush of dark mucus, black-strung red.

Pulls down her underwear.

White as cake.

"Where's the goddamn table leaf?" shouts her dad, stomping downstairs.

The Salem cousins come for dinner in an hour.

She fishes under the sink for the box of tampons and tugs out what's hidden under the Regulars and Super Pluses.

"Shut up," she tells the shiny blond infant on the box.

Thighs planted on the toilet, she tears the plastic sheath off the pee stick.

There is a loving home out there for every baby who comes into the world.

She doesn't weep or hyperventilate or text Ash a photo of the plus sign blazing on the stick. She wraps the test box and its contents in a brown paper bag, which she tucks into a rain boot at the back of her closet. She gets dressed.

The witch has a treatment, if it's early enough. And she doesn't charge money. Ash's sister's friend, who got an abortion from the witch last year, said it only works before a certain week in the pregnancy. The witch uses wild herbs that won't incriminate you if you're caught with them, because the police can't tell what they are. And the daughter doesn't plan to be caught.

Yasmine could have gone to Canada for an abortion, because the Pink Wall didn't exist yet. Or she could have given the baby to someone else.

Yasmine asked what it felt like to be adopted.

The daughter said, "Normal."

Which was true and not true.

* * *

Yasmine knew the daughter was curious about her bio mother.

Maybe she

Was too young.
Was too old—didn't have the energy.
Already had six kids.
Knew she was about to die of cancer.
Was a tweaker.
Just didn't feel like dealing.

It was a closed adoption. There is no way to find her, aside from a private detective the daughter can't afford yet.

So she dreams.

About her bio mother getting famous for developing a cure for paralysis and being on the cover of a magazine in the checkout line, where the daughter instantly recognizes her face.

About her bio mother finding *her.* The daughter comes down the school steps, the three o'clock bell is ringing, and a woman in sunglasses rushes up, shouting, "Are you mine?"

About her bio grandmother, who maybe loved to bake. She sees the ramekins her bio grandmother used for custard. A set of six, white-rimmed blue, one chipped. Her bio mother maybe always chose to eat from the chipped one.

The ramekins are smashed at the bottom of a well in the yard of the house where they all died, grandmother and grandfather and cousins and her bio mother, who was still weak from giving birth, overwhelmed with sadness, resolved to go the next day to the agency and get her baby back—she had a forty-eight-hour window; it had only been thirty hours; she would go the next day; now she just needed a little rest, but what was that smell? It was smoke, because fire, because malfunctioning space heater, but nobody was paying attention because drunk, and her bio mother, though not drunk, was too exhausted from the pain of labor to call out a warning; so they died.

An aunt, arriving later to pick through the rubble, threw all non-valuables into the well. If this well existed—if the daughter could find it—she'd climb down a rope and save the pieces of white ramekin, the spoons and knives, tin canisters of love notes, steel lockets packed with hair. That hair would have the DNA of her bio mother, sealed safe from fire and from damp.

Sixteen years ago abortion was legal in every state.

Why did she spend nine months growing the daughter if she was just going to give her up?

The Salem cousins yammer in the hall. Upon seeing the daughter, Aunt Bernadette goes, "What is it about these teenagers dressing so *unemployably?*" and Dad laughs. Mom, not laughing, tells Aunt Bernadette: "Mattie can wear whatever she wants. Last time I checked, this was America."

Mom and daughter escape to the kitchen.

"Would you wash the potatoes?"

The daughter dumps them into a colander, starts scrubbing under the faucet.

"By the way..." There's a forced-cheerful note in her voice. "I got a call from Susan Korsmo."

"Yeah?" says the daughter, scrubbing harder.

"It was an odd conversation, frankly."

"Oh really?"

"She expressed some concerns."

"About what?" Thank God for you, potato dirt. So much scrubbing you require.

"Well, I told her it was ridiculous, but she sounded—I don't know, adamant. Although she tends to sound adamant most of the time."

There is no way Mrs. K. could know. No way.

"Matilda, look at me."

She turns off the faucet, wipes her hands on her jeans. "So what was she adamant about?"

Mom's face is papery, punched in. "She says you were vomiting at her house. When you babysat last week. She heard you in the bathroom."

No.

"And she thinks you have an eating disorder."

Yes!

"This is funny to you?" says Mom.

"It's—no—because she's so wrong."

"Is she?"

The daughter reaches her arms around Mom's neck, presses a cheek into her shoulder. "I ate a bad burrito at school and threw up. Mrs. K. has too much time on her hands, so she—"

"Creates a crisis where there is none," whispers Mom. Then she draws back, cups the daughter's chin in her fingers. "You're sure, pigeon? You'd tell me if something was up?"

"I swear to you, I do not have an eating disorder."

"Thank Christ." Tears in her eyes.

The daughter is lucky to have this mother, even if she's already sixty, even if she makes jokes about pulling a mussel at a seafood disco. A young mom like Ephraim's might have said "Bulimia? I've taught you well!"

For reasons she can't figure out, the daughter almost never dreams of her bio father.

She takes an extra-big spoonful of mashed potatoes. Looks at Mom, points to the plate, winks, hates how hard Mom is smiling. She breathes through her mouth when passed the bowl of brussels sprouts, the vegetable whose odor, when cooked, most closely resembles human wind.

The Salem cousins blather and blither. "Well, what do the illegals expect, a red carpet?" Blahblahblahblah. "And then they refuse to learn English—" Blahblahblahblah. "So then why should I have to take three years of Spanish?" Blahblahblahblahblah. The invaders all look like xeroxes of each other, their beefiness repeating itself, reheating itself. Whereas the daughter is tall, and Dad is short. The daughter is pale, and Mom is sallow.

This clump of cells would have turned out tall, though maybe not pale. Ephraim tans brown in the summer.

Gravy has dried on the daughter's sleeve. She hates this shirt anyway. Maybe she'll give it to Aunt Bernadette, who hates it even more.

Mom and Dad can never know.

What if your bio mother had chosen to terminate?

"Matilda, your turn."

"Pass," says the daughter.

Think of all the happy adopted families that wouldn't exist!

Never, ever know.

"Oh, you!"

"Don't be a poop at the party."

"I can't think of any jokes," she says.

"Very funny!"

"What is it with these kids pretending to be so miserable?"

Yasmine said she'd die before telling her parents.

jumps down the sky (lightning)

sheep groaning (what narwhals sound like)

a smell grew

sea struck, ice bound

causing regret where it did not exist before

THE WIFE

Didier hums "You Are My Sunshine" and trims fat off raw breasts. He worked in kitchens for years, scorns recipes, is good with a knife. A decent restaurant job would pay better than teaching at Central Coast Regional, but he swore off food and bev because he'd miss the kids' childhoods. The wife sees a calendar of vacant blue evenings, Didier away cooking, children in bed, herself alone and accountable to no one.

"—the tinfoil?"

"What?"

"Foil, woman!" Didier trots over to snatch it. His mood is merry; he's happiest when cooking, a dish towel slung over his shoulder. Happiest, yet he rarely cooks.

"What else?" she says.

"I'm good here. Go relax."

"Really? Okay." She rubs at a smear of old yogurt on the stovetop. "Should I do a salad?"

"You should sit down."

She watches him chop, one hand herding the olives and the other bringing down the knife, fast, accurate. Eyes don't waver from the olives. Shoulders don't slump. Happy and confident, yet most of the meals fall to her, the one who "has time."

"By the way, why is Mattie still here?"

"She's putting them to bed."

Didier sets down the knife and looks at her. "We're paying twelve dollars an hour to keep our kids at home while we're at home?"

"Well, I would like, for once, to have dinner with you alone. Without the kids underfoot."

"Just saying, it's a luxury, whereas a cleaning service—"

"You mean like living rent-free is a luxury?"

He scrapes the olives off the cutting board into a bowl and lifts his beer bottle. "Is that gonna be held over my head for a*nother* six years?"

"How about, regardless, it's saving us a lot of money?"

"That's like saying 'Be grateful you live in purgatory, because it's cheaper than—' "

"Newville is hardly purgatory," says the wife. The yogurt is stubborn; she licks her finger and rubs again. "I saw this thing on the road. A burnt little animal. I thought some kid had set it on fire. It was trying to get across to the other side."

"As in the great hereafter?"

"Of the road. It was burnt within an inch of its life, but it was still moving—which felt so, I don't know, brave?—and I wanted to help it, but it was already dead."

Her husband slaps the breasts onto a foiled baking sheet. "I've never understood that saying, 'within an inch of its life.' Like there was some danger right *next* to its life but not quite touching it?"

"This little animal. It's weird. I can't stop thinking about it."

"Where's the salt?"

"I think it was a possum. It was like it wasn't accepting death—or didn't even realize death was near. It *kept going*."

"There you are, Salty McSalterton." He dusts the chicken, slides the pan into the oven. "You know what's so messed up about Ro's sperm donors?"

The wife closes her eyes. "What?"

"They can totally lie on the application. All four grandparents died of cirrhosis, but dude claims they're alive and healthy? Nobody's checking. I'm surprised that somebody as neurotic as Ro isn't worried."

"She's not neurotic." But it pleases her to hear him say it.

"You don't work with her." He sets the timer. "She's in full denial mode. Doesn't realize what a nightmare it's going to be. By herself? It's a nightmare even where there's two of you."

"Didier, I want to go to counseling."

He wipes his hands, hard, on a kitchen towel. "So go."

"*Couples* counseling."

"Told you before"—reaching for his beer—"I'm not a therapy person. Sorry."

"What does that even mean?"

"Means that I don't respond well to being blamed for things that aren't my fault."

Oh God, not his father again.

"I found someone in Salem," she says, "who's highly recommended, and they do late-afternoon appointments—"

"Did you not hear me, Susan?"

"Just because you had an incompetent therapist in Montreal thirty years ago? That's a *great* reason not to try to save—" She stops. Licks her finger again, scratches at the yogurt on the stove.

"What? Save what?"

"Can you please just *consider* it? One session?"

"Why are people in the States obsessed with therapy? There's other ways to solve problems."

"Such as?"

"Such as hiring a cleaning service."

"Oh, *okay*."

"Since you clearly don't want to do it yourself. Which"—he holds up a palm, nodding—"I *get*. I don't feel like cleaning either, especially after being at work all day."

"I'd much rather be at work all day," she says, wondering, as the words settle in the air, if this is true.

"Then get a job. No one's stopping you. Or go back to law school."

"I wish it were that easy."

"Seems pretty easy to me." He is paper-toweling translucent pink shreds of raw chicken off the cutting board. "Honestly, Susan? Things aren't that bad. I mean, yes, some things could be better. But I'm not gonna drive ninety miles to talk about how I should've bought you better presents on your birthday."

Or any presents.

"But what about the kids?" she says. "They sense things—Bex asks—"

"The kids are fine."

She takes a long breath. "Are you saying they wouldn't benefit from our relationship improving?"

"It's kind of interesting that you don't give a fuck about *my* benefit. That douchebag brainwashed my mom, and she never stopped blaming me. Me, who was basically a child."

"I know it wasn't your fault he left, but—"

"The therapist didn't even care why I hit him. Said it was 'immaterial.' Really, dude?"

"You broke your dad's nose."

"Well, he did a lot worse to me. Which is my point. The goal of therapy is to make you feel like dog shit in the name of insight. I'm gonna pay two hundred bucks an hour to feel like dog shit?"

"Mrs. Korsmo?" A small voice from the hall.

"Yes?"

"Sorry to bother you," calls Mattie, "but John scratched Bex's arm, and she's pretty upset about it."

"Did he break the skin?" shouts the wife.

"No, but—"

"Then can you please just deal with it?"

Mattie appears in the doorway, nervous. "Bex says she needs you."

"Well, she doesn't. Tell her I'll be up to check on her later."

"I'll go," says Didier. "Take the chicken out when it buzzes."

"But we weren't finished," says the wife.

He follows Mattie toward the stairs.

The wife shoves the chicken-stained cutting board into the dishwasher. Picks olives off the countertop. Wipes stray salt into her palm.

She washes her hands.

Switches the timer off but keeps the oven on.

Ignites a burner on the gas stovetop to high.

Reaches in with a pot holder for a breast, which she drops onto the burner's high open flame. It flares and spits and sizzles, the whole breast blue with fire.

Darkening, bubbling.

Charred and rubbery.

Little animal, burnt black.

Her mother's hand over hers on the knife.

The lamb's face coming off.

Upon tasting a new batch of *skerpikjøt,* her mother boasted she could name the very hillside on which the lamb had grazed. No one believed her, but it was wiser, with this mother, to applaud the sensitivity of her tongue.

This mother informed the explorer only two days before the wedding that she was to marry a man she'd never set eyes on, a widowed salmoner aged fifty-two. Eivør was old to be unmarried — nineteen.

THE BIOGRAPHER

Good Ship Chinese is full of teachers, thanks to a federal mandate that doubled the number of standardized tests in public schools. Only half the staff are needed to proctor this afternoon's exams.

The bleached-blond waitress pours their waters and says, "I'll give you a minute." A hairy mole clings to her cheek.

Didier reaches to pinch something from the biographer's collar. "You had oatmeal for breakfast."

She bats his hand away. He kicks her under the table. In front of Susan she doesn't touch Didier. Doesn't want her thinking *Does she want my husband?* because the biographer doesn't, and if she did, all the more reason not to arouse suspicion. Susan once told the biographer how the music teacher had flirted her tiny ass off with Didier at the summer picnic, and Bex, drawing at the kitchen table, said, "Did she put her tiny ass back on?" and Susan said, "I wish you'd be seen and not heard for once in your life." The biographer was pleased to know that Susan could be an unskillful parent.

"How goes your saga," says Pete, "of the lady adventurer?"

"Almost finished."

"I have no doubt." He flaps his placemat vigorously, airing himself. "Everyone needs a good hobby."

"It's not a hobby," she says.

"The hair coming out of that mole," says Didier, "has got to be three inches long."

"Of course it's a hobby," says Pete. "You do it on weekends or vacations. The act of doing it brings you amusement but no profit or gain."

"You guys want to order? I can flag down the hair taxi."

"So if something doesn't make money," says the biographer, "it's automatically relegated to hobby?"

The waitress returns. Her sprouting hair—quite long, quite black—for a moment mesmerizes all of them. The biographer, who bleaches her own upper lip every few weeks, warms with fellow feeling. She and Pete order Golden Lily platters, Didier the Emperor's Consolation.

Didier leans forward to say, low: "Why don't she just bleeding yank that thing out, eh?"

There is an egg bracing to burst out of its sac into the wet fallopian warmth. Today the ovulation predictor kit showed no smiley face; she'll test again tomorrow. Back to Kalbfleisch for sperm, once she gets the smiley face.

"Pour me some more tea, Roanoke?"

She moves the teapot six inches toward him.

"I said *pour,* woman! Can I get a ride home, by the way? I left Susan the car today."

"How were you planning on getting home if I didn't drive you?"

Didier grins, *beau-laid*. "I knew you'd drive me."

Bryan Zakile saunters over to their table and bellows, "*These* three are clearly up to no good! Want to hear my fortune? 'You will leave a trail of gratitude.'"

"'In bed,'" adds Didier.

"You said it, not me."

"Not I," mutters the biographer.

Bryan flinches. "Thank you, grammar Schutzstaffel."

She drags her fork through the Golden Lilies. "I'm not the one who teaches English."

"He don't really teach English either," says Didier. "His subject is the beautiful game."

"If only that knee had held up," says Pete, "we'd be watching Bryan on telly. Who'd you be playing for? Barça? Man United?"

"Hilarious, Peter, but I was All-Conference for three years at Maryland."

"That is tre*mend*ously impressive."

The biographer smiles at Pete. Surprised, he smiles back.

Sometimes he reminds her of her brother.

* * *

She can't use the ovulation predictor test when she wakes up, because first morning urine isn't optimal for detecting the surge of luteinizing hormone that augurs the egg's release. She has to wait four hours to let enough urine accumulate in her bladder, and in these four hours she can't drink too many fluids, lest she dilute the urine and skew the results. Instead of coffee, she toasts a frozen waffle and gnaws it unbuttered at the kitchen table. She stares at the bookstore photograph. The shelf where her book will go.

Between first and second periods, in a stall of the staff bathroom, the biographer inserts a fresh pee-catching tab into the plastic wand of the ovulation predictor kit and squats over the toilet. The instructions say you don't need to absorb the whole stream, only five seconds' worth, which is good because the opening spray goes wide of the stick. She has to keep moving the stick around under herself to find it. Count to five. Rest the stick on some toilet paper on the metal tampon receptacle, angled just so, to allow the caught pee to wend its way through the stick into whatever mechanism tests it for luteinizing hormone. Which takes a minute or longer.

She wipes her wet hands, pulls up her jeans, sits back down on the toilet. During this minute or longer, while the digital display blinks—it will turn into an empty circle or a smiley-faced circle—the biographer sings the egg-coaxing song. "I may be alone, I may be a crone, but fuck you, I can still ovulate!"

She checks: still blinking.

Woman who is thin and ugly. Withered old woman. Cruel and ugly old woman. Witch-like woman. Stock character in fairy tale. Woman over forty. From the Old Northern French *caroigne* ("carrion" or "cantankerous woman") and from the Middle Dutch *croonje* ("old ewe").

Still blinking.

Through the bathroom wall come shrieks of girls whose ovaries are young and juicy, crammed with eggs.

Still blinking.

What is the total number of human eggs in this building right now?

Still blinking.

How many of the human eggs in this building right now will get sperm pricked, cracked open, to produce another human?

She checks: smiley face!

Bloom of delight in her ribs.

I may be forty-two, but I can still fucking ovulate.

"Hello, yes, I'm calling because I got my LH surge today—Okay, sure..." Holding, holding. "Yes, hi, this is Roberta Stephens...Yes, right...And I surged today...Yeah...And I'm using donor sperm so I wanted to—Okay, sure..." Holding, holding, bell shrilling; that was the second bell; she's late for her own class. "Okay...Yes, I've got more than one donor in storage, but I'd like you to use number 9072."

Donor semen is frozen shortly after collection and thawed shortly before insemination. In between, millions of sperm lie arrested, aslant, their genetic material paused. Tomorrow morning, before she arrives, the clinic staff will thaw a vial of 9072 (Rock Climber Beautiful Sister) and spin its contents in a centrifuge to separate sperm from seminal fluid, wash the swimmers clean of prostaglandins and debris.

"See you at seven!" she tells the nurse, so excited her throat hurts.

Tomorrow at seven. At seven tomorrow. Tomorrow, in Salem, on a leafy little upmarket street, at the hands of a former tight end, the biographer will be inseminated.

If it is possible for you to come to me, little one, let you come to me.

If it is not possible, let you not come, and let me not be shattered.

She can hardly sleep. Is holding a jar of some sort of face cream that contains opiates, and is going to cook it and shoot it, and is hunting in her mother's bathroom for cotton. She needs to hide the gear from her mother. But she also *is* her mother, and the person with the jar is Archie. "What happened to the cotton balls?" he asks. "All gone. Use a filter." "But I'm out of cigarettes!" says Archie. "Maybe I have some," says the biographer.

She wakes before the alarm. Glass of water, her brother's old green parka, her mother's bike-lock key on a chain around her neck. The biographer is an atheist, but she doesn't rule out helpful ghosts.

"Archie's the charmer," said their mother. "You're the wise one."

She leaves her apartment building in the briny dark, sea crashing, car freezing. No other cars on the cliff road. Her headlights sweep the rock wall, the fir tops, the black ocean flecked with silver, same road and water the baby will see one day.

7:12 a.m.: Signs in at the front desk. Takes her place among the silent, rock-fingered women.

7:58 a.m.: Nurse Jolly leads her to an exam room, where she strips below the waist and climbs under the paper sheet. Her heart is going twice as fast. Do quickened beats affect fertilization? In last night's dream, she—as Archie—planned to shoot up into her chest, left-hand side, because she'd been told a "heart direct" made the pleasure immense.

8:49 a.m.: Kalbfleisch stands beside the biographer's spread legs and stirruped feet and shows her a vial. "Is this the correct donor?" She squints: 9072 from Athena Cryobank. Yes. "The count on this vial was quite good," he says. "Thirteen point three million moving sperm."

"Remind me what the average is?"

"We want the count to be at least five million."

He inserts a speculum into the biographer's vagina. It does not exactly hurt—more of a serious pressure—then he opens her cervix, and the pressure turns teeth clenching. A plastic catheter is guided through the speculum into the biographer's uterus. The nurse hands Kalbfleisch the syringe of washed semen, an inch of pale yellow. He injects it into the catheter, depositing the semen at the top of her uterus, near the fallopian tubes.

The whole thing takes less than a minute.

He snaps off his gloves and says "Good luck" and goes.

"Rest for a bit, hon," says Nurse Jolly. "You want any water?"

"No thanks, but thank you."

In-breath.

She is so, so scared.

Out-breath.

Either this has to work or she has to be matched with a bio mother in the next two months. After January fifteenth, when Every Child Needs Two goes into effect, no adopted kid will have to suffer from a single woman's lack of time, her low self-esteem, her inferior earning power. Every adopted kid will now reap the rewards of growing up in a two-parent home. Fewer single mothers, say the congressmen, will mean fewer criminals and addicts and welfare recipients. Fewer pomegranate farmers. Fewer talk-show hosts. Fewer cure inventors. Fewer presidents of the United States.

In-breath.

Keep your legs, Stephens.

Out-breath.

She lies perfectly still.

In high school she ran for hours every day of track season—had muscles then, had stamina. She competed in the four hundred and the eight hundred, and though not a star, she was decent, even won a few meets her senior year. Archie, tenth-grader, pressed himself against the chain-link fence and cheered. Her parents sat in the bleachers and cheered. Her mother made celebratory dinners with the biographer's favorite foods: green-chile scrambled eggs, peanut-butter pie. How she loved the laden table, the lamps, the spring-night crickets, Mama before she got sick, Archie in his skull T-shirt balancing a spoonful of pie on his head. In the beam of their attention she was tired and proud, a warrior who had slung her arrow into every heel she aimed for.

* * *

If it is possible for you to come to me, let you come to me, and I will name you Archie.

In the car, she opens the ziplock of pineapple chunks, whose bromelain is supposed to encourage a fertilized egg to implant itself in the uterine wall. It will be five days before the egg is ready to implant, but eating pineapple comforts the biographer. Its sweetness is strong and good against the bitter, spitty fear.

Five days. Two months. Forty-two years. She hates the calendar.

Please let it work this time.

She doesn't move her pelvis the whole drive home. Lifts her toes carefully on the brake and accelerator, no thigh muscle. "Hell, you could go to the gym today if you wanted," said Kalbfleisch after the first insemination, to underscore how much it didn't matter what the biographer's body did after a few minutes of lying still on the exam table; but the biographer's body is going to stay as quiet as it can.

It has to work this time.

She will sit behind her desk in class without thigh movement or pelvic commotion of any kind; and the eggs will float in the tube waters unjarred, open, amenable; and one sperm-struck egg will welcome a single invading spermatozoon into itself, ready to meld and to split. From one cell, two. From two, four. From four, eight. An eight-celled blastocyst has a chance.

I spent eighteen months in my husband's house before a storm sank his boat and him with it.

That in eighteen months I had not been gotten with child brought shame to my mother.

The red morn I left for Aberdeen, she said, "Go on, get that broken *fisa* away from us."

THE DAUGHTER

Her parents aren't religious. Their reasons are pragmatic, they say. Logical. So many people *want* to adopt. Why should people be deprived of babies they will nourish, cherish, rain love down upon, just because other people don't feel like being pregnant for a few months? When the Personhood Amendment passed, her father said it was about time the country came to its senses. He had no truck with the wackos who bombed clinics, and he thought it was going a little too far to make women pay for funerals for their miscarried fetuses; but, he said, there was a loving home out there for every baby who came into the world.

Her eighth-grade social-studies class held a mock debate on abortion. The daughter prepared bullet points for the pro-choice team. Her father proofread her work, as usual; but instead of his usual "This is top-notch!" he sat down beside her, rested a hand on her shoulder, and said he was concerned about the implications of her argument.

"What if your bio mother had chosen to terminate?"

"Well, *she* didn't, but other people should be able to."

"Think of all the happy adopted families that wouldn't exist."

"But Dad, a lot of women would still give their babies up for adoption."

"But what about the women who didn't?"

"Why can't everyone just decide for themselves?"

"When someone decides to murder a fellow human with a gun, we put them in jail, don't we?"

"Not if they're a cop."

"Think of all the families waiting for a child. Think of me and your mom, how long we waited."

"But—"

"An embryo is a living being."

"So is a dandelion."

"Well, I can't imagine the world without you, pigeon, and neither can your mother."

She doesn't want them to imagine the world without her.

Ash offers a ride home, but the daughter says no, her dad is coming; retirement means he's so bored he can pick her up anytime. It is cold, dim skied, the grass on the soccer field stiff and silver. The team has an away game today. She hasn't told Ephraim. What if he's like "Is it even mine?" Or "You made your bed; now lie in it." They passed each other last week in the cafeteria, and Ephraim in the old-school hat she once adored said, "Hey," and she said, "Hey, how are you?" but he kept moving and her non-rhetorical question was rhetorical. He was probably on his way to put his hand up Nouri Withers's shirt.

Her bio mother could have been young too. She could have been headed to medical school, then to a neurochemistry doctorate program, then to her own research lab in California. (What if she's close, at this very moment, to finding a cure for paralysis?) Keeping the daughter would have meant forfeiting her med-school scholarship.

She doesn't want the kid to wonder why he wasn't kept.

And she doesn't want to wonder what happened to him. Was he given to parents like hers or parents who scream and are bigots and don't take him to the doctor enough?

She jumps at the tsunami siren—will never get used to that nerve-scraping howl.

"Only a test, my love," says Dad.

She turns up the car radio.

"How was school?"

"Fine."

"Finished the academy application yet?"

"Almost."

"Mom's making fish tacos."

She swallows down a little spurt of vomit. "Awesome."

"Earlier today," goes the radio, *"twelve sperm whales ran aground a half mile south of Gunakadeit Point. The cause of the beaching has not yet been determined."*

"Oh my God." She turns it up.

"Eleven of the whales are dead, says the sheriff's office, though it remains unclear—"

"Remember the stranding of '79?" says Dad. "Forty-one sperms on the beach near Florence. My pop drove out to photograph them up close. He said they made—"

"Little clicking sounds while they died." She knows the gruesome details, because Dad likes to repeat them. He's told her many times that a whale can be killed by the pressure of its own flesh. Out of water, the animal's bulk is too heavy for its rib cage—the ribs break; the internal organs are crushed. And heat hurts whales. Greenpeacers brought in bedsheets to soak with seawater and throw over them; it didn't help.

But that was 1979. Hasn't somebody by now figured out a way to get them back into the ocean?

"Can we go down there, Dad?"

"They don't need the public meddling in—"

"But one is still alive."

"Are you going to roll it back down to the water yourself? Don't turn this into a morbid preoccupation."

"The heart of a sperm whale weighs almost three hundred pounds."

"How do—?"

"Me and Yasmine once made a list of how much different animals' hearts weigh."

"Yasmine and I." Dad gets tense at the mention of her. "Don't worry too much about the whales, okay, pigeon? Otherwise those lovely eyebrows might get tangled up in one another, never to untangle."

"They're not lovely, they're thick."

"Which is what makes them lovely!"

"You're not objective." She wants a cigarette but will content herself with a licorice nib, for now.

Ash isn't into the idea. So tired, etc. But she is convincible. The daughter crawls out her bedroom window onto the roof, rappels down the trellis, stands still a full minute in the porch shadow in case any noises were heard. A block away is the blue mailbox, their meeting place, where she smokes and waits.

Yasmine once asked her why white people are so obsessed with saving whales.

The beach is crowded with people shouting, dogs yapping, cameras popping, rain raining. A TV crew has aimed screeching lights on the whales, a row of twelve, their pewter-gray hides slashed with chalky white. They look like stone buses. The one at the very end is slowly lifting and dropping its flukes. Each time a fluke hits the sand, the daughter's thighs tremble.

Humans pose for photos in front of the dead.

A guy has clambered onto a massive gray tail. "Snap me!" he shouts. "Snap me!"

"Get the hell down."

"Move back, folks!"

"Did the dead man's fingers have anything to do with this?"

"Who do I talk to about reserving some of the teeth? For scrimshaw?"

"Sir, get down from there immediately."

"Were they poisoned by the seaweed?"

"Move aside, move aside."

A woman with gloves and a long knife—a scientist?—squats by the first whale in the row. Will she carve off a slice of blubber to test for disease? A madness, maybe, has infected their spines and driven them onto land, all twelve fevered with death wish. Maybe the infection can pass to humans. Newville will be quarantined.

"You need to leave, girls," says a cop not much older than they are. "We're clearing the beach. And put out that cigarette."

"Why isn't anyone putting them back in the water?" says the daughter.

The cop peers at her. "A, they're dead. B, you realize how much these goddamn things weigh?"

"But one of them *isn't* dead!"

"Go home, okay?"

She and Ash walk past the enormous bodies—one spray-painted with an orange question mark, another sprayed with OUR FAULT!—to the last breathing whale. Its flukes lie still. Blood pools on the sand by its head. The mouth is open, drenched red. The beaky lower jaw, illogically small for such a huge skull, is sown with teeth. The daughter touches one: a banana of bone.

Has moved amid this world's foundations.

"Now your hand is infected," says Ash.

She wipes it on her jeans.

The whale's eye, wedged between wrinkled lips of skin, is open and black and quivering. *Hast seen enough to split the planets.* She kneels down. Leans her cheek against the gray body. Dry, scarred leather.

"It'll be okay," she says.

Can't hear any clicking sounds.

Where are the machines? The cables, the levers?

A whale is a house in the ocean.

A womb for a person.

Whale song is heard from sea floor to star, from Icy Strait Point to Península Valdés.

"Ash, give me your hoodie."

"I'm cold."

"*Give* it." The daughter runs down to the waves and douses Ash's hoodie and her own. Runs back to throw them, dripping, onto the whale's head. The only song she can think of is "I've Been Working on the Railroad." She's in the midst of chanting "Someone's in the kitchen with Dinah" when she hears a gunshot.

Then screams.

Everyone is clustering around something up the beach.

It wasn't a gun; it was a whale. Exploding. The gray belly, split wide, leaks slimy bundles of pink intestine and purple organ meat. Fat shreds of flesh flap in the wind. "Get it off! Get it off!" yells a boy, pawing at ropes of innards stuck to his chest.

And the stink—God!—rancid blast of farts, fish rot, and sewage. The daughter pulls her shirt up over her mouth.

Black-red liquid foams at her feet.

The scientist is explaining to the cop that she'd been trying to collect samples of subcutaneous adipose tissue and visceral adipose tissue. When she sank her knife into the whale, it burst.

"Methane gas builds up in the carcass," she says. "This one must have been the first to die, possibly days ago. If he was their leader and died at sea, and his body floated to shore, the other whales would have followed. They're loyal to a fault."

"Ma'am, you can't just go around chopping up corpses," says the cop.

"This magnificent creature isn't anyone's property," says the scientist. "I intend to analyze the tissue and figure out how they ended up here."

"What lab are you with, ma'am? My captain said the OIMB guys weren't going to be here until—"

"I'm an independent researcher. But *this*"—she holds up two clear plastic bags of red flesh—"I know what to do with."

The daughter heads back to her whale.

His eye is no longer moving.

Thou saw'st the murdered mate when tossed by pirates from the midnight deck.

She presses the eye with her fingertip.

It is clammy and springy, like a hard-cooked egg.

How to make *tvøst og spik*:

1. Prepare pilot-whale meat in one of the following ways: boil fresh, fry fresh, store in dry salt, store in brine, or cut into long strips (*grindalikkja*) and hang to dry.
2. Prepare pilot-whale blubber by boiling, salting, or drying. (Do not fry.)
3. Serve meat and blubber together with boiled and salted potatoes. In some Faroese homes, dried fish is also included on the *tvøst og spik* plate.

THE MENDER

Cotter reports that Lola fell down the stairs. Was in a little coma. Better now.

New clients are supposed to leave a note at the P.O., but Lola just showed up one day, drenched. "I heard of you from my friend." The mender brought her inside, gave her a towel, inspected the red smear on her forearm.

"Is it going to scar?"

"Yes," said the mender. She pressed fresh-bruised leaves of houseleek to the damaged skin, waited, blinked at Lola's breasts, those plump puddings, then wrapped the arm with a poultice of leek juice and lard. "How did this happen?"

"It was stupid," said Lola. "I was making dinner and I caught my arm on a hot pan."

Her husband also snapped her finger bone. Left a six-colored bruise on her jaw.

Two more warts on Clementine's fig.

Clementine says, "This is kind of extremely humiliating?"

"Just a body doing what it does."

"But they're so *nasty*."

"Lots of people get them," says the mender, and she holds a compress of crushed, wet lupine seeds against the vulva. White lupine is also good for bringing down blood—a missed period, a uterus unhappily full—and for calling worms to the surface of the skin. Summers, the mender burns its seeds in stone cups to fend off gnats.

"Stick out your tongue."

Scalloped at the edges, as usual.

"Still eating pizza?"

Clementine cutely scrunches her mouth. "Not *that* much."

"Stop all dairy. Too much dampness in you."

"Hey, would you ever consider waxing your eyebrows?"

"Why?"

"I mean, not that you *need* to, because big brows are making a comeback, but a friend of mine at Snippity Doo Dah does great sugar waxes, if you ever—"

"No," says the mender. If she has such a friend, why not deal with the two-inch hair dangling from that mole? It is a misfit hair, discordant with her bleached curls and fake nails.

The mender spoons a mash of mugwort and ginger into Clementine's belly button; lays a fresh slice of ginger across the mash; holds a burning moxa stick over the ginger until she complains of the heat; and tapes the belly button with two Band-Aids to keep the mash in place for a day at least, better two.

Clementine pulls her shirt down. "Thanks for all your help, Gin." Takes small white boxes from her backpack. "Hope you like fried rice and garlic shrimp. Don't worry, it's not customer leftovers—"

"I'm not worried," says the mender.

Or hungry enough for Chinese food. Once Clementine is gone she drizzles half a slice of brown bread with sesame oil. Every Thursday Cotter leaves a loaf he baked himself, wrapped in a towel, on her cabin step.

Some supermarket breads are made with human hair dissolved in acid, part of a dough conditioner that accelerates industrial processing. The mender does not eat bread from the supermarket, and she has her own supply of hair, which instead of dissolving in acid she grinds into her mixtures. She keeps head hair in a separate box from pubic, as they're good for different things—pubic has more iron, head more magnesium and selenium. The mender's supply came from one person and is dwindling.

* * *

Long red head hairs can be used in mixtures. Brown pubic hairs can be used. But there are some hairs that can't be. The stray whiskers under the arms; the little breath of brown on the upper lip. Those hairs are iced onto the skin of the body in the freezer.

What does the girl's hair taste like, her shining flat dark hair? The girl doesn't slick or shellac it. Long enough to get caught in her satchel strap, the mender noticed when she saw her come through the blue school doors, the girl had to tug and rearrange, she was annoyed for a second, a flip of heat on her cheeks, then she forgot her hair, the mender saw, because she was looking for someone, but the someone wasn't among the burst of kids. The girl kept walking, alone, and the mender almost followed.

The brown bread is dry, because today is Tuesday.

Aunt Temple died on a Tuesday, eight winters ago.

Before Temple, when her mother forgot to buy food, the mender cooked ketchup, mustard, and mayonnaise into a hot crust.

Before Temple, she put herself to bed.

Before Temple, she took a lot of aspirin, because regular doctors were too expensive and the ER staff knew the mender's mother only too well.

Before Temple, she had never been to the movies.

She had those wild red braids and wore billowy purple pants and wasn't married. She laughed in a shrieky way. Her shop was named after a witch who lived in Massachusetts three centuries ago. The people of Newville called Temple a witch too, but they didn't mean it the same way they mean it about the mender.

* * *

When she was young, Goody Hallett loved a pirate who forsook her. Legend has it she killed their baby on the night of its birth, suffocated the thing in a barn, then was imprisoned and lost her mind and lured ships to crash on the Cape Cod rocks. In truth, said Temple, she gave the child in secret to a farmer's wife. The wife kept a diary, which preserved the fact.

The baby is the mender's great-great-great-great-great-great-great-grandfather.

The innermost chamber of her left ear notices powderpost beetles scratching in the roof joists, laying their eggs in the seams of the wood.

"Never forget," said Temple, "that you descend from Black Sam Bellamy and Maria Hallett."

But the mender would never tie a lantern to a whale. Like sailors and fishermen, she hates to swim.

The red morn betoken'd wreck to the seaman and sorrow to the shepherds, woe unto the birds, gusts and foul flaws to herdmen and to herds.

THE WIFE

Screaming screaming screaming. No stop no stop no stop.

"TURN!"

John wants her to play the record again; she will not do it. The whole morning has been records: yell scream yell scream, throw self on floor, starfish arms and legs "TURN!" no stop no.

"Mommy turn it Mommy turn it Mommy turn it Mommy..."

She has reasoned, she has implored, she has ignored, she has worried her eardrums will be actually damaged; and now she says, "Shut the *fuck* up," which makes no difference to John, still screaming and starfishing, but Didier yells from the dining room, "Don't say that to him!"

"Either come and deal with him yourself," calls the wife, "or fuck off."

Her husband stomps in, lifts the dustcover, sets the needle on the record, unleashes a bouncy guitar.

John goes quiet, wetly heaving.

"We are the dinosaurs, marching, marching.

"We are the dinosaurs. Whaddaya think of that?"

"The lesson he just learned," says the wife, "is that if he screams long enough, he'll get what he wants."

"Well, good. It's a hard world."

"We are the dinosaurs, marching, marching.

"We are the dinosaurs. We make the earth flat!"

"Could you take him for a walk?" says the wife.

"It's raining," says Didier.

"His raincoat's on the banister."

"He doesn't look like he wants to go for a walk."

"Please do this one tiny thing," she says.

"I really don't feel like it."

"I'm never alone."

"Well, me neither. I'm with those *trous du cul* all day, five days a week."

"Didier"—slowly, carefully—"will you please take him out. Bex will be back in an hour, and I'll make lunch, but until then, I would like to be alone."

"I'd like to be alone too," he says, but heads for the banister. "Come on, *Jean-voyage*."

Herd crumbs into palm.

Spray table.

Wipe down table.

Rinse cups and bowls.

Put cups and bowls in dishwasher.

Soak quinoa in bowl of water.

Rinse and chop red bell peppers.

Put strips in fridge.

Rinse quinoa in sieve.

Put clean, uncooked quinoa in fridge.

Pour water from quinoa soaking into pot of ficus tree.

Spray mist onto snake-like arms of Medusa's head plant.

Pull clothes out of dryer in basement.

Fold clothes.

Stack clothes in hamper.

Leave hamper at bottom of stairs to second floor.

Write *laundry detergent* on list in wallet.

Plip, plip, plip, says the kitchen tap.

Nobody on this hill even likes quinoa.

She pulls the kids' plastic pumpkins down off the high shelf.

Over a month since Halloween. She told them the candy ran out.

In the empty kitchen or the sewing room, she eats sugar nobody knows about.

She allows herself, now, three coconut crunches. And one almond smushie. And one packet of candy corn.

This is what you're missing, Ro! Ramming stale candy stolen from your own children down your throat.

How can the wife hope that Ro doesn't get pregnant? Doesn't publish her book on the ice scientist?

Plip, plip, plip.

As if Ro's not having a kid or a book would make the wife's life any better.

As if the wife's having a job would make Ro's any worse.

The rivalry is so shameful she can't look at it.

It flickers and hangs.

It waits.

So cold in this house.

She takes off her sweater and pushes it between the back door and the kitchen floor, which is, she notices, sandy with crumbs.

She goes for the broom but ends up with her phone.

Saturday morning: her mother will be puttering, cleaning, paging through magazines.

They see each other, of course, make visits—Thanksgiving is next week—but that's not the same as having her here, in pinches, on spurs of moments. A hundred miles is too far for an unplanned pinch.

She is thirty-seven years old and pines for her mother.

But won't she be thrilled, thirty years hence, to learn that Bex and John are pining for her?

She can see John's little face bigger but still with its translucent emotions, clean feelings surging and waning, her tidal boy. He will always want her.

Bex has too strong an instinct for self-reliance; she'll be fine on her own.

"Hi, Mom," says the wife. "What's your weather?"

"Drizzling. Yours?"

"Oh, um—just gray."

"Sweetpea . . . ?"

"The sprites are good," says the wife.

"Susan, what's going on?"

"Bex's class is doing the *Mayflower,* and John is obsessed by dinosaur songs."

"With you, I meant."

"Nothing," she says.

"What time do you want us on Thursday?" says her mother. "I'm bringing candied yams. I think they'll be a hit."

Everyone on this hill hates yams.

"Come as early as you feel like. I love you, Mom."

Plip, plip, plip.

Shell's perfect mother will drop Bex off in fifteen minutes, and the girl will be full of praise for the fun she has with that family, the plucking of wild berries, the baking of homemade berry pie sweetened only with Grade B maple syrup because refined sugar is toxic.

Then she'll want help with her worksheet. *Write down the weather for each day of the week. Was it sunny? Was it foggy? Was the ocean cheerful or angry?*

At the rim of sleep, she dreams of how Bryan would fuck her, the big thick plunge of him, the brawny thrusting, he's a shoving leopard, lord, he does not tire, all that soccer, those extra-long muscles to drive the blood heartward—

"Meuf." A pinch in the rib meat.

"Nnnnnhhhh."

Didier's breath on her neck. "It bugged me what you said today. To John."

"Nnnnnhhhh."

"Bugged me a lot."

"Are you joking?" she whispers. "You say 'fuck' in front of them all the time. I say it once?"

"But I never tell them to shut up. I don't want you talking to them like that."

"Too bad you don't get to decide," says the wife.

* * *

The next morning she walks out back, feet bare on the cold, wet grass, past the lavender bushes and the garage and the tire swing. Opens her phone and dials.

"Hello?"

"Hi, Bryan, it's Susan." Air, silence. "Didier's wife?"

"Yeah, yeah, of course. How are you?"

"Fine! I, ah, got your number from the school directory and was calling to—say hi." *What?*

"Well, hi there," says Bryan.

"Also, I wanted to invite you to Thanksgiving dinner at our place. If you don't have plans. Ro will be there. She's sort of an orphan. I mean not technically but—And my parents, which isn't—I mean—" *Cease talking. You must cease talking.*

"That's really nice," he says, "but actually I do have plans."

"Oh! Well, I thought I'd ask."

"Mmm."

"Anyway." She coughs.

"Yeah," he says.

"But you and I should have coffee sometime," she says.

Air, silence.

Eventually he says, "I'd like that."

anchor
candle
drift
fast
frazil
grease
nilas
old
pack
pancake
rafted
young

THE BIOGRAPHER

She breaks it to her father quickly, on the drive to school. He doesn't bother to conceal his displeasure. "Another Christmas by myself?"

"I'm sorry, Dad. I have so little time off, and it takes a whole day to fly—"

"I never should've moved."

"You hated Minnesota."

"Give me a blizzard any day over this humid netherworld."

The crease above her pubic bone feels vaguely bloated—or sore—different from period cramps, but the same family of sensation. It's been almost a week since the insemination; she will take a pregnancy test in eight days. Are these signs of implantation? Has a blastocyst burrowed into the red wall? Does it cling and grow with all its might? Are its chromosomes XX or XY?

"Am I ever going to see you again?" says her father.

He won't fly, on account of his back. He would send her money for a plane ticket if she asked, but he can't afford it any more than the biographer can. His income is fixed and small. "I may not have cash to leave you," he likes to say, "but you can sell my coin collection. Worth thousands!"

"You will, Dad."

"I *worry,* kiddo."

"No need! I'm fine."

"But who knows," he says, "how many more trips around the sun *I've* got?"

The boys in ninth-grade history make spitballs and ask, "Miss, in the olden days, when you were young, did they have spitballs?"

The eleventh-graders are enjoying the fruits of someone's research on archaic terms for "penis." When Ephraim yells "Bilbo!" the biographer stares him down, but he stares right back. Usually she has no issues with discipline; this outburst makes her feel like a failure.

Well, she *is* a failure. She and her uterus fail, fail, fail.

Ephraim: "Prepuce!"

The biographer: "That just means foreskin, my friend."

Giggles. Haws. *You said foreskin.*

The biographer and her ovaries fail, fail, fail.

"Baldpate friar!"

But there have been twinges—sharp little aches. Something feels like it's happening down there. Maybe *not* fail, finally? Thousands of bodies succeed every day; why not the body of a biographer from Minnesota whose favorite garment is the sweatpant?

"Nouri," she says, "you can wait to put on lipstick until after class."

"I'm not putting on, I'm refreshing."

Nouri Withers loves books about famous murders and writes the best sentences of any child the biographer has taught. Her sentences need to be typed into a search program to make sure they're not plagiarized.

"You can refresh later."

"But my lips look janky *now.*"

"Agreed!" shouts Ephraim, long legged and fidgety, who thinks himself dashing in his vintage trilby hat. A boy who moves through the world unafraid. If he weren't so fearless and handsome and good at soccer, he might have been forced to grow in more interesting directions. The only thing interesting about Ephraim, as far as the biographer can tell, is his name.

The biographer decides she will shout too. "Have you ever considered, people, how much time has been stolen from the lives of girls and women due to agonizing over their appearance?"

A few faces smile, uneasy.

Even louder: "How many minutes, hours, months, even actual *years,* of their lives do girls and women waste in agonizing? And how many billions of dollars of corporate profit are made as a result?"

Nouri, open mouthed, sets down her lipstick. It stands on the desk like a crimson finger.

"A *lot* of billions, miss?"

These kids must think she's a joke.

"The institution began," she tells the tenth-graders, "as a fiscal arrangement in which the father's household transferred land, money, and livestock to the husband's household, attached to the body of the daughter-bride. Its economic foundations have in recent centuries become shrouded by—some might even say smothered by—the veil of romantic love."

"Are you married, miss?" says Ash.

"Shut up," someone says.

"Nope," says the biographer.

"Why not?" says Ash.

"Shut up!" shouts Mattie.

Silence crackles. Even the half-asleep kids are suddenly alert.

Mattie says, more quietly, "Why did they *die?*"

From the next desk, Ash rubs her shoulder. "You mean the whales?"

"The independent researcher said their sonar could've broken. High-decibel submarine signals can make whales go deaf." Mattie cups her lunar cheeks.

"My dad said it's the witch's fault," says the son of the local navy hero, "because she lured the dead man's fingers back to Newville and they messed up the water."

Shouts and cries: "Yeah, the seaweed poisoned the whales!" "That's so dumb." "But there's been more dead whiting in the nets too—"

"Hold on, people!" says the biographer. "Maybe your dad was joking?"

"My Gramma Costello said the same thing," says Ash, "and the last time she told a joke was 1973."

"Also my dad is not dumb," says the hero's son.

The biographer contemplates digressions into marine biology and the history of witch persecution in Kingdom and States United, but she needs to end class five minutes early to get to her clinic appointment. Kalbfleisch is insisting that she come in to discuss the PCOS test results. A two-hour drive to receive what is probably—almost certainly—going to be bad news.

"There's a Buddhist temple," she says, "on a small island in Japan that used to hold requiems for whales killed by whalers. They prayed for the whales' souls. They also had a tomb for whale fetuses taken from their mothers' bodies during flensing. They would give a posthumous name to every fetus they buried, and they kept a necrology that listed the mothers' dates of capture." She pauses, scanning the room. "Do you see where I'm going with this?"

"Field trip to Japan!"

"Did the ones on the beach have any fetuses inside them?"

"Did you know a 'tus' is a male fetus?"

"We do a requiem," says Mattie. "But first we need to name them."

Good girl. Even when distraught, she pays attention.

"Okay," says the biographer, "there are twenty-four of you. Pair off. Each pair names a whale. You have three minutes. Then we'll reconvene for a recitation and a moment of silence."

"But the temple guys named the *fetuses,* not the grown-ups. You changed the ritual."

"So I did, Ash. Get to work."

She opens her notebook.

Things to do with baby:

1. Take train to Alaska
2. Burrow in blankets
3. Gorge on dried mango
4. Tell stories about the Great Sperm-Whale Stranding
5. Put toes in waves on year's shortest day

Her students christen a Moby-Dick, two Mikes, a Spermy, for God's sake. But then whales are not exotic to these kids. The coastline near Newville is known as the whale-watching capital of the American West. For decades the local economies have depended on injections from tourists eager to see a breaching, lunging, slapping, spraying, spy-hopping colossus. They pay to watch from the decks of boats and through high-powered spotting scopes from the Gunakadeit Lighthouse; or to swim with guides, in wet suits, in the whales' feeding grounds.

The biographer is closing her backpack, thinking ahead to the traffic on 22—she can miss the worst of it if she hurries—when Mattie comes to the desk. "Can I talk to you about something?"

"Of course. I mean not right *now,* because I have a doctor's appointment, but tomorrow?" If she gets out of the parking lot in three minutes, she'll be on the cliff road in seven.

"Tomorrow's Thanksgiving."

"Monday, then."

The girl nods, staring at her hands.

"I know the whales are upsetting," says the biographer, "but—"

"It's not about that."

"Have a good weekend, Mattie." Parka zipped, pack shouldered, she bolts.

She read about the stranding in the paper but has hardly thought of it since. Barnacly, fat-lidded blocks of beast—they only feel real in her book, when young Eivør watches them die in the *grindadráp*.

"How late is Dr. Kalbfleisch running?" she asks the front-desk nurse. "I've been here almost an hour."

"He's a popular guy," says the nurse.

"Could you give me a general idea?"

"It's the day before a holiday," she says.

"And?"

"Sorry?"

"Why should that make a difference?"

The nurse pretends to read something on her computer screen. "I have no way of knowing how much longer the doctor will be. If you need to reschedule, I am happy to help you with that."

"Gee, thanks," says the biographer, and returns to her fawn-colored chair. She touches the bike-lock key on her neck. Her mother rode her bike every morning, shine or rain, until she went to the doctor about shoulder pain and learned she had lung cancer.

Accusations from the world:

13. Preferring one's own company is pathological.
14. Human beings were designed for companionship.
15. Why didn't you try harder to find a mate?
16. Married people live longer, healthier lives.
17. Do you think anyone actually believes that you're happy on your own?
18. It's creepy that you relate so much to lighthouse keepers.

Kalbfleisch wears a necktie of chuckling chipmunks. "Have a seat, Roberta."

"That's your best tie yet," she says.

"As you know, I was concerned about the possibility of you having polycystic ovary syndrome. After seeing some evidence of ovarian enlargement and polycystism, we checked your testosterone levels, and I'm afraid the results confirm that you do, in fact, suffer from PCOS."

Of course.

But she will be calm and resilient. She will be a problem solver.

"Okay, which means?"

"Which means that some or many of your follicles aren't maturing properly, and therefore ovulation is significantly compromised. Even when the OPK detects an LH surge, for instance, it's very possible no egg will appear. Let's cross our fingers for your current cycle. When do you come back for the pregnancy blood test?"

"Wednesday," she says, recruiting her facial muscles into a smile. *Problem solver.* "And if it's negative, I'll use a different donor for the next cycle. Someone with more reported pregnancies than—"

"Roberta." Kalbfleisch leans forward and looks her, for once, in the eye. "There won't be a next cycle."

"What?"

"Given your age, your FSH levels, and now this diagnosis, the chance of conception via IUI is little to none."

"But if there's a chance, at least—"

"By 'little to none,' I mean more like 'none.'"

Taut pain at the back of her mouth. "Oh."

"I'm sorry. It wouldn't be ethical for me to continue the inseminations when the statistics just don't bear it out."

Do not cry in front of this man. Do not cry in front of this man.

He adds, "But let's, well, let's keep our hopes up for this cycle, okay? You never know. I've seen miracles."

She doesn't cry until the parking lot.

On the dark highway, she works the calendar.

She will take the pregnancy test, her last ever, on the first day of December.

If positive—!

If negative, she'll have six and a half weeks before January fifteenth.

Before January fifteenth, she could still be picked from the catalog, chosen by a biological mother, phoned by the caseworker: *Ms. Stephens, I've got some good news!*

On January fifteenth, the Every Child Needs Two law will restore dignity, strength, and prosperity to American families.

In the lobby of her apartment building, she checks the mailbox. A reminder card from the dentist; a catalog of long skirts and floaty tops for women of a certain age; and an envelope from Hawthorne Reproductive Medicine, which she rips open. THIS IS A BILL, it says, to the tune of $936.85.

Very possible no egg will appear.

In her kitchen, on a cookie sheet, she sets fire to the bill and watches the flames until the smoke alarm goes off. *WANH! WANH! WANH! WANH!*

"Shut up, shut up—"

WANH! WANH! WANH!

Drags a chair toward the shrieks

WANH! WANH!

and climbs on

WANH! WANH!

and punches the alarm with her fist ("Shut the *shit* up") until its plastic cover splits in two.

I took my broken *fisa* to Aberdeen. Worked
as a mangler in a shipyard laundry.

THE DAUGHTER

The three o'clock bell is still clanging when she heads up Lupatia Street toward the cliff path. In her pocket are directions to the witch's house, which Ash managed to pry from her sister.

The heart of a guinea pig weighs three ounces.

Of a giraffe, twenty-six pounds.

Yasmine, I've been adding to our list.

Where is Yasmine, at this very moment?

The daughter can hear the thumping of her own aorta as she crunches over needles and rocks and leaves, following what she prays is the right path. She left the road by the blue CAMPING 4 MI. sign, followed the hiking trail to the brown GUNAKADEIT STATE FOREST sign, then turned onto a smaller trail—but what if there's more than one brown state forest sign?

"You just drink some wild herbs," explained Ash's sister.

Her body will be clean again.

But it will be a crime.

Half Ephraim, half her.

Less of a crime than crossing into Canada for it.

But they could still lock her up in Bolt River Youth Correctional Facility.

And it might hurt.

Less than it would hurt at a termination house, where they use rusty—

The daughter walks faster. Her neck is sweating, thighs stinging, ribs loud with cramp.

Ash refused to come with. If they were caught, the police might think she was seeking one too, and she'd be charged with conspiracy to commit murder, and she's already sixteen, and at sixteen you can be prosecuted as an adult.

The daughter gets it. But Yasmine would have come with.

* * *

A cabin appears, a plain little log square, windows lit, smoke drifting from the chimney. Ash's sister said to look for chickens and goats as proof it was the witch's place and not a rapist's. Although rapists could have goats and chickens. The daughter sees what might be a coop but no chickens around—are they sleeping?—and a shed, in which (she sidles up to check) are two little goats, one black, one gray. They watch her with robot eyes. "Shhh," she says, though they haven't made a sound. Chimney puffing, lights on, the witch is home; so why is the daughter dawdling by these goats? But what if the witch hates unannounced visitors, what if she has guns? It's legal to shoot someone if you say they were invading.

Going up the cabin steps, the daughter takes long breaths like Mom taught her to do at gymnastics meets, when she was still short enough for gymnastics.

Mom would understand this whole situation better than Dad would.

Not that the daughter is ever going to tell her.

Knock, knock.

The person who opens the door isn't old. Is even almost pretty. Big green eyes, dark hair in coils around pale cheeks. Her outfit—velvet choker and coarse sack dress—is Victorian prostitute meets Cro-Magnon. Is this even the witch?

The person frowns and stares.

"Hello," says the daughter.

Is it the witch's servant, or the witch's younger sister?

"You." The person crosses her arms over her chest, begins to scratch her sack-covered shoulders. The fingernails make a whispering sound.

"I'm sorry to disturb you, but I'm looking for...I don't know if you're...Gin Percival?"

"Why?" She stares sideways at the daughter. More like an animal than a human.

"I need some gynecological help?"

"How did you come here?"

"I heard about you from Clementine?"

"Clementine." Still frowning, but now smiling too: a face pulled two ways.

"She said to tell you the, um, wart is gone?"

"Okay." The person stands back. The daughter steps in. The room is warm and smells of wood; its rafters are strung with tiny white lights, shelves packed with jars and bottles and books. There is an old-fashioned stove. No cauldron.

"I'm Mattie—Matilda."

"My name is Gin Percival."

"Nice to meet you."

The witch's throat makes a long, low gurgle. Her big eyebrows are twitching. It might be true that she's crazy.

"Sit."

"Thank you." The daughter takes a chair.

"What kind of help?"

"I need the termination herbs."

"You're pregnant and don't want to be?"

She nods.

Gin Percival stretches a hand across her forehead, as though shielding her eyes. Gives a hard, short laugh.

"I'm not here undercover," adds Mattie. "And nobody followed me." That she knows of.

"How old are you?"

"Almost sixteen."

"When's your birthday?"

"February."

"When in February?"

"The fifteenth. I'm an Aquarius."

Gin paces around the small room, fingers interlaced on top of her head. "Oh-two-one-five. You'll be sixteen."

"Do you not—" The daughter coughs, to bury her nervousness. "Is the jail sentence worse if the seeker is a minor?"

She stops pacing. Lowers her hands to her sack-smocked sides. "That has nothing to do with anything. Want some water?"

"No thanks. I'm sorry I didn't make an appointment."

"How many weeks are you?"

"I'm not *totally* sure but I think eleven or twelve? My period was supposed to come midway through September. Ish."

"Then you're around fourteen. End of first trimester. You have to include the two weeks before conception."

"But I still have time, right?"

Those *eyebrows*. Frantic brown caterpillars. Maybe because she lives by herself she has no idea how her eyebrows behave? No mirrors in the cabin that the daughter can see.

"For the kind of treatments I do? Barely. But yes. You sure you want to?"

What if your bio mother had chosen to terminate?

"Will it—" The daughter looks at the bare planks under her feet. "Hurt a lot?"

"Not a lot. You'll drink a bad-tasting tea, then later you'll bleed. You'll have to stay home for a day at least. Better two. Do your, uh, parents know?"

Think of me and your mom, how long we waited.

The daughter shakes her head. "But I can go to my friend's—Whoa! Hello!" A gray thing has leapt into her lap, a purring accordion.

"That's Malky."

"Hi, Malky." She sort of hates cats, but she wants this cat to like her and for the witch to notice that he likes her. "Friendly little guy," she adds.

"He's not friendly," says Gin. "Get on the bed. I need to look at you. Jeans and underpants off." She goes to the sink to wash.

The daughter undresses. Gin has put nothing over the bed she presumably sleeps in, no fresh towel or sheet. Cat hairs all over the brown blanket.

"Lie back," says Gin, kneeling. She smells a little like sour milk. She places both hands on the daughter's belly and starts a gentle pressure. The hands move methodically, rubbing, pushing. Above her pubic bone they pause for a while. As if listening.

Then she unscrews a jar and thumbs out a scoop of clear jelly. "I'm going to put two of my fingers into your vagina. Okay with you?"

"Yeah." The daughter shuts her eyes, concentrates on the goal of her visit.

The fingers aren't in there more than a few seconds, and it doesn't hurt. Still—

Gin washes her hands again, returns to sit on the edge of the bed. Stares at the daughter. "Your teeth are very straight," she says.

"Braces," says the daughter, not sure why Gin feels the need to point this out. "I still wear a retainer."

"You grew up in Newville?"

"Salem."

"Moved here when?"

"Last year."

Gin touches the skin above the daughter's right hip. "How'd this scar happen?"

"Fell off my bike."

"And this mole?"—pressing the apple-shaped one on her left thigh. "When did it appear?"

"I had it when I was born, I think."

Gin's finger circles the mole. Her eyebrows have quit moving, but the eyes themselves, staring moleward, are shining with tears.

It's weird that she is feeling the mole for this long.

The daughter says, loudly, "Does it look cancerous or something?"

"Nope," says Gin, getting to her feet. "You can put your clothes on." She takes something down from a shelf. The termination herbs?

Offering the jar: "Horehound candy."

"Uh, sure." The brown nub, minty and licoricey, sticks to the daughter's molars. "By the way, my gums have been bleeding when I brush my teeth. Could I have scurvy?"

"Scurvy is only on boats. Your body's making more blood now—that's why." Gin frowns, taps her cheek with one finger. "I can end the pregnancy, but not today. I need to restock some supplies."

"So, like, tomorrow?"

"Longer. I'll leave a note at the P.O."

Longer? Spasm of fear in her ribs.

"But I don't have a box at the P.O."

"Cotter will know about it. Ask him in two, three days."

"The guy with the acne?"

"Yes. And the tea will taste terrible."

The damn cat is back on her lap. She pets it. "Like kombucha?"

"A different bad. A stronger." Gin Percival smiles. Her teeth are yellow and not very straight. She isn't pretty, the daughter decides, but she is bold looking. A person uninterested in being pleasing to other persons. In this way she reminds the daughter of Ro/Miss. "Better leave now—dark's coming. You know how to go?"

Follow the track to the hiking trail, then to the cliff path, then down to Lupatia, where she will call Dad to pick her up from studying at the library. Returning home clumped as ever. She isn't stupid, but she has been stupid. Why did she think it would get taken care of today?

"I better show you." Gin is pulling on a dirt-colored sweater. The cat springs off the daughter's lap.

"You don't have to."

"Easy to get lost. I'll take you as far as the trail."

"Are you sure?"

"I'm sure, Mattie Matilda."

Among the different names for polar ice, the name I like best is "pack."

It reminds of dogs and wolves. Things that hunt.

To be chased by ice, and torn apart.

THE MENDER

The mender lied. She is well stocked with fleabane and pennyroyal, has plenty of coltsfoot. But she wanted time to think. Time, at least, to abide with the idea of reaching into a body she made to unmake a future body.

When she saw the girl outside the library, months ago, it was like looking in a mirror, not at herself but at her whole family shoved together in one face. The agency had guaranteed that the baby would be placed at least seventy-five miles away, yet here she was, dancing out of the Newville library, face full of the mender's mother and aunt.

The girl is a mirror, repeating, folding time in half. When the mender had the same problem, she didn't solve it how Temple told her to. Terminations were lawful then, but the mender wanted to know how it felt to grow a human, with her own blood and minerals, in her own red clock.

Grow, but not keep.

The girl's parents have kept her well. Her breath smells sweet, and her hair is lustrous, her tongue salmon-pink, her eyeballs moist. The moon-colored skin she comes by naturally, and, of course, the height.

At the hiking trail they say goodbye. She waits until Mattie Matilda has disappeared down the trail, one minute, in the purpling air, two minutes, below the blatting owls, three minutes, upon the frost-veined ground—then follows: she'll make sure no demons touch this girl. She steps like a cat, unheard, on soil alive with blind hexapods, who ingest fungi and roots. Malky recognized the girl from her oils; he went right into her lap because underneath the lip gloss and deodorant he smelled the oils of a Percival.

* * *

From the fir shadows the mender watches her reach the cliff path and go left, in the direction of town and people. The mender goes right, toward the sea, night seeping through holes in her sweater. Closer and closer to the cliff's edge. The shark field is resting. Stripe of moon on the flat water. Out by the horizon, a black fin. And the lighthouse. House has light so ship won't crash. Light has beam so sea won't swallow. Ship has watchers, wary squinters, men in raincoats scared of dying. Light will tell them *Don't come here;* light will steer them other ways on water black and full of bones these men don't want their bones to meet. Bad luck on ships to mention lawyers, rabbits, pigs, and churches. Don't say "drown" on ships; say "spoil."

On Parent Conference Day the teacher said, "But where's your mother?" and the mender said, "She took a ship."

But really she left in a taxi, paid for with cash stolen from the till at Goody Hallett's. And the mender, eight years old, waited by the hour. The day. The winter. Then Temple drove them to Salem and got legal guardianship.

Eight winters ago she found Temple's body flopped at the base of a silver fir, and will never be sure of the reason. Heart attack? Stroke? Out to gather miner's lettuce, her aunt had been gone so long the mender started to worry. Went looking. There she was. Her skin was bluish, but otherwise she seemed asleep.

Goody Hallett's was closed by then, because not enough tourists were buying candles and tarot packs. Temple had sold the building. They had moved from the apartment above the shop to a cabin in the forest, and Temple had told the mender, who since leaving high school had kept to herself in the library and on the cliffs: "Time for you to get to work."

The mender did not want anyone taking the body away. She couldn't give her aunt to a funeral home to be gutted and waxed; and the ground was hard; and Temple had never liked fire. So the mender clipped off her nails and her hair and her lashes, shaved the skin from each fingertip, and put her body in the chest freezer, under salmon and ice.

Last winter the mender turned thirty-two: two times sixteen (the age of the girl come February) and half of sixty-four. Sixty-four is the number of demons in the *Dictionnaire Infernal*. Of squares on a chessboard. Sixty-four is the square of eight, which is the number of regeneration and resurrection: beginning again, again.

How can she sleep when she keeps seeing the girl's face?

She used to go months, years, not thinking about it. Then something (the smell of cherries, the word "soon") would remind her. Then she would forget again, let the little fish slip away. But after seeing that face outside the library, she couldn't stop thinking. Wondering if she really was. *Are you?*

She is.

"Malky, come here."

She cuts a piece from Cotter's loaf, offers the first bite to the cat. She presses a drop of black spruce oil to the corner of the ball of her right foot.

And sleeps.

The wood is knocking, Malky's hissing, and every chicken in the family is squawking its throat off. She stands, stuporish. Clears her throat. Farts.

Her door is knocking. Malky goes from hiss to howl.

"Quiet, mo," toeing him away from the threshold.

Men in blue uniforms. A black haired, a blond.

"What," she says.

The black haired says, "I'm Officer Withers and this is Officer Smith. Are you Gin Percival?"

Did they see her watching? Will she be accused of stalking? Did the girl, on meeting her, remember seeing her in the trees by the school and tell her parents?

She only wanted to look at her face. Hear her voice. See how she turned out.

"Gin Percival," says the black haired, "I'm placing you under arrest for medical malpractice."

The mender gapes.

"Does she not speak English?" says the blond.

The black haired clears his throat. "You have the right to remain silent. Anything you say can and will be used against you in a court of law. You have the right to speak to an attorney and to have an attorney present during questioning. If you cannot afford an attorney, one will be appointed for you. Do you understand these rights as they have been read to you?"

She waits on a bench near the desk of the blond policeman. They have given her a package of elf crackers, water in a wax cup.

Who will pour grain for Pinka and Hans? Carry the halt hen to shelter? Set out fish for Malky? And what if they open—

"I want to call someone," says the mender.

"You already had your call," says the blond policeman.

"No, I didn't."

He yells over his shoulder, "Jack, did this one get a phone call?"

"I have no idea," someone the mender can't see yells back.

"Go ahead, I guess," says the blond.

She stands at the desk with her fingers on the plastic receiver.

"Go ahead, ma'am."

She hasn't used a phone since Temple was alive.

"I forgot the number," she says.

How many salmons has she thawed recently? How many are still in the freezer? How many bags of ice?

"All your contacts are on your cell, am I right?" says the policeman. "Common predicament."

"I need the number for the P.O."

"The one in Newville?"

She smiles, because a nod would shake the tears out of her eyes and down her face.

The ice that would chase me is called by the Inupiat *ivu* and by the Europeans "ice shove," and it never gives warning. It gallops to shore from the outer sea, a heave of water caught and stropped into an iron tidal wave. But I would be faster than *ivu*. I would change into a snow deer and outrun it.

THE WIFE

Walks the children down Lupatia Street, killing time. The wind is fast and blue and sharp with late November.

In front of Cone Wolf, she thinks of Bryan's dimple.

Bryan's thighs.

The way he looked at her.

"Morning, Susan!" says the passing librarian.

"Morning."

Goody Hallett's is gone, Snippity Doo Dah is new, but otherwise the shops and pub and library and church have sat here, in the salt wind, for decades.

Is the wife going to die in Newville?

As they cross Lupatia, a bicycle whips past so close her arm hairs crackle.

"Watch the fuck out!" yells the rider, slowing and turning to look at the wife. "It's bad enough you chose to procreate on a dying planet."

"Dick," she calls after him.

Admittedly she was not in the crosswalk.

Admittedly she has added more people to this steaming pile.

Warm, silky new smell of Bex's neck.

Her rapturous mouth on the wife's nipple to bring down the milk tingling in the ducts.

How John slept on her chest with measureless trust.

This planet may be choking to death, bleeding from every hole, but still she would choose them, every time.

"Momplee, is there school tomorrow?"

"Yes, sweetpea." She signals, brakes, turns off the paved road.

"Why?"

"Because tomorrow's Monday."

Up the hill beneath a waving roof of red alder and madrone.

You and I should have coffee sometime.

They could meet in Wenport. For coffee.

She used to pass through Wenport on those endless drives to get Bex to nap—infant Bex who never wanted to close her eyes—when Didier was teaching and the wife didn't know how to make her baby fall asleep.

The air in Wenport stinks like eggs, from the pulp mill.

She and Bryan could have sex in the backseat of this car.

Maybe not in the backseat; Bryan's too big.

A motel. Pay in cash.

The trees give way to an open slope, patchy with salt grass and lavender. The dirt driveway. The house.

"We're home, baby bones!" Bex tells John, who will be scarred for life because the wife told him to shut the fuck up. John, whom she'd give her own life not to scar.

Unbuckle, untangle, lift, set down.

She drops the car keys on the hall table. Her husband is prostrate on the living-room couch.

"Your shift now," she says. "I'm going for a walk."

"What about lunch?"

"I ate with the kids in town."

"But I haven't eaten."

"So—eat."

"I was waiting for you," he says. "There's nothing in the house."

"Untrue."

"What am I supposed to have, then?"

The wife starts for the kitchen, then stops. "Actually, it's not my job to figure out what you're having for lunch."

"Could you at least make a suggestion? There's like absolutely *rien* in the fridge."

"I suggest you put the kids back in the car, drive somewhere, and buy something."

"I'm exhausted," he says.

The wife kicks off her flats and puts on sneakers, yanks the laces. The clock has started on her alone time.

"Daddy, I'll cook you a cake if you want."

"I'd love a *space* cake."

"What are the ingredients of that?" says Bex.

Didier throws the wife the look, polished by years of use, that casts her as a prudish shrew and him as a guilty but unrepentant fourteen-year-old. "On second thought, Bex, would you fix me a sammie? Butter and brown sugar?"

"One sammie, upcoming!" The girl hops away.

"See you in an hour and fifty-seven minutes," says the wife.

Walks down the hill into the hushed green gloom.

Warmer in the woods than in the house. If Didier made more money, they could afford to renovate the drafty mess, but he never will, so they won't.

Why don't you *make some money, then?* screams Ro.

Why don't you go back to law school? screams the wife's younger self.

She shouldn't have dropped out.

Of course she should have.

What if she hadn't?

Her program wasn't top tier, but it was respectable. Two years in, she went drinking with a friend from her cohort. At last call the friend said she knew an all-night doughnut shop.

If the friend had not known the doughnut shop, or if the friend had been tired, or if the friend had never existed, the wife would have finished the program and sat for the bar and been hired by a firm and maybe, yes, still have had time to make children.

But maybe not. And anyway, those children, if she'd had time to make them, would not be Bex and John.

This fact outlasts all other facts.

* * *

The wife steps on a hand, soft and rubbery.

A dead hand on the floor of the woods.

A hand torn from its owner, left loose.

A dead hand is also a mushroom.

A black plastic bag is also an animal.

You can't believe your eyes.

She convinced herself at the time it was a bag because she didn't want it to be a writhing animal.

I wanted to help it, but it was already dead.

How do you help a cinder, half-alive?

Run over it fast to stop the burning.

She could stop being married to Didier.

Put John in daycare and finish the law degree.

With what money?

Put John in daycare and get a job at Cone Wolf.

Or at Central Coast Regional, where someone with a BA and no experience can teach history, and someone with a glorified-community-college degree and no experience can teach French.

She could stop being Didier's wife.

In therapy the kids will blame her for their broken childhoods and the maladaptive coping mechanisms that have ruined their adulthoods.

Their therapists will say, *Do you think you can ever forgive her?*

First a mangler in the shipyard laundry, then a maid in the house of the shipyard director. Brewed tea for the butler and cook, learned English, overheard the lessons given to the director's oldest son. Jars of creatures to pin and dissect. A volcano built of papier-mâché. Maritime navigation demonstrated with an astrolabe.

The polar explorer asked to sit in the schoolroom with them.

~~The young tutor agreed and wanted nothing in return.~~

~~The young tutor agreed but wanted half her monthly pay in return.~~

~~The young tutor agreed but wanted sex in return.~~

The young tutor, Harry Rattray, agreed if she promised to walk with him on Sundays through the purple crocus in Aberdeen's newly opened Victoria Park.

THE BIOGRAPHER

Drives for two hours to give the clinic her blood. They will measure its HCG levels and call with the results. She did not test at home beforehand, as she typically does. She wants to make everything about this last-ever pregnancy test different, so that its result can be different too.

If this cycle fails, she isn't having a biological child.

To adopt from China, your body-mass index must be under 35, your annual household income over eighty thousand. Dollars.

To adopt from Russia, your annual household income must be at least a hundred thousand. Dollars.

To adopt from the United States—as of January 15—you must be married.

Are you married, miss?

When her first caseworker at the adoption agency said "You do realize, I hope, that a child is not a replacement for a romantic partner?" the biographer almost walked out of the interview. She did not walk out, because she wanted to get onto their wait-list. That night she threw a potted cactus against her refrigerator.

The last time she had sex was almost two years ago, with Jupiter from meditation group. "Your cunt smells yummy," he said, extending the first syllable of "yummy" into a ghastly warble. Wiped semen from the dark swirls of his belly hair and said, "You sure you're not getting attached?"

"Scout's honor," said the biographer.

"Not that attachment is always a bad thing," said Jupiter, "but I don't really see us having that. I think we connect well sexually and intellectually, but not emotionally or spiritually."

"I'm getting a Klondike bar," said the biographer, rolling off the bed. "Want one?"

"Unless you're secretly using me for *this*." He held up five glistening fingers. "Are you having a *Torschlusspanik* moment?"

"I do not speak German."

"'Gate-closing panic.' The fear of diminishing opportunities as one ages. Like when women worry about getting too old to—"

"Do you want a Klondike bar or not?"

"Not," said Jupiter, and she could feel him wondering, *now that he thought about it,* if it might be true. Afraid of withering on her own vine, had she decided to steal his vegan cum?

She bit hard into the frozen chocolate, which sparkled along her tooth nerves, and he said: "Those things are so bad for you."

Though she mentions no sex in her notebooks, it's possible that Eivør Mínervudottír slept with lots of men. Lots of women. Who can say what she got up to with the other maids in Aberdeen, or with her shipmates on ocean voyages?

Also possible: she spent her whole life (apart from or including the eighteen-month marriage) without sex. Out of necessity. Out of choice.

But how many people have sailed to the Arctic Circle, slept in tents bolted to ice floes, watched a man's skin peel off from eating the toxic liver of a polar bear?

In the clinic waiting room, under the vexing tinkle of the adult-contemporary station, the biographer does a pump of hand sanitizer. The news murmurs on a wall-mounted flat-screen and a few faces watch it and nobody talks.

"What are you in for today?"

She looks up: a blond-pigtailed woman is smiling from the chair opposite. "A pregnancy test."

"Wow! So this could be it!"

"Unlikely," says the biographer. But, yes, in fact, it could be. If this cycle works, the eleventh-hour victory will be a story to tell the baby. *You showed up just in time.* She notes that the woman wears a simple band, no rocky engagement ring. "What about you?"

"Day nine check," says the woman. "This is my second cycle. My hubby says we should adopt, but I—I don't know. It's—" Eyes fill, shimmer.

The word "hubby" cancels out the lack of a diamond.

"At least you *can* adopt," says the biographer, louder than she meant to.

The woman nods, unperturbed. Maybe she's never heard of Every Child Needs Two; or forgot about it promptly after hearing it, because the law did not apply to her.

Compare and despair.

The biographer unbuttons her sleeve, hoists it, makes a fist. Nurse Crabby swabs the bruised skin. Archie was proud of his track marks and would neglect on purpose to wear long sleeves.

The nurse has trouble, as usual, finding a vein. "They're way buried."

"The one closer to the elbow usually works better—?"

"First let's see what we can get over here."

The biographer's car crests the cliff and the ocean spreads below. Vast dark luminous perilous sea, floors white with sailors' bones, tides stronger than any human effort. Sea stacks sleep like tiny mountains in the waves. She loves the sheer fact of how many millions of creatures the water holds—microscopic and gargantuan, alive and long dead.

In eyeshot of such a sea, one can pretend things are fine. Notice only the cares within reach. Coyotes on Lupatia Street. Fund-raising for lighthouse repairs. It's why the biographer liked this country of pointed firs, at first: how easily here she could forget the hurtling world. She could almost stop seeing the blue lips of her brother, the gray jaw of her mother in the hospital bed.

* * *

While the biographer was hiding out in a rainy Arcadia, they closed the women's health clinics that couldn't afford mandated renovations.

They prohibited second-trimester abortions.

They required women to wait ten days before the procedure and to complete a lengthy online tutorial on fetal pain thresholds and celebrities whose mothers had planned to abort them.

They started talking about this thing called the Personhood Amendment, which for years had been a fringe idea, a farce.

At her kitchen table she eats a bowl of pineapple chunks.

Sips water.

Waits for the call.

When Congress proposed the Twenty-Eighth Amendment to the U.S. Constitution and it was sent to the states for a vote, the biographer wrote emails to her representatives. Marched in protests in Salem and Portland. Donated to Planned Parenthood. But she wasn't all that worried. It had to be political theater, she thought, a flexing of muscle by the conservative-controlled House and Senate in league with a fetus-loving new president.

Thirty-nine states voted to ratify. A three-quarters majority. The biographer watched the computer screen splashed with this news, thought of the signs at the rallies (KEEP YOUR ROSARIES OFF MY OVARIES! THINK OUTSIDE MY BOX!) and the online petitions, the celebrity op-eds. She couldn't believe the Personhood Amendment had become real with all these citizens so against it.

Which (the disbelief) was stupid. She knew—it was her job as a teacher of history to know—how many horrors are legitimated in public daylight, against the will of most of the people.

With abortion illegal, said the congressmen, more babies would be available to adopt. It wasn't hurting anyone, they said, to ban IVF, because the people with faulty uteri and busted sperm could simply adopt all those extra babies.

Which isn't the way it turned out.

She finishes the pineapple.

Swallows the rest of the water.

Tells her ovaries: *For your patience, for your eggs, I thank you.*

Tells her uterus: *May you be happy.*

Her blood: *May you be safe.*

Her brain: *May you be free from suffering.*

Her phone rings.

"Hello, Roberta." Kalbfleisch himself is calling. Usually a nurse does.

"Hello, Doctor."

Is he calling himself because the news is different this time?

She stands with her back pressed against the refrigerator. Please please please please please please please.

Firs shake and shiver on the hill.

"I'm sorry," he says, "but your test came back negative."

"Oh," she says.

"I know this is disappointing."

"Yeah," she says.

"The odds just weren't, you know, in our favor." The doctor clears his golden throat. "I'm curious whether—Well, have you—Let me put it this way: do you travel much?"

"Florida sometimes, to see my dad."

"International travel."

Take a vacation to console herself?

Screw. You.

Wait.

No.

He's saying something else.

"So you recommend," she says haltingly, "in light of my—*difficulties,* that I should go—somewhere where IVF is legal?"

"I am *not* recommending that," he says.

"But you just said—"

"I am not giving you any advice that is against the law and for which I could lose my medical license."

Has she, without realizing it, been talking to a human being?

"Do you understand me, Roberta?"

"I think so."

"Okay then."

"Thank you for—"

"Happy holidays."

"You too." She presses END.

Fingers the tea towel draped on the oven handle.

Watches the fir-fledged hill, the deep green waving.

Maybe he genuinely, sincerely believes she has the money for "international travel."

Get in the shower, she tells herself.

Too sad to take a shower.

She wanted to study sea ice, which

begins as a cold crystal soup

Harry Rattray, the Scottish tutor, knew nothing about

forms a swaying crust ~~strong enough to hold up a puffin~~ thicker than the height of a man

can block, trap, gouge, or

                    outright crush
                    a ship

                                        too sad

THE DAUGHTER

While they take their quiz, Ro/Miss is doing a weird thing with her fingers on the sides of her face. Rubbing in a sort of violent way. Her eyes are closed. Bad headache? The daughter doesn't agree with Dad that Ro/Miss is a radical leftist; she's just smart. A smart spinster. If the daughter were to say that word in front of Ro/Miss, she'd get a sermon: *What does the word "spinster" do that "bachelor" doesn't do? Why do they carry different associations? These are language acts, people!*

The witch is a spinster too. She is bold and cold and wouldn't be agitated by the Nouri Witherses of this world. In the daughter's shoes, instead of fretting over some little melancholy jelly Ephraim prefers, Gin Percival would either quit caring or take revenge. Devise a potion that made Nouri's fingertips numb for the rest of her life, so that if she went blind in old age, she couldn't read braille.

Except she can't make potions in jail.

"Everyone finished?" goes Ro/Miss. "If not, too bad."

She hurt the principal's wife, according to the newspaper.

"Ash, stop writing. *Now.* Give me that paper."

Except she didn't seem like a person who would hurt anyone.

Do they provide tampons in jail? Gin Percival might not have brought any with her. And what if they give her the wrong size? A Slender when she needs a Super Plus?

Yasmine coached the daughter on the phone when she lost a tampon inside herself. Explained how to find the muscles that would expel it. "Pretend you're stopping yourself from peeing."

Pack ice could block, trap, gouge, or outright crush a three-hundred-fifty-ton ship. Mínervudottír wanted to acquaint herself with this brute.

THE MENDER

She is come from walking on the bottom of the sea. There the tiny eyeless and the footless walked with she. Ran with she the finned and flattened, sailed with she the lungless; swayed with she the fantom grasses, lantern fishes, wolf eels. To the north bathed viperfish, who did not even see she; to the south flew goblin sharks, who did not even eat she. Toed a wolf eel, thumbed a skate, fingered the sucker of a cockeyed squid.

And back again, on waking, to the concrete bed.

Like the cell of any hive.

"Here's your tray," says the day guard, who has six fingers on her off hand. Hyperdactylia is a sign of the visionary. "And you got a letter."

On white paper, in pencil:

> Dear Ginny,
>
> Everything will be all right. I'm feeding the animals. And I took care of the other thing. I hope you like this kind of chocolate.
>
> C.

So polite, Cotter. "I'm going to put it in now, okay?" he said, the first time they had sex. Polite till the cows come home. In, and in, and in. Her scabbard hurt after.

She had been curious to try. They did it five times, on four different days, on a blanket on the floor of Cotter's parents' basement, until she decided she didn't want to do it anymore.

* * *

Cotter was sad but still walked her home from school, and they didn't talk much, sometimes not at all. Her scabbard stopped hurting. They listened to the *scroof* and *bap* of their shoes on the sidewalk. The tsunami siren went off so loud the mender fell to her knees—"Will we drown?" She hated to swim, was frightened of sharks. "No, it's just a test," he said, and crouched to hug her.

Cotter was not her future husband, even though, back then, he sort of wanted to be. Scottish virgins used to douse charred peat with cow piss and hang it in their doorways, and whatever color the piss-moss was, next morning, would equal the color of their future husbands' hair.

Has Mattie Matilda solved her problem by now? Or is the little fish still inside?

"The letter says chocolate," she tells the guard.

"You're not allowed to have the chocolate."

"But it was sent to me."

"You're in jail, Stretch. Nothing here is yours."

"At least tell me what *kind* it was?" she yells at the guard's back.

The other guards are eating the chocolate, she knows. Smearing it all over their faces.

They took away her Aristotle's lanterns too. Her neckcloth.

"If we go to trial, it will help if you look as mainstream as you can," said the lawyer. "Studies have shown that juries are influenced by grooming and attire."

Her grooming won't change one inch of itself. She won't let him bring her any department-store clothes. Her aunt yells from the freezer: *Show those fuckshits how Percivals do!* The mender has been refusing the instant mashed potato and pork nuggets; she eats her own nails and the brickling skin around them. The lawyer has promised to bring better food. He said, "I'll have you out by Christmas."

* * *

Christmas, her favorite criminal. Stockings are hanged, trees chopped, geese shot, children threatened with coal.

Christmas is next week.

Medical malpractice: who'll believe forest weirdo over school principal? Naturally that prick became a principal—plenty of little ones to boss around. Wasn't enough for him to boss Lola. "You divorce me at your age, you'll never get another man, it's just numbers, babe, you're at the wrong end of the numbers," she told the mender he'd said.

They think the mender harmed her grievously. Think she waved her broom at the moon and saved her own menstrual blood in a cat skull and dipped a live toad in the blood and tore off one of the toad's legs and stuffed it into Lola's butthole.

Nobody knows why the dead man's fingers—poisonous to ships' hulls and oysters and fishermen's paychecks—have come back to Newville. Nobody knows, so they've decided that it's the mender's fault. She hexed the seaweed. Called it to shore with her special weed-hexing whistle. And her reason? What reason, bitches?

Some things are true; some are not.

That Lola fell down the stairs, hard.

That she fell down so hard her brain swelled up.

That she fell down because she drank a "potion."

That the "potion" she drank before falling down was directly responsible for the falling down.

That the providing of the "potion" counts as medical malpractice.

That the newspaper headline says POTION COMMOTION.

That the oil she gave Lola was for calming her scar.

That the oil was topical, not meant to be swallowed.

That, even if swallowed, elderflower, lemon, lavender, and fenugreek don't make people fall down.

That nobody will believe forest weirdo over school principal.

"Percival!"—a guard through the screen box. "Get dressed. Your lawyer's here."

The lawyer wears a suit, like last time. As if to make himself more real. As if, in a suit, he will appear forceful and real and not the plump weird trembler he is. Among humans, the mender prefers the weird and the trembling, so she likes him.

From his briefcase he produces two boxes of licorice nibs. "As requested."

The mender breaks one open. Crams her mouth thick with the black taste, holds the box out to him.

"Mmh. I don't eat those." He pulls out a bottle of hand sanitizer and squirts a palmful. "So your friend Cotter's been checking on the animals and says everyone is fine."

"Did he make sure the goats aren't going up to the trail?"

The lawyer nods. Scratches the back of his neck. "So I'm afraid I have some tough news."

Mattie Matilda?

Went to a term house—*died?*

"The prosecutor's office has appended a charge," says the lawyer.

"Appended?"

"Added. They're bringing a new charge against you."

"What charge?"

"Conspiracy to commit murder."

Silver cold burn in her belly.

"Because fertilized eggs are now classified as persons," he says, "intentionally destroying an embryo or fetus constitutes second-degree murder. Or, if you're in Oregon, 'murder' rather than 'aggravated murder.'"

"What did the music teacher tell you?"

"Who?"

"The—"

"Stop talking," he barks.

She looks at him sidelong.

"Ms. Percival, it is much better if you don't tell me whatever you were about to tell me. Understood? The charge is being added by Dolores Fivey's attorney. Mrs. Fivey claims you consented to terminate a pregnancy of hers. Any truth to that?"

"No."

"All right, good." He fusses in his briefcase for a notepad and pen. "Did she ever mention being pregnant? Or that she was seeking an abortion?"

That clock never had a kernel in it.

"Lola's lying," says the mender.

"Why would she lie?"

"Get a doctor to look at her. Womb's been silent."

The lawyer looks up from his pad. "Not a talkative womb?"

He is helping her when she has no money to pay him, so she fakes a laugh. "She was never pregnant."

"Well, she can testify that she *believed* she was." He reaches under his suit sleeve to rub a forearm, then applies more hand sanitizer. "Per our last conversation, I haven't been able to find any evidence that implicates Mr. Fivey in domestic violence. No hospital records, no police reports, no concerned friends or doctors. Zero."

"But he snapped her finger bone," she says, "and burned her arm and punched her in the jaw."

"Without any corroborating evidence, we can't present this information in court."

I am descended from a pirate. From a pirate. I am—

"Ms. Percival, I want you to understand that conspiracy to commit murder carries a mandatory minimum prison term of ninety months."

Seven years, six months.

"And that's the *minimum*. They could add more at sentencing."

"But I didn't," she says.

"I believe you," says the lawyer. "And I'm going to make the jury believe you. But we need to go over every single detail of your acquaintance with Mrs. Fivey."

He wants to know what Lola paid for the scar treatments. If the prosecution can prove that money or goods changed hands, then the jury might plausibly leap to believing that the money or goods were prepayment for a termination. By accepting the compensation, the mender conspired to commit murder.

"This is the narrative they'll build for the jury," says the lawyer. "We need to hack away at it. Anything that can throw this narrative into doubt, we'll use."

"I can't remember," says the mender. Telling about the sex would make it worse. The world's oldest method of payment.

In seven years and six months the chickens and goats will be dead, Malky will have forgotten her, and the powderpost beetles will have eaten the roof clean off.

The skin on the explorer's hands grew hard from housemaid duties.

She grew bored of the ~~payments sex~~ walks with Harry Rattray, the Scottish tutor, in Victoria Park.

THE WIFE

The high school auditorium, muggy and tinseled.

"All of the other reindeer. Used to laugh and call him names."

"Santa?" asks John.

"Soon."

"Santa doesn't *come* to holiday assembly," corrects Bex, hell-bent on accuracy.

Didier, on the other side of John: "Pipe down, *chouchous*."

The wife glances around for Bryan. Pauses at the silver-sequined breasts of Dolores Fivey, which seem smaller, like the rest of her, shrunk down in those long weeks at the hospital. Not so sixy anymore. Penny, yawning. Pete, checking his phone. Ro, sagged down in her seat, looking enraged.

"As they shouted out with glee, 'Rudolph the Red-Nosed Reindeer, you'll go down in history!'"

Applause, bowing, then Bryan strides onstage in a Grinch-green sports jacket. She can't see his dimple from here.

"Thank you, choir!" he booms. More applause. "And thanks to all of you for joining us at our, ah, seasonal celebration."

Didier leans over John to whisper: "That man is dumb as a melon in a sock."

"May everyone's holidays be merry and bright," says Bryan. Where will he be having Christmas dinner? He must eat like a shire horse, big as he is.

Outside the auditorium she stands with Didier and Pete, postponing the moment when she must snap the kids into their seats, drive back up the hill, unbuckle them, rinse apples, spread almond butter onto whole-grain bread, pour cups of milk from cows who eat wild grasses only.

Pete: "That record didn't come out until 1981."

Didier: "Excuse me, but it was 1980, exactly two months after he hanged himself."

Yet he can't remember to give the kids their fluoride supplement.

"And exactly a hundred years," adds the wife, "after our house was built."

"I bet Chinese laborers hammered every nail in it," says Pete, "for criminally low wages. My people got *fucked* in Oregon. Railroad workers especially, but also the miners. Ever heard of the Hells Canyon Massacre?"

"No," says the wife.

"Well, you should look it up."

Pete's scorn for her is always just barely concealed. Pampered white lady who doesn't have a job, lives on family property—what does she *do* all day? Whereas Didier regales him with stories of his trasherjack childhood in Montreal public housing and is revered.

Her phone vibrates: an unknown number. She prepares her telemarketer line: *Remove me from your call list immediately.*

"Susan MacInnes?" The name she had for thirty years. "It's Edward Tilghman. From law school?"

"Of course, Edward—I remember."

"Well, I should hope so." He hasn't lost his primness, or his nasal congestion. Book-smart and life-dumb Edward.

"How are you?"

"Tolerable," says Edward. "But here's the thing: I'm in your village."

She looks around, as though he might be watching from the auditorium steps.

"I'm representing a client in the area, and I wanted you to know I'm in town. It would be somewhat awkward if we just bumped into each other."

"Do you have a place to stay?" she says.

Edward would be a clean houseguest but a finicky one; he'd want extra blankets and would remark on the drafts, the dripping taps.

"The Narwhal," he says.

"Well, you're more than welcome to—"

"Thank you. I'm already ensconced."

She has followed his career, a little. He was an excellent student, could have gotten hired in a minute at a white-shoe firm. But he works at the public defender's office in Salem. Must earn practically nothing.

"You should come for dinner one of these nights."

When he sees her he'll think *She's blown up a bit. Used to be a slender thing, and now—although it happens,* he'll think, *after they reproduce. Fat hardens.*

"Mmh. That's a thought." That was one of his trademarks, she recalls: soft grunting.

There have been reports of bedbugs at the Narwhal.

"So . . . ?" but she realizes he has hung up.

Didier bumps his shoulder against hers. "Who that?"

"Guy from law school."

"Not Chad the Impaler, I hope."

"Just a nerd I worked on the law review with."

True to form, her husband asks nothing further.

John whimpers, yanking on her hand. She didn't remember to bring the porcupine book or the bag of grapes. And there are streaks of her own feces in the upstairs toilet. She's grown afraid of the toilet brush, damp and rusted in its cup.

Bryan is surrounded by eager, jostling boys; they must be his players. Isn't the season over?—but of course they wouldn't stop adoring him when the season ends.

Ro, too, is thronged by students. She has wiped the rage off her face and is gesturing theatrically, making them laugh. They love her—and why not? She's a good person. The wife would like to be a good person, a person who'll be happy if Ro gets pregnant or adopts a baby, who will not hope that she doesn't.

When Ro sees the wife's children, is she jealous? What if she never conceives? Can't adopt? What will be her life's pull light then? When the wife goes down a street, John in the stroller and Bex holding her hand, purpose is written all over them. These little animals were hatched by the wife, are being fed and cleaned and sheltered and loved by the wife, on their way to becoming persons in their own right. The wife *made persons.* No need to otherwise justify what she is doing on the planet.

Huge brown eyes, sunlit hair, perfect little chins. *All small children are cute. You know that, right?*—D.'s reliable smashing of her happiness. Okay, yes, kids are built adorable so they won't be abandoned to die before they can survive on their own; but it is also true that some kids are more adorable than others. *Jambon sur les yeux,* Didier likes to say. You've got ham over your eyes.

Lifting, settling, buckling.

Specks of rain on the windshield.

Soon, the sea.

"Starving!" calls Bex.

"Almost home," says the wife.

Almost to the sharpest bend, whose guardrail is measly. Hands off the wheel. They would plow through the branches, fly past the rocks, tear open the water.

The newspapers tomorrow: MOTHER AND CHILDREN PERISH IN CLIFF TRAGEDY.

"Momplee," says Bex, "do reindeer sleep?"

As they approach the bend, she eases her foot off the accelerator.

Didier was once jealous of Chad, the third-year student she'd gone out with a few times before meeting her husband.

If she were ever to tell him *I slept with Bryan,* would he spring into action, agree to counseling, fight to get her back? Or would he say, without looking up from the screen, *Congratulations*?

She is too chickenshit to leave her marriage.

She wants Didier to leave it first.

In the summer of 1868, aged twenty-seven, Mínervudottír left Aberdeen, taking with her an extra month's salary (the shipyard director's wife liked her) and, shoved deep in her suitcase, four silver candlesticks.

Went to London.

Sold the candlesticks.

Obtained a reader's ticket to the British Museum Reading Room, which required no membership fee.

Bought a notebook with a brown leather cover.

This notebook filled with facts.

THE DAUGHTER

Behind the Dumpsters she lights her first cigarette of the day, which is normally the best one but they haven't been tasting right lately. Soft chemical bloom on the roof of her mouth.

Why do some walruses in Washington, DC, who've never met the daughter care what she does with the clump? They don't seem bothered that baby wolves are shot to death from helicopters. Those babies were already breathing on their own, running and sleeping and eating on their own, whereas the clump is not even a baby yet. Couldn't survive two seconds outside the daughter.

The walruses are to blame for Yasmine.

Who sang at church.

Whose church was African Methodist Episcopal. Whenever the daughter went to services with the Salters after sleepovers, she felt strange.

Yasmine said: "Well, Matts, I feel strange all the time."

Ignorant white girl.

It starts to rain. The daughter lights a second cigarette and decides to skip math, even if it means annoying Mr. Xiao, whom she does not want to annoy and who'll say, next time he sees her, *What the hell, Quarles?* Nouri Withers will be in math, and who needs a glimpse of that mess. She closes her eyes, sucking, rain pittering on her lashes.

"Trying to get cancer?" Ro/Miss is standing right in front of her.

"No." The daughter grinds the cigarette under her boot.

"Pick that up, please."

The daughter tucks it into her peacoat pocket to avoid the inelegance of walking over to the Dumpster and struggling to lift its crusty lid. Her peacoat is going to reek of dead cigarette.

"Tell me what's going on, Mattie."

"Nothing."

"You've never gotten a B minus on a quiz before."

"I studied the wrong chapter."

"Are you still upset about the whales?"

The daughter spits out a laugh. Looks across the soccer field at the jagged evergreens, the sky darkening behind them.

"You can talk to me, you know. I'll help if I can."

"You can't," says the daughter.

"Try me," says Ro/Miss.

I'm too scared to go to Canada because of the Pink Wall but the witch went to jail and I need a plan and I don't have a plan and what would you do if you were me?

But what if it's in her teaching contract—mandatory reporting of child abuse and, in her case, child murder?

The daughter is not a murderer.

They're only cells, multiplying.

No face yet. No dreams or opinions.

You didn't have a face once either.

Ro/Miss reports her, and Principal Fivey kicks her out of Central Coast Regional.

Math Academy not thrilled about that.

Colleges not thrilled about that.

Mom and Dad least thrilled of all.

"I have class in a minute," she says, "and Mr. Xiao said he's going to rip the next person who's late a new turd cutter."

"Emotional health takes priority. I'll handle Mr. Xiao."

Maybe she can.

"It's nothing," says the daughter.

"*Try* me."

Ro/Miss wouldn't care if it's in her contract. She's fiercer than that.

The daughter says, still watching the trees: "I'm pregs?"

"Oh Jesus—"

"But I'm taking care of it."

"In what way?" snaps Ro/Miss, engine-red, freckles pulsing like brown stars.

She's *angry?*

"It's being dealt with," says the daughter.

"How can you be smoking?"

How can she be angry?

"It doesn't matter."

"Oh really?"

"The smoke won't—"

"What do you plan to do, Mattie?"

"Terminate," says the daughter.

Ro/Miss frowns.

"It's just an embryo, miss. It can't make an offer on a house, even though it has the legal right to."

Not even the littlest twist of a smile at hearing herself quoted. "What happens if you get caught?"

This is not the Ro/Miss she loves.

"I won't get caught," says the daughter, buttoning her peacoat. The rain is coming down harder.

"But what if you do?"

"I *won't.*"

What happened to the Ro/Miss who says we have better things to do with our lives than throw ourselves down the stairs?

"You know they'll charge you with a felony? Which means juvenile detention until you're eighteen, then—"

"I know, miss."

She would be sent to Bolt River.

Who is this monstrous imposter?

Ro/Miss pushes back her parka hood and starts raking all ten fingers through her hair, scalp to ends, scalp to ends, like an actor playing a mental-hospital patient.

"I got the name of a termination house," lies the daughter. "It's supposed to be good."

Raking, raking, scalp to ends. "Are you kidding?"

"Um, no?"

"Term houses charge a shit ton," says Ro/Miss, "and take shortcuts because nobody, obviously, is regulating them. They use out-of-date equipment, don't disinfect between patients, administer anesthesia without"—the first bell rings—"training." The fingers stop, mid-rake.

"Please don't tell my parents or Mr. Fivey?"

Tears in Ro/Miss's eyes. As if this moment needed to get any worse.

"Are you going to tell them?" bleats the daughter. "Please don't!"

It is weird to be scared of a person you've always been the opposite of scared of.

Ro/Miss pulls her hood back up. Tightens the drawstrings around her scrunched, streaming face. "I won't." She wipes her eyes with a parka sleeve. "This is just—This is really, I don't know—"

"It's okay," says the daughter, touching her elbow.

The elbow stays against her hand.

Ro/Miss blinks and shudders.

They stand hand to elbow for what feels like a long time. They are both getting soaked and the daughter's arm starts to hurt.

The second bell rings.

She says, "I have math?" and unhands the elbow.

"Sure. Yes." Sniffles. "But Mattie...?"

The daughter waits.

The teacher shakes her head.

They walk together along the soccer field, not talking, and up the steps, not talking, and through the blue doors.

She shouted "Help" in three languages.

Slit lambs hung in the shed, throats red.

THE BIOGRAPHER

There are four oranges in a bowl on her table. She throws them one at a time at the kitchen wall. Two bounce, one splits, one splatters. Opens the fridge: soft cheese, broccoli, chocolate pudding. Flings the cheese and pudding out the window into the neighboring yard, hears no splat because the wind is up. Recalls that chocolate is fatal to dogs. Has never seen a dog in that yard.

Words I hate:

33. hubby
34. sammie
35. diagnosis
36. pregs

She will leave the oranges where they are. Head off soon to this goddamn eve of Christmas Eve dinner.

Mattie will head off soon to her abortion.

That's one more married couple ahead of the biographer on the wait-list who's not getting a baby.

Which is not Mattie's problem.

She rubs her cold forearms.

Her veins are buried. Archie's were collapsed.

A friend of Archie's wore black wire-and-mesh wings to his funeral.

The biographer once watched, on television, a church group chanting "Hurray!" outside the funeral of a politician's wife who had used IVF to acquire two children and thereby had summoned (said the church's press release) her own death by cancer. She and her husband coveted things that were not theirs, they reared up in fury, decided to show God who was boss, and meddled in matters of the womb. The politician's wife was now a resident of hell. Flee her example.

The biographer's ex-therapist asked, "Are you claiming not to need a romantic relationship in order to shield yourself from disappointment and rejection?"

"Would you ask that question of a male client?"

"You're not a male client."

"But would you?"

"Maybe, sure." He folded spotty hands on a baggy corduroy lap. "I am simply wondering to what extent your campaign to have a baby is a defense against the pain of being alone."

"Did you say *campaign?*"

"I'm recalling the period when you were sleeping with—Zeus, was it?"

"Jupiter," she said.

"*Jupiter,* and you told me that you'd just as soon support the death penalty as have a relationship with him. And yet you were fucking him." He said "fucking" with a relish that disturbed the biographer even more than "campaign." "There's of course also the issue of your brother, who abandoned you in rather a gruesome fashion."

The biographer never set foot in his office again.

Things I have failed at:

1. Finishing book
2. Having baby
3. Keeping brother alive

She starts dialing Susan, to cancel. Then thinks about being alone all night, smelling the broken oranges.

Bex meets her on the porch steps. "You're not dressed up," accuses the girl, herself stuffed into a burgundy pinafore and black patent leathers. "It's Christmas Eve eve!"

"Sorry," says the biographer, clenching her fists.

"I made popcorn for the reindeer." Bex points to a salad bowl on the lawn.

In Mínervudottír's day, sleeping bags were made from reindeer hides, the hairy skin good for warming wrecked men huddled on bergs.

"For my Christmas I asked for a kitten, but my mom says Santa can't bring a kitten, which is a lie because a girl in my class got one for Hanukkah."

The biographer sits beside her on the damp step. "Well, Santa doesn't deliver Hanukkah presents, only Christmas presents."

"Why?"

"Because that's how it works."

"But I want a Hanukkah present," says Bex, fingering a burgundy button.

"You're not Jewish."

"I want to switch to Jewish. Also, what's a cunt?"

The biographer leans to examine the eye-shaped pattern carved into the railing. "Um, have you asked your mom?"

"No, because it goes in the special box."

"Did you ask your dad?"

"He said let's talk about it later. Look it up on your phone."

"My phone can't look things up; it's too old. 'Cunt' is just another word for vagina."

In Faroese: *fisa*.

"Okay," says Bex, taking her hand.

The tinsel has been hung halfheartedly; the eggnog resembles a bodily fluid; Susan looks as though she'd rather be anywhere else. They've been invited to gather because it's what you do, and Susan is a person who does what you do. At the teachers' picnic last summer she said to a fellow mother, "You don't truly become an adult until you have kids." The fellow mother said, "Totally." The biographer, standing nearby with a mustard-glopped hot dog, said, "Seriously?" but this went unheard. Susan is an expert in adulthood. Kid things, cooking things, knowing which fork to use for fish in a high-end restaurant things. And the Korsmos live in what is basically a mansion, even if it was built as a summer home, because a summer home in the 1880s was fancier than today's average winter home. Susan's parents own it, but the deed will doubtless come to her.

You don't even want a house, the biographer reminds herself.

Didier is bent over an open oven, squirting pan juices on a sizzling hunk of meat. "Get ready for some fine damn beef," he greets the biographer. John comes barreling toward the oven, but his father yanks him up in time ("No scorched babies on my watch") and sets him down ("Go find your porcupine book"), and he scampers away. "You know, I wanted to name that kid Mick. I should've argued harder. John Korsmo is a real-estate agent, but Mick Korsmo is a badass."

"Except," says the biographer, "that pretty much every one-syllable word that rhymes with Mick has a negative, lewd, or derogatory connotation. Ick. Sick. Lick. Prick."

"Wow," says Didier.

"Kick. Brick. Trick—"

"Why is brick negative, eh?" he says. "Unless it's a brick of heroin, although that, to some people, would be very positive indeed."

Straw.

Camel.

She's really in no mood.

"Didier, is there any particular reason you mention heroin so much?"

He frowns. "Do I?"

Keep your legs, Stephens.

"Well, yes, actually, and somebody important to me died from it, so I would appreciate it if you'd stop glamorizing it when I'm around."

"Oh. Sorry." He frets an oily strand of blond hair between his fingers. Purple lids hood blue-gray eyes. *Beau-laid.* "A boyfriend?"

Her face pounds with heat. "Somebody important," she says.

"Such as a boyfriend?"

"So we have a deal?" she says. "No more romanticizing?"

"Okay, but hold on, eh—I need to hear more."

"Another time."

"I'll get it out of you eventually," he says. "I'll huff, and I'll puff, and I'll blow your story down!"

Didier hapless. Penny yawning. Bex whining about kittens. Mattie's luck. The semeny eggnog. The cysts on her ovaries. Her dad eating soft vegetables at Ambrosia Ridge Retirement Village. Susan believing the biographer is not yet an adult. Every Child Needs Two coming true in three weeks.

They've tucked into Didier's roast when a late-arriving guest is ushered in, a pudgy white guy with a shaved head. "Everyone," says Susan, "this is Edward Tilghman. We were in law school together. By the way, you didn't need to dress up."

"I didn't," he says, brushing rain off his suit jacket. "These are my work clothes."

"Edward has a client in town," explains Susan.

The guest settles in between Penny and the biographer, takes a sip of water, and shakes out his napkin.

Something warm and moist hits the biographer under her left eye. She finds it in her lap: a slice of meat.

Another wet little slap—Bex is hit too.

"Cunt!" says the girl.

"Goddammit, John," says Didier, "if you can't sit at the table without throwing food, you're not going to sit at the table."

Susan stares at her husband. "Why does she know that word?"

"How should I know?"

Bex sings, "Cunty McGee was a happy little cunt."

"Goodness," says Edward.

"Not a nice word, Bexy—" But Didier is laughing.

"Does it go in the special box?" she asks.

"What special box?"

"*Nothing,* Momplee."

"Mommy," cries John, "a boy and a fish is friends."

Penny asks, "Whom are you representing, Edward?"

"He can't divulge," says Susan.

"Their *names* aren't confidential," says Edward. "This isn't Alcoholics Anonymous," and Susan takes the shock of correction square in the face.

"But the fact of representation," she insists, "is privileged in some jurisdictions—"

"A woman named Gin Percival." Edward helps himself to a plop of parsnip.

"The witch!" says Didier. "She's been doling out the wrong kind of family planning."

"Ucchh, shut *up,*" says Susan.

"Momplee, that's rude and you should say sorry."

"I think Daddy should say sorry. For being an idiot."

Didier is watching Susan with an expression the biographer has never seen on him before.

Penny stands up and claps. "Time for all children who live in this house to prepare a welcome letter for Mr. Claus! All children of the house, please come with me to the letter-writing station."

"We have to be excused first," says Bex.

"You're frigging excused," says Susan.

The kids follow Penny to the living room, and Susan carries plates to the kitchen. Didier, wordless, heads out to smoke.

The biographer feels bad that Gin Percival is in jail, but not as bad as she should. Gin can't help her anymore, and the biographer can't be sympathetic right now.

Unless a pregnant woman or girl decides, in the next three weeks, that she'd actually really love for her baby to be raised by a single mother on a high school teacher's salary, then the biographer will be removed from the agency's list. *To restore dignity, strength, and prosperity to American families.*

She can remain on the fostering list; but ECN2 stipulates that in single-parent homes, foster placement cannot lead to permanent legal adoption.

She sneezes, wipes her nose on the pink linen napkin.

Edward leans away from her and says, "Could you please cover your mouth?"

"I did cover my mouth."

He moves three chairs away.

"Really?" says the biographer.

"Sorry, but my immune system isn't strong and I can't afford to get sick right now."

The biographer pushes the tip of her napkin up one nostril.

In-breath.

She wants to go home, where no one can see her.

Out-breath.

Sneak out now without saying goodbye.

In-breath.

Susan would hold a grudge for such rudeness.

Out-breath.

But what if—

What if, instead—

Mattie gave her the baby?

What if she just gave it to her?

But that's insane.

Demento dementarium.

What if Mattie said, *Yes, okay, here—for you. Take care of him. Take care. I'll see you later, miss. I'm off to my life. Tell him about me one day.*

What if she asked, and Mattie said yes?

She would never ask, obviously.

Unethical. Malfeasant. Pathetic.

But what if?

Ice fog = pogonip
Ice crystal = frazil
Ice feathers = rime

THE WIFE

What joy to walk naked after a shower and hear your labia clap. To rise from the toilet and hear your labia clap.

The stretching and loosening is permanent, no matter what miracles they tell you Kegels can work. Kegels can't fix the lips. The wife's college roommate got the surgery after her third child. "Flappy no more!" reported the roommate in a mass email. The wife remembers thinking how odd to announce your labiaplasty to seventy-nine people—the addresses weren't hidden—but odder still were the replies. "Tell your javiva congrats." "Bet your man is lurving it!"

She buttons her jeans, flushes the toilet, returns to her children, slumped on the sofa. Didier is hiding upstairs, pretending to write lesson plans.

Bex moans: "I'm so bored."

"Then play with your Christmas presents."

"I played with everything."

"Have you read all the books Grammy gave you?"

"Yes." She is facedown on the Turkish carpet, snow-angeling.

"I doubt that." The wife watches John start to remove, one by one, the blocks she just put away.

"Where's Ro?"

"At her own house. John, leave those in the basket, please—"

"Why are you sleeping in the sewing room and not with Daddy?" Still facedown, but the girl has stopped moving, is waiting hard for the answer.

"Daddy snores."

"So do you."

"No, I do not." The wife grabs two blocks from John, bangs them into the basket with their fellows.

"Also, if you have another baby—"

"I'm not having another baby."

"But if you do have another baby, will you get a purple nurple again? And will your hair fall out and your breasts die?"

"They didn't *die*. They changed shape when John stopped nursing."

"Went flat," says Bex.

Just wait until you get here, sweetpea.

"I'm not going to hit you," she whispers.

She has never hit her sprites, and never will.

Fifteen minutes later she's alone in the car, going fast. The road is wet and dreamy with fog, but she is a good driver; her foot is steadfast and capable.

Inside the Acme she slows, lingers over her selections. In the chocolate department she has her preferred brands and flavors, the organic rainforest companies, the mints and the sea-salt-almonds; but sometimes she likes to mix it up with a hazelnut-coriander or a black-pepper-fennel-cardamom.

She sets six bars (three cardamoms, three mints) and a family-size of soft-batch chocolate-chip cookies on the conveyor belt, along with an unneeded pack of kitchen sponges.

"Looks like you're in for a fun night," says the cashier.

"It's for my daughter's class," says the wife.

"Right," says the cashier.

On the way home she pulls into the scenic overlook parking lot, whose guardrail is sturdy.

Dials Bryan.

Gets his growly message: "You know what to do and when to do it."

"Hey there," she chirps, "hope you had a good Christmas. Checking to see if you wanted to have that coffee sometime. Oh, and this is Susan. Okay, well, call me! Thanks!"

What will Bryan make of her clapping labia?

The cardamoms go in the kitchen drawer, under the maps.

The mints stay in the torn lining of her purse.

The soft batches were eaten in the eight minutes between the scenic overlook and home.

She spots husband and children through the window, tumbling in the brown grass behind the garage. He has given them a snack, at least, even if he didn't clean it up.

Herd crumbs into palm.

Spray table.

Wipe down table.

Rinse cups and bowls.

Set cups and bowls in dishwasher.

Throw empty family-size soft-batch cookie box into recycling.

If she leaves first, she breaks her family.

Knot up recycling and take out to blue bin.

Pour compost pail rinse water into pot of ficus tree.

Spray mist onto green snake arms of Medusa's head.

If she sleeps with Bryan, it won't be a relationship.

Stack books.

Push fairy costumes into trunk.

Only sex.

Ignore black dust on baseboards.

Intercourse with a shire horse.

Ignore soft yellow hair balls in every corner.

Ignore beds of children, but make own.

That little red motel on 22—

While making own bed find sock of husband in covers.

Sniff sock; be surprised that sock does not smell bad.

Run rag through dust on dresser.

She will leave the credit-card statement open on the dining-room table.

In downstairs bathroom, ignore soap heel crusted to sink.

Except that Didier wouldn't bother reading the charges.

Lift toilet seat.

Count three pubic hairs.

Slam seat back down.

Then she will just tell him, flat-out.

And he will leave first.

When London was colder, "frost fairs" were held upon the Thames. Fire pits and puppet stages, caged lions and gingerbread booths, were dragged onto the ice; there were sled races, pigs turning on spits, fortune-tellers, bull-baiters. One could see flounder and porpoise trapped mid-swim in the glass river. But not since 1814 has the ice been solid enough to withstand this revelry. I came to London too late.

THE MENDER

The jail washes its blankets with so much bleach she has to shove them in the opposite corner of the cell. She sleeps in her clothes, the mattress thin, she pretends it's the forest floor. When she wakes, her chest hurts and her nostrils are full of chemicals. The walls are still gray.

She draws the outside inside her head. Sky full of water. Clouds full of mountains. Shark field full of bones. Stoves full of trees. Trees full of smoke. Smoke full of winter. Sea full of seaweed. Fishes full of fishes.

In here they bring her nuggets and colas, but no fishes.

The bitches are squirrely. They are sending letters. They want advice remotely. Give them recipes, they demand. What about the ointments for their figs? The stinky teas for their bloods? Oh, bitches. Please can the mender provide the name of a pharmacy that carries the ingredients? No, she can't, because the pharmacy is the phorest. It is pherns, phunghi, phauna. It is hairs from dead Temple, ground up.

Mattie Matilda has not written to her. Term-house procedure gone wrong. Untrained scrapers. Dirty gear. If the girl started to hemorrhage, they would've been too nervous to take her to the hospital.

"Breakfast," calls the day guard.

"Don't want it," says the mender, not sure if she is saying this out loud.

The guard has unlocked the cell door, stands holding a tray. "Cereal and sausage."

"Poison." When she eats cereal, her scabbard gets yeasty; and truly anything could be in that sausage.

"Your trial starts next week, Stretch. I'd advise you to eat."

Can she see into next week, this guard with the sixth finger on her off hand? Can she see the mender fainting from hunger on the stand?

"Well, it's here if you change your mind." Clunks the tray down on the floor, and the little milk box jumps.

Squeeze the lemon. Grind dried lavender and fenugreek seeds in a mortar. Unscrew the jar of elderflower oil.

Then Lola's husband gets ahold of the bottle. Pours in the crushed-up drug. Makes her drink it, or she drinks willingly. Washes it all down with Scotch.

Ninety months is two thousand, seven hundred thirty-nine days. All those days in a cell like this one. Her nostril walls will turn white from bleach. Hans and Pinka and the halt hen will die. Malky will forget her.

To quit shaking, she reminds herself: *You are a Percival. Descended from a pirate.*

25 January 1875

Dear Captain Holm,

Allow me to offer my services on the upcoming voyage of *Oreius* from Copenhagen to the Polar North. I am a hydrologist with significant expertise in the behavior of pack ice. It would be my honor to assist in your collecting of magnetic and meteorological data.

Though a Scotsman by birth, I speak and write fluent Danish.

I am, Sir,
Your most obedient servant,
HARRY M. RATTRAY

THE BIOGRAPHER

You can't just say to a person, "Would you give me your baby, please?"

Allow me to offer my services.

Eivør Mínervudottír did things she wasn't supposed to. Took plunges.

"It doesn't work for everyone," said Dr. Kalbfleisch at their first appointment. "And you're well over forty."

Woman who is thin and ugly. Cruel and ugly old woman. Witch-like woman. Mínervudottír was forty-three when she died; the biographer turns forty-three in April. Crones to the bone.

"You need to cultivate acceptance," said the meditation teacher. "Maybe motherhood isn't your path."

Acceptance, thinks the biographer, is the ability to see what is. But also to see what is possible.

She puts on her running shoes. Her gloves. Dark out: she'll keep to the lit streets. She jogs up the hill, focusing, as her track coach taught her, on the balls of the feet pressing at the asphalt, press and release, press and release. Her breath is stiff. Sweat tingles in her armpits and at the top of her butt. She's too out of shape for running to feel good, but it feels correct, a corrective—slam the blood through every vein, unseat the sediment, flush the channels, ask the heart to do more.

She cuts over to Lupatia and back down toward the ocean. Passes Good Ship Chinese and the church. If she turned left here, she would end up, after a zigzag or two, on Mattie's block. She stops. Leans against the trunk of a madrone, panting. On the family trip to the nation's capital she raced her brother up the *Exorcist* steps and won. Archie said, "Only because you're older." Dad yelled, "Come the hell back down."

Mattie, can I ask you something?

The biographer doesn't know when the average person eats dinner, but she guesses by eight p.m. most dinners in Newville are done.

When Mama made a whole chicken, she claimed one drumstick for herself, and Dad and Archie fought for the other, and the biographer was the good child who ate breast.

Mattie, if I paid for all your checkups and vitamins, would you—

Her feet turn left.

If I drove you to all the appointments, would you—

She is not really doing this.

It can't hurt to ask, can it?

But how would she even get the words out?

The biographer's baby will be the good child always, even when he scribbles with permanent marker on the walls. Even when he throws his drumstick out the window into the neighbor's yard.

Bike-lock key at her throat, gloved fingers fisted tight against the cold. Her fingers ache, but not as much as the fingers of Eivør Mínervudottír once ached. All the plunges that woman took—gigantic plunges—the biographer can take one too.

She starts to sprint.

Dear baby,

You have one live grandparent. He moved to Orlando after your grandmother died. Your uncle is gone, so you're out of luck on the cousin front. As cousin stand-ins you will have Bex and Pliny the Younger.

Dear baby,

I love you already. Can't wait for you to get here. Your hometown is one of the most beautiful places I've ever known. Full of ocean and cliffs and mountains and the best trees in America. You'll see for yourself, unless you are born blind, in which case I will love you even harder.

The Quarles house is gray shingled, flanked by shore pines. Lights are on behind the curtained windows. You are not really doing this. But she is. Climbing the wooden steps to a wooden deck heavy with ceramic bowls of wintering dirt. She is. Going to convince her. She is. Whispering the sentences of her prepared speech. As she brings a finger to the doorbell, it occurs to her that a logical outcome of this plan is that she'll be fired from Central Coast Regional.

Mattie, I will take the baby on a train to Alaska.

Row a boat with the baby to the Gunakadeit Light.

Her finger hovers over the white plastic button, heart thumping frantic in her ears, rain spitting on her forehead. *Keep your legs, Stephens.*

She plunges.

Not until the steamship *Oreius* had rounded the Jutland Peninsula into the North Sea did the captain understand a woman was aboard.

He told the explorer, "We have no choice but to bear you."

THE BIOGRAPHER

Eight seconds after she presses the bell, Mattie's mother opens the door, smiling. "Miss Stephens?"

"Sorry to drop by unannounced."

"No, please, come in."

Photos of the girl overwhelm the living room—on walls, on tables, on bookshelves, their daughter's every year, it seems, well captured. "We go a little wild with the pictures," says Mrs. Quarles, noticing the biographer notice.

"You have a fabulous child, so why not?"

"I doubt Matilda would agree. She says the number of pictures is, quote, demented. Can I get you something to drink?"

"Oh no, please, I'm not staying long, I—needed to—" Breathe. "Before Christmas Mattie asked me for more comments on an essay draft, but things were so busy that—Well, now that the holidays are over, I want to give her the feedback."

"That's unusual," says Mrs. Quarles.

"When a student puts in the extra effort that she does, I'm willing to do some extra too."

"But she's not here."

"Oh?"

"She's at the conference."

The biographer is clearly meant to understand what Mrs. Quarles means by *the conference.* "Oh?"

"You knew she was going, didn't you?"

"To the—conference?"

"She told us you *nominated* her."

"Of course. I must have mixed up the dates."

"I have to say," says Mrs. Quarles, "she didn't give us many details about this thing."

"What did she tell you?"

"That it's a Cascadia history conference for high school students, and only one student from any given school is nominated to attend."

"That's right," says the biographer.

"Not as prestigious as the Math Academy, she said, but it will still look good on her applications."

Damp swoosh down the biographer's throat, into her ribs.

Is the baby gone?

Her mouth is full of bits from the planned speech—chewy clichés. *I can give it a good home. I mean her. Or him. You've got your whole life ahead of you.*

"Yes," mutters the biographer, "it'll be impressive."

"And they're all staying at the same hotel in Vancouver? Is there adult supervision?"

The biographer stands up. "I'm pretty sure they have supervision, yes. Sorry to interrupt your evening."

"You're *pretty* sure, or you're sure? Mattie hasn't been answering my calls. And I can't find anything about the conference online."

"That's because of its, um, principles? The people who run it are committed to students spending less time on computers, so they work only on paper, through the mail."

Mattie's mother is an intelligent woman, yet she appears to accept this.

The biographer walks slowly back to her apartment.

Archer Stephens may not be getting a namesake.

Her brother's blue lips on the kitchen floor.

The gravelly whine in his voice when he said he wasn't high.

"Yes, you are."

"I'm not."

"You are!"

"Jesus, I'm not—you're so paranoid."

But his pupils were the barest dots in the pale green; mouth ajar; tongue slow. She knew the signs, was becoming something of an expert;

and yet, and still, Archie's denials undid her. Dad said, "You're being duped!"—he was never much help, aside from the time he put up five grand for bail. She said, "I'm not paranoid; you're pinned!" and Archie said, "Because it's *sunny,* my friend." Possibly it was not sunny at all, but the biographer wanted to believe him. Her Archie, her dear one, no matter how buried, was still in there.

Shut up, she tells her monkey mind. Please shut up, you picker of nits, presser of bruises, counter of losses, fearer of failures, collector of grievances future and past.

At the kitchen table she opens her notebook to the *For which I am grateful* page. Adds to the list:

28. Two working legs
29. Two working hands
30. Two working eyes
31. The ocean
32. Penny on Sunday nights
33. Didier in the teachers' lounge
34.

But fuck this shitty list. She's sick of being grateful. Why the fuck should she be grateful? She is *angry*—at the amendment laws, the agencies, Dr. Kalbfleisch, her ovaries, the married couples, the term-house procedures. At Mattie for getting pregnant at the drop of a trilby. At Archie for dying. At their mother for dying. At Roberta Louise Stephens for trying so hard.

Rips the gratitude list out of her notebook, lights it in the sink with a match. She hasn't yet fixed the smoke alarm.

Mattie told her mother the conference was in Vancouver. She could have said Portland or Seattle.

By now she will have reached the border. If she manages to get across, manages to find the clinic, manages to produce a convincing Canadian ID, the abortion will happen tomorrow.

She might not get across, of course.

She might be stopped.

Don't hope she's stopped, you monstress.

But she does.

I have been lifted off the earth to sit on the ocean with men whose lives are nothing like mine yet whose waking dreams are identical: clumsy suits of caribou hide, our fingers numb, the flame-red gash of sunrise. If wrecked in this vessel, we wreck together.

THE DAUGHTER

Stares out a rain-lashed bus window at Washington State. Trees and trees and trees. A wet meadow or two. For the hundredth time she opens her passport. Date of expiration still valid. She is merely traveling, which is not a crime.

According to the online forums, you should carry evidence of your purpose in Canada. She and Ash created an email account for Delphine Gray—a sweet person but not the best speller—and sent several messages to the daughter. *Can't wait to see u Mattie, girl your going to love Raincouver, we will check out all the sites!*

For the clinic, she has a British Columbia driver's license bought from Clementine's boyfriend. Ash is lucky to have an older sister to advise her, giant brothers to defend her. A big rowdy fish-scented gang.

She keeps her bag on the aisle seat so that no friendly passenger can inquire about her destination. Rolls a licorice nib on her tongue. The sugar and chemicals ride her veins to the clump. Half Ephraim, half her.

She went to Vancouver once with Yasmine's family. Mrs. Salter, who represented Portland (District 43) in the Oregon State Legislature, was giving a speech on housing rights. The daughter remembers a city in a bowl of mountains and dark silver water. Bored at the hotel, she and Yas started their list of cardiac weights. The heart of a Canada goose weighs seven ounces. Of a caribou, seven pounds.

The bus judders to a halt. The daughter opens her eyes. Dark-green forest, steel-colored sky, a chain of tollbooths crowned with red maple leaves.

"Everyone off," shouts the driver. "Take all belongings with you and remove your suitcases from the luggage compartment."

A woman calls, "Can I leave a sweater to save my seat?"

"No, ma'am, you may not."

"What is this," she says, "the Soviet Union?"

The passengers are herded through the icy air into a low wooden building next to the tollbooths. Pale young men in olive-green uniforms sit behind the desks. A muscular dog led by an officer trots across the linoleum, nails clicking.

Do they have pregnancy-sniffing dogs?

Seekers are transported back in Canadian police cars, or buses—the daughter isn't sure. When they arrive in their home states, they are charged with conspiracy to commit murder.

An officer scans her passport. "What's your destination in Canada?"

"Vancouver."

"Reason for your trip?"

"Visiting a friend."

"For what purpose?"

"Vacation," says the daughter.

The officer looks at the passport again. Looks at her forehead, then at her chest. "You're how old, miss?"

"Almost sixteen. My birthday's in February."

"And you're traveling alone to Vancouver—for a vacation?"

Her face is getting hot. "My friend lives there. She used to go to my school in Oregon but moved to Canada a few years ago and I'm visiting her."

Don't offer too many details, say the forums.

"What's your friend's name and address?"

"Delphine Gray. She's picking me up from the bus station."

"You don't know her address?"

"Sorry, yes, I do. Four-six-one-eight Laburnum Street, Vancouver."

"Phone number?"

"We always talk online, so I don't—I don't need her number. It's so much cheaper to talk online. But I have an email from her printed out, if you want to see it?"

"Why did you print out her email?"

"It has her address on it."

"You said she was picking you up from the bus station."

"I know, but just in case? Like if I need to take a cab."

"Wait here, okay?" says the officer.

You can't say it was rape or incest—nobody cares how it got into you.

The daughter watches the Soviet sweater woman and her husband pass their check. A middle-aged white couple breezes through after them. Older Asian woman: breeze. Younger black guy: less of a breeze. They ask him extra questions, which he answers in a flat, irritated voice. But he, too, finally heads back outside.

"Matilda Quarles?" says an officer with frizzy blond curls. "Would you come with me?"

"Where?"

"Just come with me, please."

"My bus is leaving in a minute."

"I understand that. You need to come with me."

"But what if I miss my bus?"

The officer crosses her big arms. "Do we have a problem here?"

"No, ma'am."

Meant to be slitting lambs and hanging them to drain over washtubs.

Instead: riding a ship to gather facts in the boreal wilderness.

THE MENDER

Was disappointed to learn the girl's name—such a well-behaved name. The mender's own is no better. People have asked, over the years, Is it actually Virginia? Jennifer? No, just Gin. Are you named for a relative? No, for the alcohol. Oh, how funny, but really, where does it come from? But really it came from the alcohol, her mother's preferred.

The mender would have named the girl Temple Jr.

She doesn't remember the pain but knows there was pain; and Temple saying "Over soon, over soon" while she rocked the mender; and eating cherries Temple had dug the pits out of; and her stomach feeling spongy and collapsed. She doesn't remember the baby. They kept it elsewhere in the hospital. Every two hours the nurses brought in a manual pump to express colostrum, then milk, from her engorged breasts. The agency woman came with papers to sign.

People used to believe that new roses were born from the cinders of burnt roses, new frogs from rotting dead ones. Which is no stranger than believing the mender gave Lola a potion that made her fall down the stairs, or that the mender's mother is out there, somewhere, alive.

When the mender was a baby, her mother stayed clean. "She never used drugs while she was breastfeeding," said Temple. "Which doesn't exactly warrant a medal, but—you were important to her. Don't forget that, okay?"

A bad mother who was sometimes not bad. Who could still be out there, living off flowers in a tower, yarn in a barn.

Mother and mender and girl: descended from Goody Hallett of Eastham, Massachusetts, who tied lanterns to the flukes of whales.

A "lead" is the finger of open water between floes of sea ice. I have a theory: the shape and texture of a lead can foretell its behavior. How likely it is to freeze shut or open wider.

THE WIFE

On her way to meet Bryan, the tsunami siren goes off. She pulls over on the cliff road. The wail, forlorn and animal, lifts and crests, swings down and up and over again. A haunted wolf. Once a month it goes for three minutes, followed by chimes (all clear) or a piercing blast (evacuate). If an earthquake blows up the sea, a sucking wall of water will come at them, and minutes will matter.

The sprites are on the hill, higher than any wave could reach, playing camping with their father.

The ocean is a green pane. Pillars of rock shaped like chimneys, seals, and haystacks rise from the water.

She hears the chimes. Safe, sound.

She could be caught: a text sent to the wrong phone.

Or she could confess. Watch her husband's face when she says *I slept with Bryan.*

She keeps the house and he gets an apartment in town, carpools to school with Ro. The apartment will have a second bedroom for the sprites, who'll stay with him on weekends. During the week things won't be much different, no help with bath and bedtime as usual; same with the mornings, when she alone handles the boiling of oatmeal and dressing of bodies and brushing of teeth. But the weekends—the wife will have those to herself.

Or Didier could stay in the house, for now. The drafts and dripping taps and ugly wallpaper. The house has been in her family for generations; she read her first chapter book in its dining room, got her first period in its bathroom, watched Bex take her first steps on its porch. But for a while now she's been letting it go.

Too chickenshit to leave first, she will blow up her life instead.

* * *

Wenport is a dreary townlet adjacent to a pulp mill, and no one from Newville goes there except to buy drugs. Sometimes the wife asks herself which of her children is more likely to buy drugs one day, and the answer is always: Didier.

She parks right in front of the coffee shop. It wouldn't be Didier himself spotting the car, of course—he is crouched in a tent of blankets in the living room, being fed marshmallows fakely cooked on a fake fire—but Ro? Pete Xiao? Mrs. Costello?

I thought I saw Susan's car the other day...

Was Susan in Wenport with Bryan Zakile?

The coffee shop is too warm. The wife slips off her jacket and sweat darts to her cheeks. It is three minutes after two. The only other customers are two trench-coated boys playing cards.

"Can I getcha?" says the barista.

Almond pastries glisten under the glass.

"Tall skim latte, please," says the wife.

"For your info, ma'am, we are an independent business with no ties to multinational corporations. I.e., a mermaid-free zone."

"What?" The wife has one eye on the door, one eye on the boys. They could be Didier's students. Or Bryan's.

"You need to order a *small,*" says the barista.

"Then can I have a small skim latte. And a water."

"Water is self-serve."

She settles at the table farthest from the boys, facing the door. Ten minutes after two.

One boy cries, "Your griffin spell doesn't frighten me, sir!"

Seventeen minutes after. No texts or missed calls.

At twenty after, she will leave.

At twenty after, she finishes all the water in her cup.

She will leave in one minute.

At 2:24, Bryan appears. Not in a hurry at all. "Well, *hi* there," he says. "How's your day going?"

"Great, yours?"

While he's at the counter, the wife, facing the door, hears him ask the barista if she knows where the word "cappuccino" comes from; and she hears the barista giggle and say, "Um, Italy?" and Bryan say, "Well, for starters."

When he sits down across from her, she remembers that his face is not beautiful, despite the dimple. A fair to middling face. But the body that follows—

"Your hair looks awesome," he says.

"Oh—thanks!"

Slurping milk foam: "Get it cut?"

"Ah, no, actually. So how were your holidays?"

"Good, good. Went to see my folks in La Jolla. Nice to be in civilization again."

"Do you find this area uncivilized?"

He shrugs. Napkins the foam off his lip.

"Or too remote?"

"How do you mean?"

"Well, in terms of, I don't know—"

Bryan smiles. "Do you mean is it hard to meet women?"

"Or whatever. Yes."

"Not to sound conceited?—but that's never been a problem of mine."

"I'm sure it hasn't."

He pushes one fist slowly down the length of his thigh. "*Are* you?"

"What?"

"Sure. That it hasn't."

A clod of dried mascara falls off the lashes of her right eye, landing on her forearm.

"Look," says Bryan, "the way I see it, the scarcity model is a bunch of crap. When people are worried about not finding anyone, they pick the first person who comes along."

She flicks the mascara away. Her mouth is so dry.

"That's what happened to one of my cousins," he continues. "Married a total dick because she didn't think she could do better. And maybe she *couldn't* have, but, hey, I'd take lonely over beaten to a paste."

"Beaten?"

"Like I said, he's a dick."

"But that's—?"

"We all wish she would leave him. They don't have any kids."

"Even if they did."

"Well, maybe. Although children really need both parents at home."

The wife can see and hear and feel but is no longer thinking.

She wants to feel the thigh sitting two inches from her knee. Feel the fingers resting on the thigh.

Long, hard fingers.

Long, hard thigh.

"What about you, Susan? Do you find Newville remote?"

"I find it..." She twists her mouth to one side, which Didier used to say was sexy. "Boring."

"I wonder what we could do to make it less boring."

"I wonder."

"I can think of a few things."

"Can you?" Wet flare in her pit.

"I can."

"For instance?"

"Well..." Bryan leans forward, elbows on table, and holds his face in his palms. The wife leans in too, but the angle is awkward with her legs crossed. He stares at her. She stares back. Something is about to happen. He is going to kiss her right here, amid griffins and steam, twelve miles away from the house on the hill. She is going to blow up her life.

"Mini-golf team!" he says, grinning so wide she can see the black fillings in his teeth.

"What?"

"It's a thing now, competitive mini golf. There's a place right off 22. They run teams of four. I'm thinking you, me, Didier, and Xiao. You can actually win decent money."

As though a giant hand had released its grip, the wife sags in her chair. "I suck at golf," she says.

"Come now!"

"Get Ro to be on your team."

"The grammar police? *No gracias.*"

He does not want her.

Why did she think he wanted her?

"Hey," says Bryan, "let's share an original sin amen bun. They're fantastic here."

Black fillings all over his mouth.

"Why the hell not," says the wife.

In November of 1875, in the Arctic Ocean north of Siberia, pack ice started closing in on *Oreius*. The belts of open water grew farther apart; the leads shrank to black ribbons. Mínervudottír saw that the straighter leads seemed to stay open longer than the wavy, eel-shaped ones: was there something about the irregular margins that sped the knitting of the ice?

She suggested as much to the captain, who said, "And will you be pointing out the snow fairies too?"

THE BIOGRAPHER

Notices today how large Mr. Fivey's desk is. He grips its burnished surface with his hands wide apart, as a mogul might. Hanging behind him are the Ivy League diploma and several photos of Mrs. Fivey, which prompt the biographer to say: "I'm glad your wife is doing so much better."

"That's nice, Ro. But let's get down to the marrow. Since the school year began, you have been late no less than fourteen times."

No fewer.

"And absent five times."

"Four, actually."

"Tomato, tomahto—it's become a problem. These kids aren't going to teach themselves. Instead of learning history they're memorizing the anti-meth posters in study hall. I'd like to know how you intend to solve this problem."

"Well," says the biographer.

"Unless you'd prefer not to teach here at all?"

She uncrosses and recrosses her legs. "I do want to teach here. Very much. The thing is, I've been having some health issues, which—"

"Whatever it is, Ro, it can't go on. Either take a medical leave, quit, or get to work on time." His saliva lands on her face.

Has he gotten more dickish because his wife was in a coma? Or because Gin Percival's trial starts soon? Fivey will have to sit in the courtroom and hear how his wife allegedly sought an abortion from the witch, though she wasn't allegedly pregnant in the first place. And how his wife allegedly had an affair with Cotter at the P.O. And how her breasts are allegedly real. Even the biographer, whose finger is not on the pulse, has heard these rumors.

"I won't be late again," she says.

"No, you won't, because I'm giving you an official warning. One more violation and you'll need to call your union rep."

"We don't have a union."

"It's an expression. I don't mean to be a hard-ass," he adds. "You're good at your job, when you're around."

Fivey is a bush-league fish in a bush-league pond.

And these kids *are* going to teach themselves.

She's only here to give them some nudges and clues. She is here to tell them they don't have to get married or buy a house or read the list of shipwrecks at the pub every Saturday night.

Ten days until Every Child Needs Two comes true.

She should have asked Mattie sooner.

Plunged faster.

When told, last year, of the biographer's desire for a child, the meditation teacher suggested that she get a dog.

With a knife she stirs cream into her third cup of coffee. She inherited the family silverware, which Dad was not interested in carrying to Ambrosia Ridge, but most of the spoons had to be thrown away. The same spoons that had once entered the mouths of the biographer and Archie freighted with ice cream or pudding or soup were later used to heat the heroin and water that was sucked through a shred of cotton into a needle that went into Archie's skin. The charred spoons were useful to stumble upon (under beds, in creases of couches) when the biographer needed to confront him with irrefutable, unarguable evidence—though he did, in fact, to her amazement, sometimes argue.

"Ever heard of a dishwasher? They mess up spoons."

Or "That's probably been there for two years; it's not a current event, my friend."

Archie was a dumb fuck.

And her favorite person of all.

She will name her kid after him, if she ever has a kid.

Why does she even want one?

How can she tell her students to reject the myth that their happiness depends on having a mate if she believes the same myth about having a child?

Why isn't she glad, as Eivør Mínervudottír was glad, to be free?

She sips coffee. Drums her heel to the throbbing clank of the kitchen radiator. Opens her notebook. Writes on a new page: *Reasons I am envious of Susan.* It embarrasses her to write the word "envious," but a good researcher can't be stopped by ugly data.

1. Convenient/free source of sperm
2. Has two

The biographer's family once looked like the Korsmos—mother father sister brother, a foursquare American family. They had a weedy yard, a house. The biographer doesn't want a house, but she wants a kid. She can't explain why. She can only say *Because I do.*

Which doesn't seem like a good enough reason for all of this suffering effort.

Maybe she has flat-out been programmed by marketing. Awash in images of mother and child, mama bear and baby bear, she learned, without knowing she was learning it, to desire them.

Maybe there are better things she could be doing with the life she already has.

She glances down at the pasty insides of her elbows: the tracks are fading. Resemblance to Archie evaporating. Weeks since her last blood draw, since she last laid eyes on Kalbfleisch's indifferent golden cheeks.

Reasons I ~~am envious of~~ hate Susan:

1. Convenient/free source of sperm
2. Has two
3. Doesn't pay rent

4. Told me to distract self at movies
5. Has two
6. Said you don't truly become an adult until, etc.
7. Has two

A less envious, less hateful person would not be hoping that Mattie Quarles was arrested at the Canadian border.

The ice is a solid floor around our ship. No amount of chopping and sawing and hacking cracks its grip. The rudder hangs useless. *Oreius* is beset.

THE DAUGHTER

Follows the officer into a closet room with a brown table, brown chairs, and no windows. Sits down before being asked. The officer stays standing, hands on hips. "Can you tell me the real reason for your visit?"

"Going to see a friend in Vancouver."

"I said the real reason."

The door is closed.

Nobody knows she's here, aside from Ash, and what the hell is Ash going to do?

"That is the real reason, ma'am."

"We see a lot of girls like you trying to cross. Problem is, Canada has an official agreement with the United States. We've agreed to stop you from breaking *your* country's laws in *our* country."

"But I'm not breaking—"

"The nice thing about pregnancy tests? Results in one minute."

"I don't know what you're talking about, ma'am."

"Section 10.31 of the Canadian Border Services Agency Regulations states: 'If an unaccompanied minor registers a positive result on a FIRST RESPONSE Rapid Result Pregnancy Test, and cannot verify a legitimate personal or professional purpose in a Canadian province, she shall be taken into custody and returned to U.S. law enforcement officials.' "

"But I *can* verify my purpose. My friend Delphine?" The daughter opens her satchel and pulls out the email.

The officer glances at it. "Seriously?" Hands the page back.

The daughter presses her thighs together.

"This is what's going to happen, Matilda. I'm going to give you a cup, and you're going to go down the hall to the bathroom and urinate in the cup."

"You can't randomly drug-test me. That's illegal."

"Nice try."

The daughter decides to look this woman in the eye. "I can—I can pay you."

"For what?"

"For letting me get back on the bus."

"You mean a *bribe?*"

"No. Just—" Her mouth is quivering. "Ma'am, please?"

"Hey, you know who loves being called ma'am?"

"Who?"

"Nobody."

"I have a hundred dollars," says the daughter. She can sleep in the bus station and eat when she's back in Oregon.

"Keep it, eh?" The officer takes a plastic-wrapped cup from her jacket pocket and plunks it on the brown table. "Ready to pee, or do you need water?"

"Water," says the daughter, because it means delay.

Yasmine said she didn't intend to be anyone's stereotype. Black teen mother slurping welfare off the backs of hardworking citizens, etc.

And Mrs. Salter was the only woman of color in the Oregon State Legislature. She didn't intend to jeopardize her mother's career.

She gave herself a homemade abortion.

Blond Frizzy comes back without any water, followed by a man officer, blue eyed and in charge. He smiles at the daughter. "I'll take it from here, Alice."

"I was almost—"

"Why don't you go on your lunch?"

The subordinate officer does a long blink at the daughter. Wrinkles her mouth. "You betcha." And leaves.

"How are you today, Miss Quarles?" says the guy, propping one black boot on a chair. His crotch is at eye level.

She shrugs, too scared to be polite.

"So you're visiting the True North for pleasure? For fun?"

She nods.

"You know, we may be nice up here, but we still don't enjoy being lied to."

"I'm not—"

"Your face is *very* expressive. It betrays a lot."

Fear pricks up along her arms, across her chest.

"Some folks have unreadable faces. They're the tough ones, you know? The ones you second-guess yourself with. Not you, Miss Quarles. But"—he lifts up the propped foot, bangs it down on the floor—"I'm not going to arrest you."

"You're not?"

"I've got two daughters aboot your age. Let's say I've got a soft spot."

"That's—wow. Thank you."

"You'll need to go back where you came from, though. Next bus south gets here in three and a half hours. I will personally ensure that you're on it. If you don't already have a return ticket, you can pay the driver."

Back? Soft gray hole in her throat.

"Your photo and driver's license," says the guy, "will be distributed to every border patrol office in Canada, so don't even think aboot trying to cross again."

You can't tell from looking (scarves, big sweaters), but her stomach is thicker and harder. Soon it will be too late.

"I want you to learn a lesson from this. Don't repeat your mistakes. Like I tell my daughters: be the cow they have to buy."

"Sorry?"

"Don't be the free milk."

In the chilly waiting room, she eats chocolate-covered peanuts from the machine.

Mom has called twice to ask about the conference. Listening to her messages ("So proud of you, pigeon!") makes the daughter's nose run.

The daughter is ashamed to be ashamed of Mom when cashiers say "You and your grandma find everything you were looking for?"

This is the worst day of her life.

Second worst: when her father mistook Representative Salter for the school bus driver.

Is the failure of this trip a sign? She has tried twice now. Maybe she should just stay pregnant. Skip the Math Academy and push it out and give it to some couple with gray hair and good hearts. It's the legal way. The safe way. *Think of all the happy adopted families that wouldn't exist.*

She could skip the Math Academy and push it out and quit Central Coast Regional. Finish high school online. Let her mom help her wash and dress and feed it. When the daughter tries to picture herself as a mother, she sees the wall of trees by the soccer field, swaying and faceless.

She doesn't want to skip the Math Academy.

(She kicks Nouri's gothsickle ass at calculus.)

Or to push it out.

She doesn't want to wonder; and she would.

The kid too— *Why wasn't I kept?*

Was his mother too young? Too old? Too hot? Too cold?

She doesn't want him wondering, or herself wondering.

Are you mine?

And she doesn't want to worry she'll be found.

Selfish.

But she has a self. Why not use it?

Oreius would be trapped in the ice for seven months.

THE WIFE

Thanks Mrs. Costello for coming early. Kisses John's perfect ear. Gets on the road.

Twice almost turns the car around.

She hasn't been inside a courtroom since law school. This one is sultry with rain drippings raised to a boil by the heaters. At the front table sit Edward and Gin Percival. The wife can't see their faces. Fluorescent light bounces off Edward's shaved head. No sign of Mrs. Fivey, but Mr. is in the front row, checking his watch. Eight forty-five a.m.

The wife takes a seat against the back wall. In the jury box are seven women, five men, middle-aged and elderly, all white. Edward should have asked for a bench trial. Temple's niece won't make a good impression on any jury around here.

"Gin Percival," says the gnomish judge, "you will stand while the charges against you are read."

She gets to her feet. Dark hair in a bun, orange jumpsuit loose at her waist. She's gotten thinner since the wife last saw her, on the low metal stool at the library.

The bailiff intones:

"One misdemeanor count of Medical Malpractice by Commission against Sarah Dolores Fivey.

"One felony count of Conspiracy to Commit Murder in acceding to terminate the pregnancy of Sarah Dolores Fivey."

How much time could she get? The wife can't recall anything about sentence lengths.

She can recall reading aloud "manslaughter" as "man's laughter," and Edward being the only person in class to agree it was funny.

Unable to see Mr. Fivey's face, she pictures its mortification. Everyone knows his business now. The principal's wife and her backwoods abortion. No matter how this case turns out, the Fiveys will leave tarnished.

From the prosecution table rises a slender red-haired attorney in a pinstriped suit. She takes her time strolling to the jury box, palms together at her throat as though in prayer. She looks younger than the wife.

"Fellow Oregonians, you've heard the charges against Gin Percival. Your job is simple: to decide whether there is sufficient evidence to convict Ms. Percival of these crimes. During the course of this trial, you'll be shown a vast array of facts that establish her guilt on both counts. Listen to the facts. Base your verdict on the facts. I know that the facts will lead you to conclude beyond a reasonable doubt that Gin Percival is guilty of the crimes she's been charged with."

"Vast array"—lazy phrase. Repetition of "crimes," "charge," "guilt," and "facts"—predictable move. Edward can take her.

He clears his throat. "Thank you, Judge Stoughton, and thank you, members of the jury—you're performing an important civic duty." He pauses to scratch the back of his neck, under the collar. "Mmh. My counterpart has told you that your job is simple, and I would agree. But I beg to differ with her assertion that the evidence will clearly show you much of anything. Because there is virtually no evidence. You will be presented with hearsay, speculation, and circumstantial evidence, but no *direct* evidence. And your job, which is, indeed, simple, is to see that there is not enough evidence to convict my client beyond a reasonable doubt of these spurious charges."

His sentences are too long. He should have said "bogus" instead of "spurious." This is rural Oregon.

"Thank you, and I look forward to working with you over the coming days." He sits, wipes his face with a handkerchief.

Gin Percival keeps staring at the wall. Will Edward dare to put her on the stand? By all accounts—and from what the wife has smelled at the library—she's a bit unhinged.

Has the wife become a person who believes all accounts?

Sort of, yes, she has.

She has been too tired to care.

The Personhood Amendment, the overturning of *Roe v. Wade,* the calls for abortion providers to face the death penalty—the person she planned to be would care about this mess, would bother to be furious.

Too tired to be furious.

The past future Susan MacInnes could have been a battling litigator who brought milestone cases to the higher courts. Edward is battling; he has marched into the mess. The wife can hardly bring herself to read about the case.

Bring yourself.

At the library, Gin Percival's hair sometimes had twigs in it, and she gave off an oniony scent. The wife felt repelled by her animal dishevelment; yet she is coming to see the value in being repellent.

Bryan was a pitiful diversion, an excuse. This is an inside job.

Whatever frees Gin Percival to leave her hair twiggy and wear shapeless sack dresses and smell unwashed—the wife wants that.

Two days, two nights every week to herself.

Tell Didier you are leaving.

Before having kids, she envisioned motherhood as a jubilant merging. She never thought she would long to spend time away from them. It is hideous to admit she can't bear the merging 24-7. Same guilt that's kept her from putting John in daycare: she doesn't want it to be true that she wants to be apart.

The judge says, "Prosecution may call its first witness."

Mrs. Costello, never one to put much faith in science, believes Gin Percival cursed the waters, charmed the tides, and brought the seaweed back. Half of these jurors may think the same. And if a witch can charm the tides, what else is she capable of?

The pin-striped suit stands up. "Your Honor, we call Dolores Fivey."

In law school, the wife excelled at trial performance. She used to get rounds of applause. But here in the gallery, watching the judicial choreography, she feels no desire to go back to law school. If she puts John in daycare it will be for other reasons, as yet unknown.

What is the flavor of human meat? The men in Franklin's expedition, lost in the Canadian Arctic, turned to cannibalism, according to Inuit reports.

THE MENDER

Lola's tits aren't so fat anymore, they look drained, cells collapsing like houses of butter. She's wearing them thrust up hell-for-leather, but they are ghosts of their former selves. Butter ghosts. She sits in the box in her push-up bra and a blue suit with long sleeves to hide the scar—less of a scar (thanks to the mender) than it would have been.

"Mrs. Fivey," says the prosecutor, "please tell us how you came to be acquainted with the accused."

The lawyer leaps up. "Objection. Your Honor, I ask that the prosecution refer to Ms. Percival using the less inflammatory term 'defendant.'"

Drowning in his robes, the walnut-faced judge says, "Sustained."

"How did you meet the defendant?"

Lola won't stop staring at her hands. The mender loves those hands, small and graceful, the nails filed square. They held the mender's ass timidly at first; then not timidly. They found their way into her wet scabbard.

"Mrs. Fivey?"

In a frightened voice: "I went to her for medical treatment."

"Even though the acc—sorry, *defendant* is not a medical doctor? Or any kind of doctor, in fact? Even though she does not even have a high school diploma?"

"Objection," says the lawyer. "The prosecution is testifying."

"Withdrawn. Why did you seek medical treatment from the, ah, defendant?"

"I needed," says Lola, then stops.

"Mrs. Fivey?" says the prosecutor. "What did you need?"

"Medical treatment."

"Yes, that's been established. What specific treatment was it?"

Lola shrugs. Twists her hands on the rail of the witness box.

"Mrs. Fivey?"

"You will answer the question, Mrs. Fivey," says the judge.

"A termination."

"A termination of what?"

"Of..."

"Please speak up, Mrs. Fivey."

"Of a pregnancy? I thought I was pregnant but I wasn't."

In exchange for testifying, the lawyer explained, Lola gets immunity. Won't be charged with conspiring to murder.

"And did Ms. Percival agree to provide an abortion?"

She looks at the prosecutor with her beautiful, painted-on eyes. Then back down at her hands. "Yeah, she did."

Lola has reason to lie. She's a cornered animal. The life she saves will be her own.

There is nobody to contradict her but the mender herself, who is a forest weirdo, a seaweed-hexing kook.

This predicament is not new. The mender is one of many. They aren't allowed to burn her, at least, though they can send her to a room for ninety months. Officials of the Spanish Inquisition roasted them alive. If the witch was lactating, her breasts exploded when the fire grew high.

The blacksmith harpooned a polar bear. Cook made stew from the liver and heart. I did not take a portion, though it was agony to smell the rich broth. After supper the sailors grew sluggish — slept poorly — by morning, the skin around their mouths was peeling. The skin on their hands, bellies, and thighs began to slough away. They did not believe me that vitamin A occurs at toxic levels in polar-bear livers. They are saying I cursed the stew.

THE DAUGHTER

Doesn't need to be convinced. What's one absence? She has always been the good girl. Spotless record. Besides, she can't think—her eyes keep closing. She wants to sleep for a year.

"Cool," says Ash. "I've never seen a testimony before."

When the Quarles family moved to Newville, Ash was the only person willing to hang out with the daughter. She warned her that Good Ship uses ghost pepper (which can numb your lips permanently) in its hot and sour soup. She took her to the lighthouse. She taught her to find creatures in the tide pools—ass-mouthed anemones, ribbed limpets whose shells fit into dents in the rock called home scars.

They drive north in slashing sleet. Order mochas at the drive-through espresso hut. Lick the quaking towers of whip.

"New scarf?"

"Christmas," says the daughter.

"The purple one looked better."

Yasmine wouldn't like Ash much; but she is all the daughter has.

She lights a cigarette. Everything out the window is gray, the sky and the cliffs and the water, the cold curtains of rain. The cops at the hospital kept asking "How did she do it? What did she use?" and the daughter couldn't answer.

"So, um, I have a question," she says.

Ash holds out two fingers. The daughter puts her cigarette between them.

"Can you ask your sister for the number of a term house?"

Ash exhales, hands the cigarette back. "No way."

"But the ones online, you can't tell if they're real or traps. Can't you just *ask?*"

"Fuck no. Clementine wouldn't tell me, anyhow."

"She might, if she knew I didn't—have much time left?"

"Yeah, but no. Too dangerous. Clem knows a girl who got such a bad infection at this place in Seattle she had to get emergency surgery and almost died."

"Was she arrested?"

"Of course." Ash reaches for the cigarette again. "But her dad hired this famous lawyer. The girl told my sister the term house was sickening. She saw a plastic bucket of another girl's stuff just sitting there. A *clear* plastic bucket."

Hot spike in the daughter's ribs. Taste of pennies on her teeth.

Yasmine didn't die either. But she lost so much blood she needed transfusions. All night the daughter and her parents waited at the ER with Mrs. Salter, who rocked back and forth in her pink ski jacket. The lights squeaked. The daughter had to pee horribly but wanted to be there when the doctor brought news.

Yasmine's uterus was so badly damaged it had to be removed.

The cops came while she was still in the hospital.

The witch wears an orange prisoner suit, not the stitched sack, and her hair looks brushed, which in the forest cabin it did not. Good thing she can't see Gin Percival's face, in case the face looks scared. The daughter, scared all the time now, wants there to be people who aren't.

Clementine is scheduled to testify as a character witness. The rest of Ash's family thinks Gin Percival contaminated the waters. More fish are turning up dead in the nets, and the dead man's fingers are messing up the hulls of boats.

"Please silence your electronic devices," says the little judge.

At this moment Ro/Miss is taking attendance and doing the bit where she repeats the names of the missing ("Quarles . . . ? Quarles . . . ? *Quarles . . . ?*") in reference to an old movie the daughter hasn't seen.

"Doctor," says the lemon-mouthed prosecutor, "before we adjourned yesterday you said Dolores Fivey suffered a grade-three mild traumatic brain injury as the result of falling down a flight of stairs of twelve vertical feet, which—"

"Objection," says Gin Percival's lawyer, bald and round. "The doctor has already testified to these details; I can't imagine why we need to hear them again."

"Withdrawn. Can you please tell the court the results of a tox screen administered to Mrs. Fivey shortly after her arrival at Umpqua General Hospital?"

"Sure can," says the doctor. "We found alcohol and colarozam in her system."

"As you know, terminating a pregnancy is a felony."

Her clothes are too tight. The room is too hot.

A plastic bucket of another girl's stuff.

"Objection."

"Can cause dizziness and falling."

"When mixed with alcohol."

"When mixed with lemon, lavender, fenugreek, and elderflower oil."

"A felony."

"Seeking a termination."

"A felony."

She needs to find a bathroom—

"Dizzy, disoriented, prone to stumbling."

"When Dolores Fivey was admitted."

"Standard procedure."

Websites say nausea is only first trimester—

"And what were the results of."

"Women of childbearing age."

The daughter needs a bathroom. Can't think. Too hot.

Colarozam.

A plastic bucket.

The shunning of a boar.

Claimed to believe.

When mixed with alcohol.

A boar shun.

So tight this hoodie this room too hot—

Ash's mocha breath on her cheek: "Girl, are you okay?"

"What."

"You're sweating like a freak. Let's get some water."

"Bathroom."

"Hush," says Ash, and shoves her down the slippery bench toward the door.

Mínervudottír saw a narwhal come to breathe at one of the holes cut in the ice near the ship, for quick water in case a fire broke out. He was soon joined by others, their helical tusks spearing the air. The sailors watched the fire holes too and would shout "Unicorn!" when a whale appeared.

THE BIOGRAPHER

From narwhals she moves to notes on the Greely Expedition. In August of 1881 the American explorer Adolphus Greely and his team of twenty-five men and forty-two dogs arrived at Lady Franklin Bay, west of Greenland. They were to gather astronomical and magnetic data from the Arctic Circle and to attain a new "Farthest North" record.

The second summer, the expedition waited on the supply ship that was scheduled to bring food and letters. It never appeared. (*Neptune* had been blocked by ice.)

The third summer: no ship. (*Proteus* had been crushed by ice.)

Between 1882 and 1884, several vessels went in search of Greely and his crew—at first to restock them, then to save them.

Each time she types the word "ice," the biographer thinks *trial.*

Boots. Parka. Gloves. Rain has rinsed the frost from her windshield. Instead of driving down the hill toward school, she drives up: toward the cliff road and highway, the county seat. If Fivey tries to fire her, she'll hire Edward to contest it.

She has been in a courtroom twice before, in Minnesota, for Archie's possession charges. "How can you tell when a lawyer's lying?" he turned to whisper. "When he opens his mouth," she said, dismayed by how obvious the joke was.

Fiveys at the front; Cotter from the P.O. behind them; Susan in a middle row; Mattie and Ash at the very back. Mattie looks haggard and dazed. Having never needed to terminate a pregnancy, the biographer doesn't know how long it takes to recover. A hard little glass splinter in her hopes the girl is miserable.

The new laws turn the girl into a criminal, Gin Percival into a criminal, the biographer herself—had she asked for Mattie's baby, forged its birth certificate—into a criminal.

If not for her comparing mind and covetous heart, the biographer could feel compassion for her fellow criminals.

Instead she feels a splinter of glass.

In the witness box Gin Percival sits absolutely still. Expression flat as a knife.

PROSECUTOR: Ms. Percival, on Monday we heard sworn testimony from Dolores Fivey that you caused significant injuries to her. That you gave her a powerful drug that you claimed would terminate her pregnancy but which resulted in her falling down a flight of stairs and—

EDWARD: Objection. Is there a *question* hidden in there?

PROSECUTOR: Withdrawn. Did you administer a mixture of colarozam, fenugreek, lavender, lemon, and elderflower oil to Dolores Fivey?

GIN: No.

PROSECUTOR: I'll remind you that you are under oath, Ms. Percival. A bottle containing traces of those ingredients was found in Mrs. Fivey's home, with your fingerprints all over it.

GIN: That was my bottle. Oil for scars. Only the last four things. Not the first thing.

PROSECUTOR: Sorry, Ms. Percival, you're not making much sense.

EDWARD: Objection.

JUDGE: Sustained.

PROSECUTOR: Ms. Percival, tell me: are you a witch?

EDWARD: Objection!

PROSECUTOR: It's a reasonable question, Your Honor. Goes to the defendant's proficiency with herbal medicines and to her state of mind. If she self-identifies, even if delusionally, as a health-care provider—

JUDGE: I will allow it.

PROSECUTOR: Are you a witch?

GIN: [Silent]

PROSECUTOR: How long have you identified as a witch?

GIN: [Silent]

JUDGE: The defendant will answer.

GIN: If you knew about the *real* powers, if you knew, you'd be—

EDWARD: Your Honor, I request a short recess.

PROSECUTOR: Your Honor, I demand to finish my line of questioning.

JUDGE: "Demand"? You are in no position to demand anything here, Ms. Checkley. We will adjourn for thirty minutes.

Accused witches in the seventeenth century were dunked in rivers or ponds. The innocent drowned. The guilty floated, surviving to be tortured or killed some other way.

This isn't 1693! the biographer wants to yell.

She shakes her head.

Don't just shake your head.

While she hid out in Newville, they closed the clinics and defunded Planned Parenthood and amended the Constitution. She watched on her computer screen.

Don't just sit there watching.

While she hid out in her book, imagining the nineteenth-century deaths of Nordic pilot whales, twelve sperm whales perished, for reasons unknown, on the Oregon coast.

She looks for Mattie, but she and Ash and their coats are gone.

"Hey, Ro," calls Susan from the aisle.

"Hi," says the biographer, engrossed in her ancient flip phone, which can't even go online. She doesn't want to talk to Susan the non-criminal, the good adult.

Out in the marble-floored hallway she sees Mattie come out of the women's bathroom and head for the exit.

"Wait!" The biographer jogs after her.

Mattie doesn't stop. "Ash is getting the car."

Snow is flurrying down. On the courthouse steps they stand blinking at the little wet stars.

"How are you feeling?" says the biographer. "How was the procedure?"

The girl pulls on blue mittens. "I have to go."

"Wait, okay? I'm not going to tell anyone. Pretend I don't work at school."

"You do work at school."

"Did you go to Vancouver?"

Mattie's lips are purplish in the snow light. Her eyes are lake-green. "Didn't happen."

"Why not?"

"The Pink Wall."

You mean—The biographer gleams inside. "But why—did they not arrest you?"

"One was going to. Then I thought another one was about to, like, sexually assault me in exchange for letting me go. But he actually just let me go."

The baby is not gone?

The splinter is thrilled.

"Were you scared?"

Mattie wipes snow from her upper lip. "Yeah. But honestly?" Inhales a shredded breath. "I'm more scared now."

I will take the baby on a train to Alaska.

Row a boat with the baby to the Gunakadeit Light.

Ask her.

"Did they notify your parents?"

"No." A stricken look. "And you won't either, right?"

"Scout's honor."

"I better go—there's Ash."

Ask her now.

But the biographer is halted, held mute.

She pats Mattie's shoulder.

The baby will see the black ocean flecked with silver.

I will eat dinner with the baby every night.

FUCKING. ASK. HER.

Her mouth can't make those words.

"Well, if you need anything, let me know?"

"Thanks, miss."

The girl descends the steps, blue scarf rippling behind; and the biographer sees blue-swaddled babies shot from cannons across the Canadian border, then tossed back, still wrapped and cooing, onto American soil.

~~The significance of Eivør Mínervudottír's research was~~

~~Mínervudottír was important because~~

Was she important?

From the Latin: to be of consequence; weigh. To carry in, to bring in.

She brought in:

1. Refusal to submit to cottage life
2. Measurements of ice chlorides and Arctic sea temperatures
3. Metric analyses of ice responses to wind speed and tide speed
4. A theory of refreezing predictors in sea-ice leads, invaluable for navigating ice-choked waters

And thus helped to bring in:

1. Shipping and trade through the Northeast Passage, once considered impenetrable
2. More ways for white pirates to steal from the not-white, the not-rich, or the not-human
3. Oil, gas, and mineral drilling in the Arctic
4. The shrinking of the ice

Mínervudottír may have felt free; but she was a cog in a land-snatching, resource-sucking, climate-fucking imperialist machine.

~~Wasn't she?~~

~~Was she?~~

I DON'T KNOW
WHAT I AM
EVEN SAYING
ABOUT THIS PERSON THERE IS NOT
A SINGLE KNOWN PHOTOGRAPH OF

or why I couldn't bring
myself to ask for

my lips aren't working

THE WIFE

Labiaplasty surgeons earn up to $250,000 per month.

A little animal—possum? porcupine?—tries to cross the cliff road.

Sooty, burnt, charred to rubber.

Shivering, trying to cross.

Already so dead.

After federal and state taxes, social security, retirement, and health insurance, Didier brings home $2,573 per month. They don't have rent or mortgage payments, but it's still not enough.

Clap, clap, say the labia.

If the wife were a better budgeter, it would be enough. If she were more organized.

The wife has been letting the house "go."

And letting herself "go."

We'll go if you let us.

Wife and house run away together, hand in door. Hand in dormer window.

I'd take lonely over beaten to a paste.

She pictures Bryan's cousin, whoever she is, in a shack in the woods, hurled against a moldy particleboard wall. The husband is long bearded, wild haired. He rarely comes out of the woods or lets his wife come out. They drive to town once a month for supplies. On these trips Bryan's cousin wears sunglasses and a wide-brimmed hat.

Why does Bryan stand by and let it happen? Shouldn't he run into those woods and find the shack and put a stop to the beatings? Shouldn't he and the mother he visits in La Jolla, if they care so much, call the police?

Can't think of Bryan without broiling with shame.

"Mommy."

"Yes, sprite?"

"Cold," he says, her dear boy who isn't interested in saying much, who is so different from his chattery sister.

"Let's go put on a sweater," hoisting him onto her hip.

After they separate, will Didier buy pot gumdrops and leave them out on the coffee table for the children to find?

You need to tell him.

Upstairs, she finds a blue wool pullover.

Can pot be overdosed on?

"No!" shouts John.

"I forgot, you hate this one—sorry." She pulls off the blue wool and picks a red cotton, less itchy, from the drawer.

Will he remember to give them their vitamin D?

Tell him.

Downstairs the wife sits at the dining room table with her eyes closed.

"Momplee!"

"Don't yell, Bex."

"Then pay attention."

"What?"

"I *said,* what will you get Daddy for Valentine's Day?"

"That's over a month away."

"I know but I already know which cards I'm giving to people. The turtle ones, remember, that we saw?"

"Well, I'm not going to get Daddy anything."

"Why?"

"It's not a holiday we celebrate."

"But it's the day of love."

"Not for us," says the wife.

"Do you love Daddy?"

"Of course I do, Bex."

"Then why don't you celebrate it?"

"Because it's silly."

"Oh." The girl looks at her interlaced fingers and is thinking of the turtle cards, signed and sealed in small white envelopes, one for each classmate.

"I meant for grown-ups," adds the wife. "Not for kids—it's great for kids."

"Okay," says Bex, wandering off.

Two days and nights of solitude every week. The house to herself.

But first you need to tell him.

She'll feel so much better from the solitude that she will teach John to like foods other than buttered spaghetti and chicken nuggets. She'll bake those barley walnut muffins Bex eats at the Perfects'. She will start cleaning again, keep the rooms scrubbed and dusted, wipe the toilet rims weekly, buy a dehumidifier for the attic, make an appointment to test the kids' bloodstreams for lead.

Or she won't be living in this house at all: she will rent an apartment that requires virtually no cleaning.

Maybe the apartment will be in Salem.

After you tell him.

"Daddy's here!" shrieks Bex, galloping onto the porch.

"Daddy," sniffles John.

"Fee fi fo fon," calls Didier.

Children need two parents at home. Every child needs two.

So say the legislators and the commercials and Bryan, the child-free boy whose aim in life is to win money at competitive mini golf.

Jessica Perfect will have a field day. *Oh my God, did you hear? The Korsmos are separating. I feel so bad for the kids*—they're *the ones who really pay.*

The wife's mother, never a Didier fan, is going to say: *I saw this coming a mile away.*

She rummages in the kitchen drawer to see how many chocolate bars she has left.

"Momplee?"

Two.

"Yeah?"

"I lost my homework sheet."

"Look in your room."

"Incinerate! All homework sheets!" sings Didier.

Last summer at the teachers' picnic Ro asked her why she'd taken Korsmo, and the wife said, "Because I wanted us all to have the same last name."

"But why?"

"Because."

"It's the twenty-first century."

"I'm not going to sit here and justify my choices to you," said the wife.

"Why not?"

"Because I don't need to."

Ro kept her teeth on the bone. "How come nobody's allowed to criticize a woman's decision to give up her name for a man's name? Just because it's her *choice?* I can think of some other bad choices that—"

"Shut up, please," said the wife, and that was the beginning of the end of her friendship with Ro.

On the kitchen calendar, in Saturday's square, she writes a *T.*

Tell him.

She can't cheat her way out.

She can't wait her way out, head in the sand.

She has to say it herself.

"Momplee?"

"Jesus, Bex—it must be in your room. Have you checked under the bed?"

"Not about that," says the girl.

"Then *what?*" The wife stands holding the ballpoint pen with which she has just written herself a reminder to inform her husband she is leaving him. She wants to ram the pen into her own neck.

"Am I fat?"

"No!"

Voice wobbly: "I weigh eight pounds more than Shell."

"Oh, sweetpea." She kneels down on the kitchen floor, gathering Bex into her lap. "You're exactly the right size for *you*. Who cares how much Shell weighs? You're beautiful and perfect just the way you are."

The wife fails, as a parent, on so many fronts.

"You're my perfect darling gorgeous girl."

But she will do this one thing right.

I hate the chewy lard meat called pemmican; and I admit to fearing the attack of a sea bear; and my fingers hurt all the time; but I prefer immurement in these spectral wastes to a seat at the warmest hearth.

THE MENDER

A witch who says no to her lover and no to the law must be suffocated in a cell of the hive. She who says no to her lover and no to the law shall bleed salt from the face. Two eyes of salt in the face of a witch who says no to her lover and no to the law shall be seen by policemen who come to the cabin. Faces of witches who say no do resemble those of owls tied by leashes to stakes. *Venefica mellifera, Venefica diabolus.* If a town be plagued by a witch who says *No, I won't stop mending* and who says *No, you can't hide in my house,* and the lover Lola does feel sorrow and shame, and the hard-fisted husband of Lola does discover the betrayal of his wife, and the lover Lola, to save her own life, tells a lie about the witch, the witch's body shall be lashed to a stake. Her owl teeth shall catch flame first, sparks of blue at the white before the red tongue catches too. A witch's body when burning does smell of blistered milk; the odor makes onlookers vomit, yet still they look on.

My fingers hurt so much I am always humming.

Boatswain says he will punch my mouth if I don't stop.

THE BIOGRAPHER

The adoption caseworker's cubicle is festooned with evergreen boughs and reindeer cards on a string. She wears peppermint barrettes in her hair. "How was your Yuletide?"

"Fine," says the biographer. "I made this appointment because—Sorry, how was *your* Yuletide?"

"Super fun. We went up to my sister's in Scapoose. I drank way too much spiked nog, of course, but when in Rome!"

This caseworker is the biographer's fourth; turnover is high at the agency. She is straight out of college and has a tiny attention span and thinks "Fer sher" is an appropriate response to an emotionally charged disclosure. But she's better than the one who asked the biographer if she knew that a child is not a replacement for a romantic partner.

"Next week is January fifteenth. I am here to quite literally beg you to get me matched before then."

It takes the caseworker a few frowning seconds to grasp the date's significance. "I understand your concern," she says. "Let's see what's been happening in your file." She types, waits, stares. The screen is hidden from the biographer. "Okay. Since you last updated your profile, on September second, your landing page has received six views and zero Tell Me More clicks."

"Six? Jesus."

"It's difficult for some birth mothers to get past the age. You're older than some of their own parents, which—"

"Okay, yeah, thanks, I know. But you guys said if I played up my teaching career, and the fact that I'm about to finish a book, I'd have more hits?"

"I thought it would help, fer sher. We notice, though, that status and income associated with occupation can make a difference, which for you would not necessarily be great? Compounded with the singleness."

"What if you only showed them one profile?"

"What do you mean?"

"The next birth mother. You could show her my profile and no one else's. Those married people on the wait-list, they've got plenty of time ahead of them, but I only have a week left."

The caseworker smiles. "What you're suggesting is unethical."

"It's *very* ethical, actually. You'd be bending the rules in a minor, temporary way to create an opportunity for someone who is worthy but otherwise wouldn't have a snowball's chance. You'd be making a moral choice. Think of all the change makers throughout history who—"

"I'm not one of your students, Ms. Stephens."

"What? Sorry. I wasn't trying to lecture you."

"Well, you kind of were."

"I apologize. It would just be such a microscopic drop in the—"

"A drop I could lose my job over."

"What if..." The biographer has no idea how to phrase this, so she grabs language from the movies. "What if I made it worth your while?"

"What does that mean?"

"If I offered you an *incentive* to take the risk."

"Sorry, what?"

"As in, a financial incentive."

Light of no understanding on the caseworker's face.

"What if I gave you, personally, a thousand dollars," whispers the biographer, naming a sum she could realistically borrow. Her father, Penny, Didier—

"Oh my God, are you bribing me? This is my first bribe! I'm the only person in the office who hasn't been offered one. Until today."

Heartened by the lack of outrage, the biographer says, "Congratulations?"

"That's wild. I mean, of course I can't take it, but thank you."

"Why not? Nobody would find out. I give you cash, you show my profile to a birth mother before the fifteenth, I get matched with a baby, you get on with your life."

"Ms. Stephens, I totally sympathize with your situation, but I can't take part in an illegal transaction."

"You *can,* you just don't want to." The biographer is trying to breathe normally, but her lungs feel damp and fibrous, like rained-on wood. "Please? It would—it would change my life. I would never tell anyone. I'd lie on the stand if it went to court." Wrong thing to say: the caseworker's eyes crinkle up. "Which it *wouldn't,* of course, it never would, nobody will find out, I don't know why I said that but I guess it was to emphasize how much this would mean to me, and to the baby, who would have a good home with me, a really good home."

The black silver, flecked with ocean.

On a train to the Gunakadeit Light.

"Please?" she says. *"Please?"*

Breathe, Stephens.

"My supervisor's out today," says the caseworker, slowly, carefully, "but would you like me to have her call you?"

"Can she give me an extension on the deadline?"

"Every Child Needs Two is a federal law. Even if *we* made exceptions for unmarried applicants, the adoptions wouldn't be valid. Which would create more misery for all involved." She adds, "But you can stay on the fostering wait-list, fer sher."

The biographer's sodden lungs fight to take a full breath.

She drives back to Newville, gasping.

On the beach the wind drives hair into her eyes. She hurls a sneaker at a low-flying gull. Curses her aim. Retrieves her shoe. Jumps on an old log. The beach is a good place for rage: the sky and sea can take it. Her screams are absorbed by the booming waves, the heaped fields of oyster cloud. Because this is Oregon in January, nobody human is around to hear.

Doctor reported his medicine chest stolen. It was found in the snow a few yards from the tents, missing its morphine and opium pills. An able seaman was blamed for the theft, and shot dead.

THE DAUGHTER

"The jury's going to convict," says Dad.

"Are you now a fortune-teller?" says the daughter.

"She completely lost it on the stand, I hear. Looks as if she'll go to prison for a good little bit."

"Why are you *cheerful* about it?" She is extra seasick tonight.

"It's only fair she pay her debt."

Sipping water to mute the queasiness: "What if she didn't do what they said she did? What if—"

"More rice, Mattie?"

"It's like you're accepting whatever the news says. You weren't even at the trial."

"Your mother asked if you would like more rice."

"No thank you."

Mom, still holding the bowl: "You sure, pigeon?"

"Has Miss Stephens been telling you this woman is innocent? It's not her place to bring politics into the classroom, and if she is, then—"

"I can think of my own ideas. Miss Stephens didn't say shit."

"Language?" says Mom.

"Tons of injustices happen in broad daylight," adds the daughter, "when ordinary citizens are aware but do nothing."

"For instance," says Dad.

"The bystander effect. Nobody helping a crime victim when other people are around because everyone thinks someone else is going to do it."

"Fair enough. What else?"

Her father has trained her to give more than one example in any debate; and that numbers not ending in zero are more convincing in a negotiation, because they sound less arbitrary.

"For instance," she says, "the whole world knows about the pilot-whale slaughter in the Faroe Islands, but nobody's been able to—"

"People have every right to practice their own cultural rituals." He saws at his little pink pork chop. "The Faroese have been hunting whales that way for centuries."

"Pilot whales are technically dolphins. Oceanic dolphins."

"I don't know about that."

"Well, Dad, I do, and they are."

"Point is, they eat what they kill, and they only kill as much as they can eat. The haul is shared out fairly among the community."

"Good for them," mutters the daughter.

"Are you coming down with something?" says Mom. "You look—"

"I'm *fine*."

"I don't want you stressing out about the Math Academy," she says. "If you get in, you get in. If not, you try again next year."

"No reason she shouldn't get in this year," says Dad.

"May I be excused," says the daughter.

She has to get her body clean. Stop being seasick. Stop the blue veins from branching across her tightening breasts. *Don't be the free milk.*

Terribly she misses Yasmine.

Bolt River Youth Correctional Facility is a medium-security state prison for females twelve to twenty years old.

Number of letters, cards, and care packages the daughter mailed to Bolt River the first year Yasmine was inside: sixty-four.

Number of words she heard back from Yasmine: zero.

Whenever she phoned the front office, she was told, "The offender is refusing your call."

Yasmine's mother said, "I've got no idea, Matts. I simply don't."

After a year, the daughter stopped trying.

The frostbitten skin, which at first itched intolerably, has gone waxen and lifeless. Black-purple blisters seep rank-smelling pus. The doctor offered to cut the fingers off, but without morphine or opium, he said, it will be the worst pain I've ever known. I declined the offer.

THE WIFE

Puts away clean clothes while the girls play Amelia Earhart on Bex's bed. Didier is at the pub with Pete, home by dinnertime. Dinner will be taco casserole, and Shell is going to ask whether the beans were home soaked or from a can.

"What's that sound!"

"Oh no, the plane's running out of gas!"

"My only choice is to fall into the sea!"

"I'm falling! *Flump*."

"Flump."

In a non-game voice Shell says, "Gross, why is there dust all over your floor?"

Bex looks at the floor, then up at the wife.

"My mom says," adds Shell, "that a clean house is the only house worth living in."

That's enough, Perfect. That is enough.

"I guess your mom doesn't know much about dust," says the wife. "Because if she did, then she'd know that dust has pollen fibers, which are very good for you."

Bex smiles.

"How are they good for you?" says Shell.

This wallpaper is horrendous. Dark purple flowers on a brown ground. It shouldn't be the first thing her girl sees every morning.

"When you breathe them in, they create more white blood cells in your body, which keep you from getting sick. Dust is *extremely* nutritious."

By dinnertime her husband hasn't appeared, so she serves the kids their casserole, slides the dish back into a two-hundred-degree oven, hustles Shell out to Blake Perfect's car, gives Bex and John a bath, tries to recall

* * *

She looks at the kitchen calendar, where *T* has been written and crossed out, written and crossed out, written and crossed out.

Stands at the sink, scrubbing the casserole dish.

Didier and Pete come back in from their cigarettes.

"Want a beer, Peetle-juice?"

Little animal burnt black, trying to cross. Rubber and shivering.

"Can you believe she's never heard of them?"

"Dude, the sum total of Ro's musical knowledge would fit into Bryan Zakile's jockstrap."

Rubber and shivering.

"Do they make those in extra-small?"

Strapped jock. Jock of Bryan. Balls. Family jewels. Father. Mother. Cousin. *Cousin*—

"He actually uses a kids' size."

They don't have any kids, so why not leave?

Cousin beaten to a paste.

Oh no.

The wife drops the casserole dish. It clatters at the bottom of the sink.

Where is her phone—where is—"Where's my *phone?*" Furiously shaking water off her hands.

"Right here on the table," says Didier. "Jesus."

She snatches it up and hurries into the dark dining room, dialing.

He picks up on the first ring. "Susan?"

Blood beats hard in her neck. "Listen, Edward"—talking faster than she ever talks—"you need to interview a new witness, his name's Bryan Zakile, he told me firsthand that his cousin's husband hits her, and his cousin is Dolores Fivey. I think he could—"

"Hold on," says Edward.

She is light-headed. Can't find her breath.

"Did he witness the hitting himself?"

"Okay, *second*hand, but—"

"Also known as hearsay," he says.

"Which is admissible if it constitutes materially exculpatory evidence, and if corroborating circumstances clearly support the hearsay's trustworthiness."

"Damn, Susan. After seven years?"

Splashing glow in her chest. She rushes on: "It would introduce some compelling *doubt,* at least—"

"Hold it. Mmh."

Silence, while he thinks.

Her whole body is throbbing. This matters.

Edward says, "It would corroborate Ms. Percival's claim that Mrs. Fivey disclosed her husband's physical abuse. Which would in turn suggest a motive for Mrs. Fivey to lie about the—mmh."

"You should talk to Bryan tonight," she says. "I'll text you his number."

"Wait a minute. You said, 'He told me his cousin's husband hits her.' Most people have more than one cousin."

"He didn't specify, but it *is* Mrs. Fivey, Edward. It has to be."

"When did he give you this information?"

"A couple of weeks ago."

"And you're only telling me now?"

The glow cools. "I didn't—connect them."

"Mmh. I don't know that any of this will make a difference. But give me his number. Good night."

She sends the text and sits, twitching and exhilarated, in her grandmother's chair in the dark.

Upon *Oreius*'s return to Copenhagen, in the summer of 1876, the gangrenous ring finger and pinky on Eivør Mínervudottír's left hand were amputated. Her notebook does not brood long on the loss: "Two taken, under anesthesia. I have eight others."

With her right hand she wrote up the *Oreius* data. Even before she had finished a draft of the article, she knew her title: "On the Contours and Tendencies of Arctic Sea Ice."

THE MENDER

Keeps asking for different blankets, but they say work with what you have, Stretch. She hasn't been sleeping. Her throat hurts. She misses Temple, who would burn the bleachy blankets and boil a throat syrup of marshmallow root and say *Show them you're not afraid.*

Except she is.

There is one man on the jury whose eyes are alive. He looks at the mender like she's a person. He smiled when Clementine told the courtroom "Gin Percival saved my vagina." The other eleven watch her like she's batshit.

Kook. *People like to throw around labels.*

Kooky. *Don't let them define you.*

Kookaburra. *You are exactly yourself, that's who.*

Temple, wish you weren't gone.

The lawyer is excited today. His face is moving faster. He's brought licorice nibs and lettuce, a brown loaf from Cotter, butter in a ziplock. He explains about the new witness he's calling—Lola's cousin—who doesn't want to testify, so must be considered hostile.

"He'll just lie," says the mender, ripping bread with her teeth.

"Not if I approach him the right way." He takes the butter-smeared hunk she hands him and sets it on the metal bench, too polite to say no. "And if he says what I think he's going to say, then we recall Dolores Fivey to the stand."

"Also me? I could tell them what she told me. After he broke her finger he said she better start taking calcium supplements."

"You—" The lawyer smiles. "Not you."

"Why?"

"You are so much your own person, Gin. And some people on the jury may feel...unnerved by that? People tend to be more comfortable with speech and behavior that does what they already expect it to do. Yours doesn't, and I respect that it doesn't. But I have to think about the jury's perceptions."

She side-eyes him. Being fake? Talking down? With this lawyer, not easy to tell.

Clementine waves at her from the gallery. Cotter's there too, and the pissed-off blond lady from the library who doesn't lower her voice when talking to the librarian.

The mender can't remember seeing Lola's cousin ever before. He looks like your basic man in a suit, dark hair cruelly combed.

"Mr. Zakile," says her lawyer, "it is true you were a soccer star in college?"

The cousin's mouth opens in surprise. "I don't know about 'star,' but yeah, I made a contribution."

"More than a contribution, I would say! According to the University of Maryland student newspaper, *The Diamondback,* you earned All-Conference honors with your 'exquisite ball control and panther-like aggressiveness.' "

"Objection," says the prosecutor. "Where is Mr. Tilghman going with this?"

"Your Honor, I'm establishing context and background for this witness. Mr. Zakile, the *Washington Post* described you as 'a revelation' in a win over Georgetown, during which you scored three goals."

Hesitant smile from the cousin. "That was a great game."

"Plainly, then, Central Coast Regional was fortunate to hire you as their boys' soccer coach. I'm told you are an effective coach—would you agree?"

"We went fourteen and four last season. I'm proud of my guys."

"Your Honor, *what?*" says the prosecutor.

The mender watches her lawyer lead Bryan Zakile to water. As the story of his own awesomeness—as athlete, coach, English teacher, and citizen of the world—unfolds, the witness grows animated. Talkative. Of course he loves his family. Of course he wants to tell the truth as an example to his students. Of course he has no reason to slander Mr. Fivey. On the contrary (as her lawyer meekly points out) he has a motive to *protect* him, even if that would require lying, because Mr. Fivey has the power to fire him. At least, he *had* the power. Now, of course, Mr. Fivey cannot fire him, no matter what Bryan says on the stand. That would look biased, wouldn't it? That would look, frankly, *actionable.* So if Bryan had the freedom, as he now does, to tell the whole truth and nothing but the truth—the freedom to act as befits a man of his character—what would he tell us about his cousin Lola's relationship with her husband?

19 February 1878

Dear Miss Mínervudottír,

I am in receipt of your submission, "On the Contours and Tendencies of Arctic Sea Ice," a paper which, it is patently clear, you did not write. Notwithstanding the stirring discoveries it contains, unless its true author is acknowledged, the Royal Society cannot publish it.

Yours Sincerely,
SIR GEORGE GABRIEL STOKES
Physical Sciences Secretary
The Royal Society of London
for Improving Natural
Knowledge

THE BIOGRAPHER

At two forty p.m. on January fifteenth she waits, sweating and trembling, outside the door of eighth-period Latin.

It will need to be a home birth, to circumvent hospital records. Mattie is young and strong and shouldn't be in any danger. The biographer can drive her to the ER if something goes awry. She'll find a midwife to help them. They will doctor the birth certificate.

The girl will have all summer to recover.

The biographer will handle Mr. and Mrs. Quarles somehow.

Mattie emerges, knotting the blue scarf at her throat. Her cheeks are fuller, but you can't otherwise tell—scarves and big sweatshirts and winter coats do a fine job of hiding her.

"Quick word?" says the biographer.

Too cold for a walk. They duck into the music room, used for storage ever since the music program was canceled. Posters of tubas and flutes hang over broken chairs, reams of copy paper.

"Are you checking to see if I'm all right?" says Mattie.

"Well, are you?"

"It smells like ham in here."

The biographer only smells her own watery dread.

"Nothing has changed," says Mattie, "since you asked me the other day."

The biographer opens her mouth.

Give it to me.

Air moves lightly on her tongue and teeth. Dries her lips. "Mattie?"

"Yeah, miss?"

"I want to help you."

"Then don't tell anyone, okay? Not even Mr. Korsmo. I know you're pals."

She prepares to shape the words: *Pay for your vitamins. Drive you to every checkup. If you give it to me.*

The girl coughs, swallows a curd of phlegm. "By the way, I made an appointment at a—a place in Portland. I need to do it soon because I'm almost twenty-one weeks."

Twenty-one weeks means nineteen left. Four and a half months.

Only four and a half months, Mattie!

"That far along," says the biographer, "the procedure could be dangerous." The glass splinter is choosing these words. "A lot of term houses have no idea what they're doing. They just want to make money."

"I don't care," says Mattie.

"I've heard of—" The biographer's whole self is a splinter. "Fatal errors."

"I don't care! Even if the place is foul and they have other girls' stuff in the buckets, I don't care, I want this to be *over*." Hands in fists, she starts hitting herself on either side of the head, bam bam bam bam bam bam bam, until the biographer pulls her arms, gently, down.

"I'm just saying"—holding Mattie's wrists—"you have other choices."

You can wait four and a half short months.

"Choices?" A new edge in her voice.

"Well, like adoption."

"Don't want to do that." Mattie jerks out of her grasp, turns away.

"Why not?" *Give it to me.*

"Just don't."

"But why?" *Give it to me. I've been waiting.*

"You always tell us"—the girl's voice flicks up into a whine—"that we make our own roads and we don't have to justify or explain them to anyone."

"I do say that," says the biographer.

Mattie glares.

"However, I'd like to make sure you've thought this through."

The girl slumps down against a green filing cabinet. Holds her head in both hands, knees up to her chest, rocking a little. "I just want it out of my body. I want to stop being *infiltrated*. God, please get this out of my body. Make this stop." Rocking, rocking.

She is terrified, realizes the biographer.

"And I don't want to put someone on the planet," whispers Mattie, "who I'll always wonder about my whole life. Like where *is* the someone? Are they okay?"

"What if you knew who was raising them?" The biographer sees a vast, sunny cliff top, blue sky and blue ocean beyond; and Mattie in a flowered dress, shielding her eyes; and the biographer crouching beside the baby, saying, "There's your Aunt Mattie!" and the baby toddling toward her.

"I just *can't,*" rasps the girl. "I'm sorry."

Horror thuds in the biographer's chest: she has made her apologize for something that needs no apology.

Mattie is a kid, light boned and soft cheeked. She can't even legally drive.

Four and a half months.

Of swelling and aching and burning and straining and worrying and waiting and feeling her body burst its banks. Of hiding from the stares in town, the questions at school. Of seeing the faces, each day, of her parents as they watch the grandchild who won't be their grandchild be grown. Having to wonder, later on, where is the someone she grew.

The glass splinter says: *Who gives a fuck?*

Mattie says: "Would you go with me?"

To the checkups and the prenatal yoga.

To the store for dark leafy greens.

To the clean, comfortable birthing bed set up in the biographer's apartment, when it's time.

For a dazzling instant she has her baby, who will be tall and dark haired, good at soccer and math. She will take the baby on a rowboat to the lighthouse, on a train to Alaska, practice math problems with the baby on a soccer field. She will love the baby so much.

Except that's not, of course, what Mattie means.

Down her spine, an itching wire.

If the biographer were to admit her own *Torschlusspanik* motives, clarify that the baby would be for her, Mattie might end up agreeing. She wants to please—to be pleasing. She wants to make her favorite teacher happy.

The biographer would be asking something of her that she doesn't believe should be asked of anyone. Deepest convictions, trampled.

Yet here she is, about to tell a sniffly child to give her what she's growing.

The glass splinter says: *This is your last chance.*

Plunge.

The biographer says: "Okay."

Mattie looks up, green eyes red and spilling. "You'll go with me?"

"I will." She feels like vomiting.

"I'm sorry to—There's nobody who—Ash won't—"

"I get it, Mattie."

"Thank you," she says. Then: "Is there more than one girls' juvenile correctional facility in Oregon, do you know?"

"Are you—" But of course she's scared. The biographer pats, clumsily, the top of Mattie's head. "We'll be all right."

We will? They could both get arrested. The biographer could become a headline. SHIFTY SCHOOLMARM IS ABORTER'S ACCOMPLICE. She feels a rush of raw love for those who are caught, and for those who know they could be.

The girl stands up, shoulders her satchel, adjusts her scarf. Won't meet the biographer's eye. "I'll see you tomorrow?" And she is out the door.

Seed and soil. Egg and shell.

A plug of bile is bobbing at the foot of her throat.

"The key to happiness is hopelessness," says the meditation teacher.

Like a shark: keep moving.

The biographer walks up to a poster for the music club (WHY ARE PIRATES SUCH GOOD SINGERS? THEY CAN HIT THE HIGH Cs!) and claws it off the wall and rips it in half.

The explorer wrote to the tutor, Harry Rattray, who still worked for the shipyard director in Aberdeen:

> After many weeks of reflection on my difficulties with the Royal Society I have taken the painful decision to request that you publish my findings under your own name. Otherwise the world will never know them.

THE MENDER

Cousin Bryan's testimony, while damning of Mr. Fivey, only matters if Lola corroborates it. When the lawyer explains this to the mender, warning that it may have been a pointless detour, she smiles and says: "Not for Lola."

"How do you mean?"

"Other people know now," she says. "Outside her family. She's free."

The lawyer thoughtfully pets the clean pink skin over his skull. Murmurs, "There we go."

Today Lola isn't wearing as much eye makeup, so her face looks farther away.

"Mrs. Fivey," says the lawyer, "thank you for coming back to the stand."

"Well, I was subpoenaed." But she's looking at the lawyer. Last time she only looked at her hands.

"You heard the testimony of your cousin, Bryan Zakile. I want to ask you, Mrs. Fivey—"

"I prefer Lola?"

Yes, her family members have witnessed arguments between her and her husband. Yes, these arguments can get heated. No, her cousin was not wrong when he described an altercation on Thanksgiving that involved her husband clapping his hand across her mouth in an extremely forceful manner. He was not wrong when he testified that her mandible had been bruised by her husband. Or that, on another occasion, she confided to him that her phalanx had been snapped by her husband. And, yes, the scar on her right forearm was caused when her husband held a hot skillet against the skin. She did not report any of these incidents because it takes two to tango. She's not perfect either. A few family members have expressed concern, yes, but as her mother says, you don't go into other people's marriages uninvited.

When Mr. Fivey found the scar oil in Lola's purse, he pestered her until she admitted going to Ms. Percival about the burn. Hadn't that been a better idea than going to Umpqua General, where they might ask questions? Mr. Fivey didn't agree. He saw a bonkers witchy-woo too deranged to graduate from high school who had no business ministering to his wife.

Lola went to pack her suitcase. She planned to drive to New Mexico (she has a friend there who makes piñon kokopellis) to think things over.

Mr. Fivey came into the bedroom with a glass of vodka and the bottle of scar oil. He had crushed up (she learned later) several tabs of colarozam and mixed them into the oil. He handed her the oil and said, "Drink." When she said no, he slapped her. She drank. And chased the oil with the vodka. And got so wasted that on her way to the kitchen, she fell down the stairs.

She was not—nor did she believe she was—pregnant when she consulted Ms. Percival. That was the last thing on her mind.

Has she ever been pregnant?

Once, thirteen years ago, before she met her husband. She would prefer not to talk about that.

Why is she recanting her previous testimony?

This question makes her quiet. The judge has to remind her she is obliged to answer.

Finally Lola says, "Because I'm done doing his laundry."

They wait in the transition room while the jury deliberates. The lawyer's assistant brings in a box of chocolate-covered blueberries and says, "Fortitude?"

The mender tastes: delicious.

Lola didn't say: *I'm recanting because it wouldn't be fair to make Gin Percival spend seven years in prison.* Barely mentioned Gin Percival at all.

The lawyer is scratching, as usual: wrists, ears, the back of his neck.

"Eczema?" says the mender.

"Bedbugs," he says. "Courtesy of the Narwhal Inn. My apartment in Salem now has them too. I'm on my second fumigation."

"I know some good banishments. If I get out—"

"When." He lifts his arms to air out the drenched pits.

"Where will Lola go?" she asks. "She can't stay at home."

"Her attorney said she's already moved to her parents'. The question remains, where will *Mr.* Fivey be staying?"

The mender eats the last blueberry. "You mean, which cell?"

When the jury foreman rises, she shuts her eyes.

"Ladiesanjinnelminnuv."

"Haveyoureached."

"Have yeronner."

"Whatsayyou?"

Stop shaking. You're a Percival.

"We find the defendant—"

Descended from a pirate.

"—not guilty on both counts."

A whoop from the audience. She is shaking too hard to look, but it sounded like the voice of the pissed-off library lady.

She takes the lawyer's damp hand.

In the first fairy tale Uncle taught me, a glass splinter in the eye would make all the world ugly and bad. I have such a splinter now. I see Harry's name on my paper in *Philosophical Transactions of the Royal Society of London* and curl with rage. It is mine but no one knows. They know the facts imparted, which have more value than my small self; yet with this splinter lodged in me, I can't rest. I would like to run up to Sir George Gabriel Stokes at the Royal Society and show him my finger stumps and say, "I gave these in exchange for my facts."

THE DAUGHTER

Friday night she scours the Math Academy website, rereading the seminar descriptions and inserting her own face into photos of nerds laughing around tables. If she even gets in. The application was hard. All the nominees will have top grades and test scores, said Mr. Xiao: "You have to stand out. Make yourself come alive in the essay answers."

How do you see mathematics figuring into your future?

~~My future will include~~
~~Math will be important in my future because~~
~~In my future, I see~~
~~I notice there is a pun in this question~~

If she gets in, she plans to take the seminar on recursion. Self-similar structures. Variability through repetition. Fractals. Chaos theory.

Think about fractals, not about suction and sloshing tubes and the term-house door smashed open by a cop's battering ram.

She won't be sixteen for almost a month; she wouldn't be tried as an adult. But even non-adults can be sent away.

When Yasmine operated on her own clump, most termination houses didn't exist yet. It was right after the federal ban had gone into effect. To help the ban take hold, the attorney general ordered district attorneys nationwide to go after the harshest possible sentences for seekers. Send a message. Girls as young as thirteen were incarcerated for three to five years. Even the daughter of Erica Salter, member of the Oregon House of Representatives, was locked up in Bolt River Youth Correctional Facility. A message had to be sent.

* * *

A day before the self-operation, Yasmine said nobody could know she'd been pregnant, and if the daughter told anyone, she wouldn't speak to her ever again.

"I'm not giving them another reason to think I'm not smart."

"Why would anyone think you're not smart?"

"Is that a joke?"

"No," said the daughter.

"You are a very ignorant white girl," said Yasmine.

She counts every tile in the upstairs bathroom so she won't think about it.

Saturday morning she reminds Mom that after the aquarium she'll spend the night at Ash's—see you tomorrow. Yes, she packed her retainer.

When Ash delivers her to the church parking lot, it seems Ro/Miss is not in the greatest mood. Cold faced, quiet. The daughter offers money for gas and Ro/Miss rolls her eyes. How will they find topics for conversation? Thankfully Ro/Miss turns the radio on. The daughter sinks down in the seat as they drive through town: what would it look like, a student in a teacher's car? Think about Newville gossip, not about the procedure.

Passing a logged hillside, gashed and barren, the stumps like headstones, the daughter sees the shining fir floors in her house. Smells smoke on herself. Chimneylina. One day she'll quit, after she's gotten her marine-biology degree and is working in cetacean situations. Her future will include a study of whale-harming toxins dumped by humans into the sea. A trip to the Faroe Islands to disrupt the slaughter of pilot whales, who are technically dolphins. A trip to a Japanese temple that sings requiems for the whales' souls, gives names to the fetuses inside the captured mothers.

She digs both thumbs into her belly, house of the tufting, clumping, unnamed infiltrator. Please let them not leave it sitting around in a bucket.

The motto of the Royal Society of London: NULLIUS IN VERBA. Take nobody's word for it.

THE BIOGRAPHER

Mattie's directions bring them to a quiet narrow street in southeast Portland. Flat-roofed ranch homes, yellow lawns. The house they want is hidden by vine-clogged chain link and a live oak dangling with metal figurines. The front door can't be seen through the bushes. The fence gate is padlocked.

"Let's go around back." The biographer trudges ahead, up the gravel driveway. Between the garage and the house is a high wooden gate, locked as well.

"Did I mess up?" says Mattie. "I double-checked the address five times."

"Let's knock, at least."

Before either of them can, the gate opens. "I saw you on the security cameras," says a young woman with long-tailed cat eyeliner, ink-swirled arms. "You're Delphine?"

"Yeah," says Mattie. "And this is my—"

"Mom," blurts the biographer. They'll take better care of her if the mother is watching.

Mattie stares red-faced at the ground.

"I'm L. Let's get into the van." The woman nods at the garage.

"Van?" they say together.

"We don't do the procedures here at headquarters. We use temporary sites that keep changing. For safety reasons. And I need to ask you to wear masks during the drive."

The biographer laughs. "Are you serious?"

L. drags up the garage's roll door. "Yeah, we take the surveillance state and male-supremacist legislation pretty seriously. Call us crazy."

"No, it's fine," says Mattie.

"Seat belts, please. Then I'll give you the masks. Did you lock your car?"

"Aye, aye!" says the biographer.

Mattie turns from the passenger seat to give her a little frown, and the world is flipped, the order reversed.

The cotton eye mask feels absurd. The van's windows are tinted dark already. But the biographer wishes not to embarrass Mattie further.

"In your phone intake," says L., "you estimated you'd be about twenty-one weeks by now?" The van rattles over a speed bump. "Under optimal conditions, a late second-trimester abortion would require a minimum of two days, to dilate your cervix adequately before the evacuation, but these are not optimal conditions."

A bedside manner almost as delightful as Kalbfleisch's.

L. goes over a few more things—ultrasound, sedative, anesthesia. The biographer scarcely listens: she would really love to be elsewhere. The best she can do is be a body near Mattie, a body able to drive her home. At the word "speculum" she flinches, feeling the many specula Kalbfleisch slid into her. She counts her in-breaths, counts her out-breaths.

Mattie has no questions for L.

Cash only. Pay after. No forms to sign, for obvious reasons, but they do keep confidential patient records, using aliases.

"Delphine, your name for our files will be Ida."

"Okay," says Mattie.

"Hey, Mom," calls L., "any questions back there?"

"Not right now," says the biographer.

They take off their masks and step out of the van into the overgrown backyard of a bungalow. The sky is high and quiet. L.'s hands on their backs, hurrying them. Next to the screen door hangs a piece of wood painted with black letters: POLYPHONTE COLLECTIVE. The biographer strains to summon her Greek mythology. Polyphonte—Aphrodite—Artemis?

L. opens three locks with three keys and ushers them into a bright, purple-walled kitchen that smells like chili. Books, spice jars, pots of cactus, a boardful of yellow peppers in mid-chop.

"Upstairs," says their ferrywoman.

A bedroom's bed has been replaced by an exam table whose stirrups wear red knitted socks. Next to it stands an ultrasound machine. For an eerie beat the biographer thinks it is she who will climb on the table, press her heels into the stirrups, wait for the blue-lubed wand to read the shapes inside her. *You will feel a slight pressure.*

"This is Delphine and her mom," announces L.

"I'm Dr. V.," says a small, beautiful woman in a green medical smock. "I'm gonna take care of you, okay?" She looks South Asian and sounds like the ladies from Queens who live at Dad's retirement village. "Let's get started with your vitals."

"Have you done many of these before?" asks the biographer.

Dr. V. wipes back a strand of silver-black hair. "Thousands." Wraps a blood-pressure cuff around Mattie's biceps. "I worked at Planned Parenthood for almost twenty years. Until the day they shut it down."

Mattie says, "You can go now, um, Mom."

Their providers are skilled. They do not charge a shit ton.

She wants Mattie to be happy. To be safe. To be free from suffering.

Also: she can't stand her.

She hates her for getting to experience the twenty-one weeks of pregnancy she'll never get to experience herself.

There are millions of things the biographer will never do that she doesn't pity herself for missing. (Climbing a mountain, cracking a code, attending her own wedding.) So why *this* thing?

She came prepared to wait, brought a stack of tests to grade, but faced with the prospect of all day in this room of wicker couches and zebra pillows, hot bean smell blowing in from the kitchen, the biographer feels itchy. She wanders into a front hallway, where posters and pamphlets describe the other services offered by the Polyphonte Collective. Sliding-scale mental-health counseling. Sliding-scale legal services for women who are unhoused, undocumented, battered, addicted. Free childcare during court appearances. Cop watching at protests. This house must be their headquarters. It was the first address, in fact, that was a decoy.

The largest poster says:

REPEAL THE 28TH AMENDMENT!

SIT IN / RISE UP FOR REPRODUCTIVE RIGHTS

FEATURED SPEAKERS:

REP. ERICA SALTER (D-PORTLAND)

& DOCTORS FROM WOMEN ON WAVES

MAY 1, OREGON STATE CAPITOL

Up through the gummy darkness in her chest, through the self-pity and resentment, poke thin stalks of gratitude. The Polyphontes aren't just shaking their heads.

She starts to read blue books, pen in hand. *The events that led up to the American Revolutionary War included.* What about events on the second floor? Is Mattie scared? *Three main causes of the war were.* Should the biographer go and check? *The colonists really hated taxes—and still do!*

From the coffee table she picks up a graphic novel about women in the Cretan resistance during World War II. Dark-eyed schoolgirls and crones in cartridge belts lug packs of ammunition up craggy mountainsides. They shoot at German parachutists as they land. They don't just sit there watching.

The biographer falls asleep with her face in a zebra pillow.

Dr. V. shakes her awake. "Time to go, Mom."

"Who?"

"Delphine's fine. All went well. You can be on your way."

The future baby, the kid-to-be, her own—

It was never yours.

"L. will drive you back to your car. The sooner you're gone, the safer everyone is. Let's see—she'll be loopy for a bit, from the painkillers. Bleeding is expected, including clots. She can take ibuprofen for cramps. No alcohol, tampons, or sex for at least a week. She's Rh-positive, luckily, and won't need an immune globulin shot. She should be doing a course of antibiotics, but the Collective can't afford them and we certainly can't write scripts—so keep an eye out, okay? Any fever above a hundred, take her straight to the ER. Is this your bag?" Dr. V. passes the biographer her backpack and gestures to the door. "They're waiting."

In the kitchen Mattie sits bundled in her peacoat, drinking a glass of water. She looks sleepy and bleary and younger. Seeing the biographer, she grins wide. "Well," she says, her relief unmistakable, "*that* happened."

L. can't drop them off fast enough. The midnight street makes chirring sounds. Are they being surveilled from a parked car?

"You hungry?" The biographer helps Mattie negotiate the seat belt.

"Nix nought nein."

It comes to her: Polyphonte was one of Artemis's virgin followers. Punished by Aphrodite for—something.

No cars follow them out.

The police probably don't even know the Collective exists.

Unless she's being stupid. Naively ascribing common decency to people in power, as she did before the Personhood Amendment showed all of its teeth.

Aphrodite made Polyphonte fall in love with a bear.

WE NEED COP WATCHERS ON MAY 1ST, said a flyer in the front hall. PLEASE VOLUNTEER!

Don't be stupid anymore, she once wrote in her notebook, under *Immediate action required.*

By the time they get to Newville, it will be almost three a.m.

After giving birth to twin bear sons, Polyphonte was turned into an owl.

Is this even the right road?

"Miss?" comes a drowsy little voice.

"Yeah?" She thought this road was taking them to the highway access ramp, but it just keeps going, ramplessly.

"I'm sorry but I have to go to the bathroom."

"Can you hold it for a little while?" The biographer strains to read a sign, faint in the dark. Could there be *one* goddamn streetlight in this city?

"Well it's actually kind of an emergency unless it's another feeling from the, you know, and I don't actually need to but it *feels* like I do?"

Please don't let them be lost. Her phone knows nothing.

The Canadian government is funding a new search mission for Lt. Adolphus Greely and his men. Their survival is not assured: resupply ships have failed to reach the expedition two years in a row. A steam-powered icebreaker named *Khione* leaves from Newfoundland in two months. I will be on that boat, I promise you.

THE DAUGHTER

The heart of a Canada goose weighs seven ounces. Of a caribou, seven pounds.

The daughter's own heart weighs nothing. Not tonight, at least—no blood in it. All her upper blood is down, replacing what's gone. She's got on a pad and thick sweatpants, and has spread a towel across Ro/Miss's bed. The towel is beige, but a stained towel seems easier to pardon than a sheet. The pad is a little blood diaper. At home there's a picture of her baby self getting changed, fat legs in the air, and Mom, wipe in hand, making a face at the camera.

Are you mine?

The daughter is emptying.

She saw no bucket.

It feels weird to be in a teacher's bedroom. Like eavesdropping. This room doesn't give much away, though. No posters or stereo. The only thing on the wall is an old-fashioned map—the kind with dragons drawn in the waves—of the North Pole. On the dresser, two framed photos: her parents, must be, then a younger Ro/Miss next to a handsome guy in a skull T-shirt. Boyfriend? Ex-fiancé?

Saltines and a peeled orange on the bedside table; but her mouth doesn't want anything in it, not even a cigarette. She can't decide what to call this feeling. It isn't sadness. More like a wilting. A deflation. The skin of a balloon after all the air except a breath or two has seeped out.

Zero weeks, zero days.

A soft knock. Ro/Miss's face in the door crack. "How're you feeling?"

"Crampy."

"Want more ibuprofen?"

"Sure you don't mind me taking your bed?"

"My couch is so comfortable." Ro/Miss shakes two caplets onto her palm; the daughter swallows them waterless. "You ready to sleep? It's *really* late."

"What do you call a time-traveling flower shop?"

Ro/Miss raises one eyebrow.

"Back to the Fuchsia," says the daughter.

"Time to sleep?"

"I have an idea for an invention," says the daughter. "Which might not work but would be so incredible if it did. Want to hear it?"

Ro/Miss folds her arms across her chest. "Sure."

"Okay, so, you know how the world is going to run out of energy unless we stop burning oil and make more wind farms?"

"Well, among other things."

"So my idea is to harness whales. You could make very light but strong harnesses, like out of steel thread, and hook them up to super-long steel reins. The reins would be attached to turbines, which would be on their own floating platforms, capturing the energy. There would also be generators on the platforms to convert the energy to electricity."

"That's . . . huh."

The daughter winces at a pinch of dark heat above her pubic bone. "I haven't worked out the details yet. The point is, the whales won't be killed if they're making energy. They'll be treasured."

"Not by Big Coal or Big Oil, but yeah—interesting."

"You think it's dumb."

"Nope, I do not. I think you should probably go to sleep, my dear."

She doesn't want her to leave.

"Would you read to me first?"

Ro/Miss sighs. "What should I read?"

"Anything. Except not poetry or self-help."

"I'll have you know there is not a single self-help book in this house! Okay, that's not true; there might be a few." She tugs the blanket up higher, to the daughter's shoulders. "Warm enough?"

She nods.

Ro/Miss goes out, comes back. Turns the overhead light off and bedside lamp on. "Close your eyes."

All the News down in Newville sleep deep by the sea.

Your name for our files will be Ida.

Throat clearing. Paper rustling. "'As a girl, I loved (but why?) to watch the *grindadráp.* It was a death dance. I couldn't stop looking. To smell the bonfires lit on the cliffs calling men to the hunt. To see the boats herd the pod into the cove, the whales thrashing faster as they panic. Men and boys wade into the water with knives to cut their spinal cords. They touch the whale's eye to make sure it is dead. And the water . . .'"

Who is this water—girl—Ida—knife—

"' . . . foams up red.'"

She sleeps.

Off the coast of Greenland they saw the Crimson Cliffs: enormous shoulders of red-stained snow.

"God's blood," said the blacksmith.

"Algae," corrected Mínervudottír.

THE WIFE

Early to the pub, she stands at the wall reading names of sunk ships. *Antelope. Fearless. Phoebe Fay.*

Please let her stop being a coward.

Pilots Bride. Gem. Perpetua.

Please let her children not be scarred.

Onward. Czarina. Chinook.

Didier arrives from school, believing their purpose is beer and fried-fish sandwiches. The wife suggests they wait for the after-work crowd to thin. In the little park behind the church, they walk between flower beds thrusting with young stems. Early buds in a warm February. The soil is black and soft from yesterday's rain.

She is a selfish coward.

"Up for darts tonight?" says Didier. "You had an off night last time, true, but—"

"We need to talk about something." She stops walking. *Say it, Susan.*

"Do you have cash for Costello?"

"I think—" *Say it.*

"Because I have none. We can stop on the way home."

"I think we should take a break."

"Huh?"

"From each other."

He narrows his eyes.

"Like a separation," she adds.

"Why?"

"Because it's not"—no breath in her lungs—"good anymore."

Too frightened to look at his face, she concentrates on the blue leather toes of her clogs.

"Susan, I'm looking for the joke with a microscope."

She shakes her head.

"We have stuff that could improve, okay, but everyone does. We can work on it."

"You didn't *want* to work on it," she says.

"You mean the therapy? But that's—"

"It's better this way, anyway."

"Why?" he says softly.

"I'm sorry," says the wife.

Didier's face has gone rubbery. Eyes tight in their shadowed sockets. She sees how he will look as an old man.

He takes out his cigarettes.

"If you keep squinting like that," says the wife, "your eyes might get stuck."

"And if you keep eating like that, your ass might get stuck. In every door."

"I'm going to my parents' tomorrow," she says. "You can stay in the house, for now."

"Oh really? I can stay? In that broke-down bourgeois firetrap?"

But he will. That's the thing. He will judge and dismiss, he will scorn and rage; yet out of sheer laziness, he will stay.

Sucking on his cigarette: "We don't have to decide now."

"Didier."

"Let's talk about it tomorrow, yeah?" On the last word his voice quavers.

"Nothing will be different tomorrow."

She has no plan.

For telling the kids, for making a custody schedule, for finding a job.

Her mother said on the phone this morning, "You've at least opened your own bank account, I hope?" and the wife had to lie.

The only idea in her sore, stalled brain has been: *Tell him.*

He stamps out the cigarette on the gravel path. "You know what I won't miss?"

Me.

"Your shitty cooking."

"And I won't miss having three children," says the wife.

"Fuck you, Susan."

The wife kneels on the path.

Rent a car. Open a bank account. Bring yourself to care.

She reaches for the black earth.

Her body yearns, inexplicably, to taste it.

Brings a handful to her lips. The minerals sizzle on her tongue, rich with the gists of flower and bone.

"Hell are you doing?" says Didier.

Bright minerals. Powdered feathers. Ancient shells.

"Jesus, *stop* that!"

She keeps tasting. The soil is bark and needle and flecks of brain, little animal burnt and dead.

Goodbye, shipwrecks.

Goodbye, house.

Goodbye, wife.

Greely's men shot the rest of the sled dogs. They had kept alive their favorites as long as they could; but there was no food. The starving animals had already eaten their leather harnesses. They killed first the one called King, a rascal and a gentleman. His brothers waiting in the dogloo knew they, too, would be killed. Badger, Scruffles, Cricket, Howler, Odysseus, Samson — a bullet for each. The youngest sailor cried, and by the time they reached his meager beard, the tears were buttons of ice. When the Greely expedition was rescued, in June of 1884, this youngest sailor would be dead of

THE BIOGRAPHER

Knocks cup and cup tips and coffee runs across table onto floor.

When the youngest sailor died, of starvation and exposure, his shipmates probably ate him. She can only speculate. *I am inserting the speculum into your vagina; you will feel a slight pressure.* After the return to civilization of its six survivors, rumors arose that the Greely expedition had practiced cannibalism. The coffin of one of its dead, a Frederick Kislingbury, was exhumed. The body had no skin on it; the arms and legs were attached by ligaments alone. Greely claimed they had carved up Kislingbury for bait in shrimp and fish traps, not for themselves.

She paper-towels her brown spill.

Susan once told her she shouldn't be so quick to claim that Mínervudottír's life was more meaningful for having left the Faroe Islands. "That's the predictable narrative," said Susan. "But couldn't she have had an equally meaningful life if she'd stayed?"

"Depends what you mean by 'meaningful,'" said the biographer. "I don't see how gutting fish and washing six kids' underwear by hand is equal to doing research in the Arctic Circle."

"Why not?"

"One is repetitive and mindless, and the other is thrilling, courageous, and beneficial to the lives of many people."

"If she'd raised six kids," said Susan, "she would've been beneficial to *their* lives."

Mínervudottír had no wool-capped, lamb-fed children to grow.

And Susan has no book. No law career. No job, in fact, at all.

The biographer, strictly speaking, has no book either. Her kitchen table is loaded with overdue library loans about whale hunts and ice—she has read the translation of Mínervudottír's journals a dozen times—yet her manuscript has more holes than words. She wants to tell the story of a woman the world should have known about long before this; so why can't she get done telling it?

The biographer eats the dry rim off a blueberry muffin she found at the back of the teachers' lounge fridge. Forces herself to say: "We haven't talked about your good news."

Penny beams. "Ms. Tristan Auerbach wants the privilege of selling *Rapture on Black Sand* to the highest bidder."

She could be a published author before her seventieth birthday. And if this manuscript sells, the other eight she's written could follow.

"I'm happy for you."

"Listen, honey, you should send Tristan *your* book. I'll recommend you personally."

She should have congratulated Penny sooner—it's been weeks. Mired in her own sludge, she's been avoiding the lounge, begging off Masterpiece mystery nights. Had the biographer found an agent for *Mínervudottír: A Life,* Penny would have baked her a cake the same day.

"I'm not sure a romance agent would be interested in a book with no romance."

"The romance of crushed ships!" says Penny. "The romance of gangrene."

Penny loved her now-dead husband. Loves her little house. Loves writing her entertainments. Didn't have kids because she never felt like it. When the biographer compares such fulfillment with her own sticky craving, it is tempting to despair.

"I apologize, Pen."

"What for?"

"Being a bad friend."

Penny nods. "You've had better years."

"I'm really sorry."

She starts buttoning her turquoise cardigan. "I forgive you. But you better not miss my book party."

"Won't, swear."

"And I think you should apply for Fivey's job."

"Hardy har."

"I do not happen to be joking. You're a good candidate."

The biographer laughs anyway, spewing blue bits of muffin across the lounge.

Climbs to the top of the east stairwell. Sits down against a wall.

The excitement she once felt about a nineteen-year-old biology major's sperm, her willingness to drink a foul but magical tea, her wild hope on that run to Mattie's house—

Gone.

She picks at the laces of her sneakers.

All the doors have closed.

The ones, at least, she tried to open.

How much of her ferocious longing is cellular instinct, and how much is socially installed? Whose urges is she listening to?

Her life, like anyone's, could go a way she never wanted, never planned, and turn out marvelous.

Fingering her shoelaces, she hears the first bell.

Thinks of her brother getting accepted into his first-choice college and gloating, "I'm set."

WE NEED COP WATCHERS! said the flyer at the Polyphonte Collective.

The second bell.

By walking, she tells her students, is how you make the road.

The morning after Portland, Mattie pointed to the photo on her dresser. "He's cute. Who is he?"

"My favorite and only brother," she said.

He wore that skull T-shirt for years, she told Mattie. It was the shirt of a band he loved; she forgets which one. The biographer never had a head for band names or song titles or the music itself, which worried her when she was younger—was she missing something crucial?

She did not tell Mattie that even though Archie graduated with honors from his first-choice college, he was not set.

She did not tell Mattie about finding him, eight years ago, in the kitchen of his apartment. He wore black jeans and no shirt. Lips blue, cheeks flat and white. On the counter was a half-eaten bowl of cereal, bearful of honey, burnt spoon, lighter, glassine packet. The needle lay on the floor beside him.

"Hey, kiddo," says her father. "To what do I owe?"

"Spring break is soon," she says, "and I was thinking of visiting."

"Visiting whom?"

"*You,* genius."

"The Duke of Denturetown? The King of Hemorrhoidia?"

"Can't you just say 'Daughter, I'd love to see you'?"

"I'd love to see you. But bear in mind that spring break in Orlando is a hellscape."

"I'll bear it," she says.

Ice too heavy to proceed. Crew hammering at the pack to save the lead. We are more than a hundred kilometers from Fort Conger, where Greely's expedition is believed to be.

Lead gone. Food and gear dragged onto a floe, tents pitched by the sledges. Cook fills mugs with pea soup and boiled bacon.

We woke to the floes rafting up around the ship. Massive blue-white shelves, thrust vertical by wind and tide, jumped roaring out of the water and smashed at the keel. To my hoard of knowledge I may now add the sound ice makes when it destroys a ship. Booming gun cracks, then a smaller yelping; and from the vibration the ship's bells began ghoulishly to ring. Within hours, says the captain, *Khione* will be sunk.

THE MENDER

After her motionless weeks in jail, the walk to town feels awful. Her knees are buckling by the time she reaches the Acme.

She keeps her head down against the lights, the stares. One box of licorice nibs. One bottle of sesame oil. Is she inventing the stares? Maybe her mind is buckling too. She hasn't been sleeping well; the memory of bleach keeps waking her.

When they released her, the lawyer was there to take her home. "Hold on to my arm, okay?" he said. "Don't let go." They came out of County Corrections into a chattering snarl of cameras and microphones, and all the microphones were being pushed into her face. Some of them hit her face.

"How's it feel to be free, Ms. Percival?"

"Are you angry at your accusers?"

The lawyer put his mouth on her ear: "Don't say a word."

"Do you plan to sue Dolores Fivey?"

Clicks and flashes.

"What's the next step for you?"

"Any opinion on the local seaweed infestation and the economic losses it's caused?"

"Have you ever provided an abortion?"

Click flash click flash click flash.

"At your accusers?"

"To be free?"

Click. Flash.

"Hello? Gin?" A bright voice behind her.

The mender stops in the aisle. Canned tomatoes make loud red suns across her vision.

"It's me—Mattie."

She turns and blinks at the girl, who is steering a shopping cart; and her mother, who has long gray hair, big teeth when she smiles. The mender has watched them together on Lupatia Street.

"Mom, this is Gin. Gin, this is my mom."

"Pleased to meet you," says the astonished mother. She holds out her hand and the mender shakes it; the skin is dry. "How do you two...?"

"We met at the library," says Mattie Matilda.

"Oh." The mother's eyes relax a little. Kind brown eyes. She has kept the girl safe and well.

"Hello," says the mender stiffly.

She glances at the girl's midsection: flat in a close-fitting sweater. Her hair: less lustrous. Her skin: no darkening patches. How and where did she take care of it? She managed not to get caught. She went a different path. She won't be wondering and forgetting, forgetting and wondering again. Or she will wonder—but not the same way the mender did.

"I'm so glad about your verdict," says Mattie Matilda.

The green of her irises is not the same green as the mender's.

Mine and not mine.

"What a terrible thing to go through," says the mother.

The mender nods.

"They fired Principal Fivey," says Mattie Matilda.

The mender nods.

"We should be on our way," says the mother, "but it was nice to meet you, Ms. Percival." Her cart starts rolling.

"Bye!" The girl waves.

The mender waves back.

Soon it will be February fifteenth: the Roman festival of Lupercalia. And the girl's birthday.

* * *

She and Cotter started the girl. The mender, with her body, continued the girl. For a time her clock was full of water and blood and a kicking fish. Which is both important and not important.

He may figure it out himself, once he sees her enough times in town. But he may not. Should she tell him? All that Cotter does for her. The bread on her step each week; the nutmeg pie at Christmas. Hauling Temple's plastic-wrapped body in his truck bed to the harbor, hoisting the body onto a borrowed boat, maneuvering the boat in darkness out of the slip and past the breakwater and into open ocean. Without hesitation he did these things.

The girl is continuing herself. Has no need of Cotter, or of the mender.

But if she ever returns to the cabin of her own accord, she will be welcomed in. Given tea that tastes good. Introduced to Hans and Pinka and the halt hen. (She is already acquainted with Malky.)

The mender pays for the nibs and sesame oil.

Walks back to the forest.

When the track narrows to a footpath, canopied by chain fern and rhododendron and Oregon manroot, she looks for the silver fir with the hourglass resin blister.

Hello, Temple.

Alive in the women who've swallowed mixtures made with her skin, her hairs, her eyelashes.

Buried in the sea.

* * *

The mender rubs leopard's-bane salve into her burning calves. Lies in the dark with the cat on her chest. No more human voices the rest of the day. She wants only Malky's growl and the *mehhh* of Hans and Pinka. The bleat of the owl, chirp of the bat, squeak of the ghost of the varying hare. This is how Percivals do.

She packed her rucksack with the anemometer and aneroid barometer, a flask of tea, two biscuits. Informed a tentful of card-playing crew she would be back in a few hours.

"If not, we'll whistle for you," said the boatswain, to groggy laughter.

She hadn't been walking long when the fog flew in.

There are many names for fog. Pogonip. Brume. Ground clouds. Gloom. Mínervudottír had written every name in her brown leather notebook. She stood now in a dense, creamy mist, the worst ice fog she'd ever known.

Was her compass damaged? Had she forgotten to bring it?

Bells and sledgehammer = fog signal

She shouted "Help" in three languages.

When her legs were too numb and trembling to lift themselves, she sat down.

No reindeer bag to crawl into.

She thought she heard the ship's bells, but couldn't place their direction.

She drank ten sips of tea.

It was like sitting in a cloud.

Brother, where are the bells?

Eivør tried walking again but could see nothing in front of her except whiteness. She was afraid of stepping in a crack in the ice and dropping into the sea.

She sat down again.

Slit lambs hung in the shed, throats red.

I know which hillside.

She had no reindeer bag.

This lamb fed from.

Survival was not assured. Her eyes were closing. She lay down ~~and slept until~~. She tasted milk-boiled puffin — she was chewing her own cheeks.

Brother Gunni, bells are the where?

If she didn't move, her blood would stop.

Persist, Eivør told herself.

She stood and staggered on.

THE DAUGHTER

Dearest Yasmine,

I'm writing this letter from the Math Academy. It's not as amazing as we envisioned, but it's good.

I miss you. Always wondering how you are. What kind of school situation do they have there? Do you still want to do pre-med? My plan is marine biology. I touched a whale's eye on the beach.

Please believe me, Yas: I didn't want to tell anyone. I thought you were going to die so I called them. That was the only reason.

Also: I had ~~a procedure~~ something happen. Three months ago.

When you get out of Bolt River, can we be friends again?

Love,
MATTS

Mínervudottír was found under a pane of ice. They saw her face first, as if pressed up to glass, one cheek flat and white. The blacksmith wrote later, to his wife: *I have never seen an eye opened wider.* She had removed her coat to free herself to fight the current and break the ice. Her fingernails, from scratching, were almost gone.

The search party did not chop open the water to claim the explorer's corpse. They may have crossed themselves, or said prayers, or simply been relieved that one less mouth was alive to feed. *It is odious to lose a woman's body to this wilderness,* wrote the blacksmith to his wife, *but we hadn't the strength to retrieve it.*

THE BIOGRAPHER

Where does the book end?

It has to stop somewhere.

She has to step out of it.

Mínervudottír: A Hole.

Most whales, when they die, don't wash up on beaches. Their carcasses fall to the ocean floor, where they are consumed over time by foragers big and small. A deep-sea whale fall can feed scavengers for fifty years or more.

Osedax, types the biographer into her computer, *is a bone-eating worm.*

She peers through the slatted blinds at the heat-slicked lawns and palmettos and fire bush. The air-conditioning is jacked so high she shivers. Dad's condo is a stucco box fastened to a row of other boxes, each with a tiny lanai overlooking the community center. It's not all bad, he says. The community center has a barbershop and shows movies. Every Fourth of July, they serve a decent whiskey punch.

Archie never set foot in Florida. The idea of a retirement village appalled him, and Ambrosia Ridge sounded like a porn name. One of their last arguments was about his refusal to visit. The biographer didn't love retirement villages either, but Dad was here now. Archie called her a pious bureaucrat and hung up.

She calls toward the bedroom: "I'm turning down the AC, okay?"

"Be out in a sec." His bedsprings jounce.

"Don't rush. Breakfast is still in progress."

It will take him time to emerge. When he walks, his pain is conspicuous—the hunched-over shuffling, the pausing every few feet. He waves off the biographer's questions about treatment options. She needs to call his doctor herself.

* * *

Once her father has shambled in, she explains the Faroese meal laid out on the coral-laminate countertop: boiled puffin eggs (chicken eggs), wind-dried whale blubber (pork bacon), and Shrovetide buns (canned-dough biscuits).

"My doctor says I can't have bacon"—he crams a strip into his mouth—"but blubber is allowed."

"Why can't you?"

"When you're old, they like to prohibit things. How else are they going to fill up those twelve-minute appointments? No bacon, no sugar. And no amorous exertion."

"Dad."

"Oh, relax."

The biographer chews and stares out at the man-made pond. Like many things at Ambrosia Ridge, the pond is depressing and soothing in equal measure. The aerator generates a round-the-clock fountain, proof of fraudulence; yet the little fountain, throwing beads of green sunlight, is actually kind of pretty.

"Let's toast to your mother."

She lifts her cup. "To Mama."

Dad lifts his. "To my dear heart."

The refrigerator whirs. A distant lawnmower revs its motor.

"Should we also," says the biographer.

He nods.

"To Archie," she says.

"To Archer, who was the sweetest little boy." Clears his throat. "To go from such sweetness to—"

Pawning their dead mother's jewelry.

Pushing a steak knife into the fat of Dad's upper arm.

"Peace," says the biographer.

They raise their cups.

Dad eases himself down off the high stool. "This goddamn chair is hell on my back. I'll just stand."

She really needs to call his doctor.

"So today is my birthday," she says.

He slaps his forehead. "What? Jesus, did I forget?"

"We don't need to celebrate, I just—"

"Answer: I did *not*." He takes a folded envelope from his shirt pocket. "Happy birthday, sweetheart."

"Wow, Dad, thank you!"

Inside the envelope is a gift certificate for Rose City Singles, good for two months of online membership and three speed-dating evenings. MEET SINGLES IN OREGON AGES 40+.

"Okay." She takes a long sip of coffee.

"An unconventional gift, I realize, but it might prove useful?"

He lives at Ambrosia Ridge. He's in acute physical pain much of the time. She says mildly, "Thanks," and sets the certificate next to her plate.

"I am a fan of the Shrovetide bun," says Dad, buttering his third.

"I'll buy more dough before I leave. You just twist open the canister and they bake themselves."

"I wish you could stay longer, kiddo."

"Me too." Despite the gift certificate, this isn't a lie.

Reasons I can't:

1. Job

The school term ends in June. But she might apply for Fivey's position. There are some changes she wouldn't mind making. Fewer bubble tests, more music classes. Social-justice and meditation curricula. *Principal Stephens.* A good job for a pious bureaucrat?

Or she could work outside the apparatus, as the Polyphontes do.

After the body of Eivør Mínervudottír sank to the bottom of Baffin Bay, west of Greenland, it entered into many other bodies.

* * *

She is menstruating when she dies. Strips of burlap wadded into her crotch unfurl in the water, making a brief red cloud. A Greenland shark smells the blood from two miles off; turns in a slow, silent arc; and aims his sleek bulk in the blood's direction.

Crumbs of her skin drift up into the brine channels. Reindeer fur and flannel threads catch on ice dendrites reaching down from the undershelf.

After the apex predators have had their fill, the smaller ones feast: hagfish, lobsters, limpets, clams, brittle stars. Then the amphipods, the bone-eating worms, the bacteria.

A narwhal hunting for air holes drags its shadow across her.

Krill gnaw green blooms of algae off the ceiling of ice.

The explorer comes, over time, apart.

Weeks after digesting Mínervudottír's flesh, the Greenland shark is caught near the western coast of Iceland. The fishermen lop off his head and bury his body in gravel and sand, heap it with stones that press out the shark's natural poisons (urea and trimethylamine oxide). After two or three months, the fish—by now fermented—is sliced and hung in a shed to dry. The pieces grow a brown crust, a shocking smell. When citizens of Reykjavík eat the shark on December 25, 1885, they are eating Eivør Mínervudottír.

She did not leave behind money or property or a book or a child, but her corpse kept alive creatures who, in turn, kept other creatures alive.

Into other bodies she went, but also other brains. The people who read "On the Contours and Tendencies of Arctic Sea Ice" in *Philosophical*

Transactions of the Royal Society of London were changed by the explorer. The English translator of her notebooks was changed by her. Mattie, hearing her tell of the *grindadráp,* was changed. The biographer, of course. And if her book has any readers, Mínervudottír will persist in them.

She brought in research that helped pirate ships penetrate the North, guns cocked, drills whetted.

And she brought: *If wrecked in this vessel, we wreck together.*

And she brought: *The name I like best is "pack."*

Instead of applying for the principal job, the biographer could spend the summer at Ambrosia Ridge baking Shrovetide buns, calling doctors, and starting her next book. Go as Dad's date to the Fourth of July picnic.

She could stay in the fog-smoked mountains, applying or not applying, breathing in the Douglas-fir and Scotch pine. The waves thumping, spilling, sucking back.

She wants more than one thing.

To write the last sentence of *Mínervudottír.*
To write the first sentence of something else.
To be courteous but fierce with her father's doctors.
To be a foster mom.
To be the next principal.
To be neither.
She wants to stretch her mind wider than "to have one."
Wider than "not to have one."
To quit shrinking life to a checked box, a calendar square.
To quit shaking her head.

To go to the protest in May.
To do more than go to a protest.
To be okay with not knowing.
Keep your legs, Stephens.
To see what is. And to see what is possible.

ACKNOWLEDGEMENTS

I am grateful beyond measure to Lee Boudreaux, whose brilliant editing led this book into bolder, deeper territory; and to the phenomenal Meredith Kaffel Simonoff, who has been my dream agent in every way. Huge thanks also to Suzie Dooré, my editor in the UK, for her astute suggestions and excellent sense of humor.

For their artistry and expertise, I'm indebted to Carina Guiterman at Lee Boudreaux Books; Charlotte Cray at The Borough Press; Lauren Harms, Karen Landry, Sabrina Callahan, Katharine Myers, and Julie Ertl at Little, Brown; the keen-eyed Dianna Stirpe; Alice Lawson at Gersh; and Reiko Davis, Colin Farstad, Linda Kaplan, and Gabbie Piraino at DeFiore and Company.

Thanks to the Money for Women / Barbara Deming Memorial Fund and the Regional Arts and Culture Council for their generosity, as well as to the editors of *Columbia: A Journal of Literature and Art* and *Winged: New Writing on Bees,* where excerpts from this novel appeared, in very different form.

For their encouragement, support, and inspiration, I thank Heather Abel, John Beer, Liz Ceppi, Paul Collins, Sarah Ensor, Brian Evenson, Jennifer Firestone, Michele Glazer, Adria Goodness, Amy Eliza Greenstadt, Noy Holland, Alastair Hunt, Michelle Latiolais, Elena Leyva, Nanci McCloskey, Tony Perez, Peter Robbins, Shauna Seliy, Sophia Pfaff Shalmiyev, Anna Joy Springer, and Adam Zucker. Special gratitude to the early readers of this manuscript: Zelda Alpern, Kate Blackwell, Eugene Lim, and Diana Zumas.

Thank you to my family: Kate, Felix, Diana, Casey, Bridget, Greg, and little Charles. E grazie ai miei amici e alla mia famiglia in Italia: Lucia Bertagnolli, Pietro Dipierro, Chiara Berattino, e Federico Zanatta.

Above all else, thank you to Luca, for his fierce and marvelous love; and to Nicholas, for being exactly himself.

NOTES

Some details of European animal trials are taken from E. P. Evans's *The Criminal Prosecution and Capital Punishment of Animals* (London: William Heinemann, 1906).

"City born of the terror of the vastness of space": W. G. Sebald, "And If I Remained by the Outermost Sea," in *After Nature,* translated by Michael Hamburger (New York: Random House, 2003; first published in German by Eichborn AG [Frankfurt am Main], 1988).

Details of blindness curing and drum shattering are taken from Francesco Maria Guazzo's *Compendium Maleficarum,* translated by E. A. Ashwin (London: John Rodker, 1929; first published in Latin by Apud Haeredes August [Milan], 1608).

"Of all divers, thou hast dived the deepest... And not one syllable is thine"; "Has moved amid this world's foundations... when tossed by pirates from the midnight deck": Herman Melville, *Moby-Dick; or, The Whale* (London: Richard Bentley, 1851).

"When I lay with my bouncing Nell, I gave her an inch, but she took an Ell: But... it was damnable hard, When I gave her an inch, she'd want more than a Yard": John Davies of Hereford, "Wits Bedlam" (1617), in *A Dictionary of Sexual Language and Imagery in Shakespearean and Stuart Literature,* vol. 1, by Gordon Williams (London: Athlone Press, 1994).

"They rob the poor under the cover of law... and we plunder the rich under the protection of our own courage": Captain Samuel Bellamy, as recorded in *A General History of the Robberies and Murders of the Most Notorious Pyrates,* by Captain Charles Johnson [pseud.] (Guilford, CT: Lyons Press, 2010; originally published in 1724).

"I love the old way best, the simple way / Of poison, where we too are strong as men": *The Medea of Euripides,* translated by Gilbert Murray (New York: Oxford University Press [American Branch], 1907; first performed in 431 BC).

NOTES

"Geography has made us neighbors.... Those whom nature hath so joined together, let no man put asunder": John F. Kennedy, "Address Before the Canadian Parliament in Ottawa" [speech], May 17, 1961, online transcript, The American Presidency Project website, http://www.presidency.ucsb.edu/ws/?pid=8136.

"The red morn betoken'd wreck... to herdmen and to herds": William Shakespeare, "Venus and Adonis," in *The Works of William Shakespeare,* vol. 2, edited by Charles Knight (London: George Routledge and Sons, 1875), ebook.

"We are the dinosaurs, marching, marching... We are the dinosaurs. We make the earth flat!": Laurie Berkner Band, "We Are the Dinosaurs," *Whaddaya Think of That?* (New York: Two Tomatoes Records, 1997).

"I have been lifted off the earth to sit on the ocean..." borrows from a line in Virginia Woolf's *The Voyage Out* (London: Duckworth, 1915): "how strangely they had been lifted off the earth to sit next each other in mid ocean..."

"Warm as toast, smaller than most": Margaret Wise Brown, *Little Fur Family* (New York: Harper Brothers, 1946).

Some particulars of Mínervudottír's ice research are taken from Adolphus Washington Greely's *Handbook of Arctic Discoveries* (Boston: Roberts Brothers, 1896).